WHAT FREES
THE HEART

Karen A. Wyle

ISBN 978-0-9980604-7-7
Published 2020 in the United States of America
Oblique Angles Press

Cover design by Kelly A. Martin of KAM Design

Author photo by Holy Smoke Photography

Dedication

To my daughters
And the creative paths they follow.

Chapter 1

TOM BARLOW leaned against the fence for support and tossed the last sack of fall potatoes into the wagon. He could still load a wagon, at least. Not the first time he tried, or the second — and the way he fell the second time, landing on his arm, had made him even more useless for the next week. But he'd got the hang of it now.

Pa came out of the house, putting on his hat as he walked to the wagon. "Coming with me, son?"

That was a puzzle with no good answer. Tom could use the rail of the fence and a handy stump to climb into the wagon without Pa's help, but getting back down was more of a trick. He could try it, and maybe fall down for folks to laugh about, or stay perched up on the wagon like a cigar store Indian for passersby to stare at.

"I'll come." At least, whatever happened, he'd get to see something different for a change, if only the little bit of difference between the farm and town. It was bad enough being stuck around here before, when he could at least sneak off with one of the horses between chores and ride around a bit.

Sometimes, he could hardly believe he couldn't just hop onto a horse — or a wagon — the way he used to. Other days, he could hardly believe he'd ever done it at all.

After they dropped off the sacks at the train station, Pa drove to the square and parked in a shady spot near the dry goods store, within reach of the water trough. "Keep an eye on the horse and wagon for me, will you, while I go in?" Pa had been thinking along the same lines as Tom, seemingly. And maybe he didn't much fancy having the people in town see his son stumbling around like a barely-born colt.

Tom gave Pa a short nod just a hair shy of rude. Pa paused, his eyebrows going lower like he was thinking of fetching a strap, before he shook his head a little and headed toward the general store.

Now Tom had nothing to do but feel conspicuous and look around him. The first thing he noticed was a cardinal, landing in the nearest tree with a twig in its beak, bright red against the bare branches. That bird could fly most anywhere, but here it was in Cowbird Creek. It must feel a whole lot different than he did these days.

Tom saw himself working into an even worse mood, and tried to steer another way. It was sunny, at least, and sunshine always boosted his spirits some. And that tree with the cardinal might be bare still, but right under it was a forsythia bush well along in its blooming, the first of many to come.

Then something moving caught his eye from down the street. He turned to see a girl walking up — no, walking didn't do justice to it. She sort of bounced along, stepping out strong and lively, her yellow hair bouncing too, bright in the sun under a little nothing of a hat. There was plenty of her, all put together just right, and a pretty face to finish off with — not what you'd call refined, but a straight-ahead honest sort of good-looking.

Why hadn't he seen her before, at a dance or a church social? Or had she been some little stick of a kid and just lately blossomed out?

He'd already got a nice long look at the front of her, and now she headed into the store and let him enjoy the view from behind. He sighed to see her pass through the door and out of sight.

Coming into town did beat sitting at home watching cows, at that.

Another woman came walking past, older, with a little boy skipping alongside her. Skipping, like any child did, like Tom had often enough. He closed his eyes and waited for the pain to ease. But before he got to opening them, he heard the boy's voice. "Why's that man got a wooden leg? Was he a soldier, like Uncle Jake?"

Tom ground his teeth, cussing in his head. What with the way he was growing out of his trousers, and sitting high up on the wagon, anyone could see the wood between his trouser leg and his boot.

Meanwhile, the woman was saying, "No, Johnny. He's too young. He'd have been maybe your age when the war ended."

"Then what *happened* to him, Ma?"

The woman glanced up at Tom, looking embarrassed and sorry, as she grabbed her son's hand and pulled him along, saying something Tom couldn't hear. But right behind came two men, the barber and some other fellow, who acted like they'd heard it. Because the barber said to the other man, not troubling to be quiet, as if Tom was deaf along with crippled: "Poor lad. At least a soldier who lost his leg gets a pension, and knows he's a hero. And an old man with a game leg was a young man with two good legs once."

And all Tom could do was sit there on the wagon like a log, thinking how the barber was right. No honorable war wound for him, no life full of memories. One clumsy moment, and his life was more or less over before he'd done much of anything with it.

And there, finally, came Pa carrying a big sack of

provisions, smiling like someone just told him a joke, taking big steps. But when he reached the wagon and got a look at Tom's face, he all of a sudden seemed to shrink shorter.

They didn't talk on the ride home.

* * * * *

Tom remembered the first time Pa said he was big enough to groom the horses. He'd been so proud! and then mortified when that big horse went and kicked him into the straw.

Years later, now, and the horse Tom had named and raised from a colt wouldn't dream of kicking him, and here he was, sprawled in the straw again.

He crawled over to the side of the stall and pulled himself upright, Cochise nickering at him all the while. The big gelding hadn't meant it. He'd just been nuzzling. He couldn't know how easy Tom lost his balance these days.

Tom took the brush down from its hook and set to grooming. Cochise leaned into it, but Tom had seen that coming and braced himself against the wall.

"You like that, don't you? Enjoy it, then. Got to take your pleasures where you can get 'em. You and me both. You like me brushing you, and I like your company."

Cochise, not to be left out, decided it was time to groom Tom right back, licking at his hair. Tom laughed for the first time all day. "Won't Ma think I look pretty, once you're done with me!"

But Cochise was getting restless, shifting his weight around from hoof to hoof. "Easy, now. Almost done."

Maybe Cochise would have liked a different sort of life. Rounding up cattle, say, with a cowboy on his back. "I thought of going for a cowboy, did you know? Sounded mighty fine to me, chasing cattle across the prairie. How'd you like that kind of life? But I'm afraid you aren't the right kind of horse for it, not hardly."

Tom's chest was tightening up again, like it did when he thought too much about things. "No, not the right kind of horse at all. No more'n I'm the right kind of man, any more. You'll keep on pulling plows and wagons, and I — well, I'll find something I'm fit for, if I can." There had to be *something*.

Which was why he'd be heading to town to talk to Finch.

Not the easiest fellow to talk to. But Doc Gibbs had said Finch might have work for him, work he could do sitting down, mostly. And Tom had stalled as long as he could stand to, telling himself it'd be too tricky to walk into town on days the road had snow or ice, or that he needed to work up to walking that far every day. Now he'd out-stalled winter, and he was more perishing sick of the farm than fretted about dealing with Finch. And today, it wasn't even raining. So off he'd go.

But first, he'd better comb his hair.

It was a pretty morning for a walk, and warm enough for early spring. And his leg held up better'n he'd feared. Still, he was limping pretty good by the time he passed the Gibbs place, where the widow Blum used to live before she hared off with that medicine show fellow. Mrs. Gibbs, Clara Brook that was, hailed him from the window. "A good morning to you, Tom! Care for some coffee?"

She might be offering so's he had a reason to rest his leg, but he had managed to work up a thirst. "Thank you kindly, ma'am. I'd like that fine." He made his way to her front step and eased himself down. She came to sit next to him with two mugs and handed him one.

"Would your errand today be with Mr. Finch?"

He hadn't slept specially well last night, and coffee would help him gather his wits. He gulped a third of it down before he answered her. "That's right, ma'am. He said he'd come out to the farm if I . . . if more convenient. Which was good of him, busy as he keeps. But I could hardly work for him if I couldn't get myself to his shop, so I may as well start out as I'll need to keep on."

She nodded and drank her coffee, leaning on one arm, head back to soak in the sun. He snuck a look at her. She'd always been on the skinny side, but she was fattening up some now that she was married. Must be eating plenty of her own cooking.

But then she put her hand on her belly, gentle-like, the way he remembered Ma doing before he'd known he had a sib coming.

She caught him looking at her and flushed a little. "Yes, I'm in the family way. Old for it, but at least I've got a doctor handy."

She'd always had that way of just coming out with things other folks wouldn't say, or would say roundabout. He found himself blurting out, "Do you think I can work for Finch? Satisfy him? He don't seem easy to please."

She sat up straighter and turned toward him, studying on what to say, Tom on tenterhooks. He drank some more coffee, waiting. Finally, she nodded and said, "I think you can. He's not one to put people down just to make himself feel bigger. And I know you'll work hard for him, harder than someone with less to prove."

There she went again, throwing truth at him. But that meant he could trust she meant what she said. Something wound tight inside him eased up. "I surely will."

He finished the coffee and put down the mug. She watched him haul himself upright, not offering to help. He bowed in the careful way he'd learned to do, and got back on the road.

Finch was taking his ease, leaning against the wall out in front of his shop, when Tom showed up. That wasn't the best sign — it might mean he wasn't busy enough to need help after all. But as soon as the cordwainer spotted Tom, he straightened up and called, "Come along in, youngster! I've got a job I haven't been hankering to do, and if you sound like you'll suit, you can get started on it."

Finch headed back inside and Tom stumped along after. The smell of leather hit him as soon as he went through the door, a good thick smell that lifted his mood right away. Then a breeze from somewhere shifted, carrying a less agreeable stink — the horse piss the hides were soaking in to soften them and make it easier to get the hair out. No matter. You didn't grow up on a farm and stay prissy about smells.

Finch walked over to a barrel where the piss smell came from. "This hide's been soaking long enough. Next step is to scrape it. You could use that table to lay it out, and set yourself on the stool, but you'd have to stand up to reach some of it." He looked Tom up and down. "Seeing as you're here, and I don't see a wagon that could've brung you, I guess you can manage it.

"I'll pay you eighty-five cents a day, Sundays off. Deal?"

Eighty-five cents was better than nothing. And it wasn't as if Tom was all that much help on the farm. But there were times Pa and Billy could use a hand. "When things get busy on the farm, I'd want to take another day now and again. Deal?"

Finch chuckled. "All right, deal for now. If you need more time than I can spare, we'll see if we can go on with each other somehow, or no. Anyone expecting you at home real soon?"

If they were, they'd know where to come look. "No, sir. I can get to work. You want I should get that hide out?"

Finch took down two aprons from a hook in the wall and tossed one to Tom. The toss could've been aimed better, but Tom managed to catch it. "I'll show you how to lay it out and what tool to use. Then it's all yours."

Smell and all.

Chapter 2

JENNY climbed the stairs trying to look carefree, in case any of the other girls was watching. Not much point to it — they all knew. It was never good news if Madam Mamie called you up to her office. If she was pleased with you, she'd come and find you and give you a kind word or a side-hug or maybe a cash bonus. The office was for scolding a girl, or even warning her that she'd come to her last chance and might be out on her ear soon.

Jenny had a pretty good idea what the trouble was. It wore a fancy frock coat, smoked cigars too smelly for what they cost, and had looked down his nose at her when he left that afternoon.

Mamie's door was open, but as soon as Jenny showed up, Mamie waved her in, stood up, and closed it. Jenny's belly went cold. Would Mamie kick her out, just because one client didn't find her as much to his taste as he'd reckoned? Where could she go? The sheriff would never let her walk the street for customers, even if she could stand to do it.

Mamie grabbed Jenny's shoulder and steered her into the chair close to Mamie's desk. "Sit down, girl. And don't look so petrified. You're not in that much trouble. You just need reminding of some things." Mamie sat back down at the desk, thumped her elbows on it, and leaned forward. "In fact, I bet you can tell me what those things are."

Jenny knew she must have a sour-looking pout on her

face as she recited, "Make the gentleman feel welcome. Follow his lead, unless he don't know what he's doing. Make him feel special. Laugh at his jokes —"

"Which is *not* the same as telling jokes of your own, now, is it? It is especially important to avoid coarse humor. Our patrons do not consider themselves to be coarse individuals. And you should have learned better than to use slang expressions to our more refined gentlemen."

Jenny stuck out her lip. "Why'd he pick me if I'm so common, then?"

Mamie got her *I shouldn't have to explain this* look. "Probably because he knew that *all* my girls are supposed to have some *class*. You didn't just leave a customer dissatisfied —"

Jenny tossed her hair. "Oh, he sounded satisfied enough to *me*. He bellowed like a hog!"

Mamie stood up behind her desk, leaned over it, picked up the nearest bit of Jenny's hair, and gave it a sharp tug. "You know that's not what I'm saying. You didn't just leave a customer dissatisfied with the quality of our service, you damaged my reputation by doing it." She did a double take, looking at the hair. "Right here, this is part of the problem. That color looks cheap. You'd have done better leaving it brown." She turned the strands of hair this way and that. "On the other hand, now that it's lighter, you could . . . how'd you like to go red? Plenty of men consider red hair exotic, and even believe red-haired women are more passionate by nature."

Jenny tried to remember what she'd heard about turning hair red. "Do you mean henna? Won't it rub off or nothing?"

Mamie let go of Jenny's hair, sat back down, and tapped her long fancy fingernail on the desk. "No henna for my girls. We'd use the latest dye, that I ordered a while back from a factory in Massachusetts." Prob'ly like what Mamie used herself. Jenny had to admit Mamie's hair was a prettier blonde than Jenny had managed. "I figured I'd be wanting a redhead sooner or later, if one didn't wander in. Of course, dye like that is expensive. You'd have to share the cost."

That would mean a smaller payment for every customer until she paid off however much Mamie wanted out of her. But what choice did she have? After she'd gone and ticked off that stuffy old coot, she had better do whatever would make sure Mamie gave her another chance. "All right. I'd like that fine."

Mamie finally smiled. "And fine is just how you'll look. Meanwhile, you need to spend more time with some of our best-mannered girls. Listen to them, try to talk more like them, watch how they handle men. Girls like Lucette and Penny, they could almost skip bedding the customers and still send them out happy."

I'd sure like to skip bedding some of them as come in here. She knew not to say anything of the kind. "Yes, ma'am."

"Have them teach you some songs. You've a pretty voice, if you learn what to do with it."

Jenny winced before she could catch herself. Her brother would laugh himself sick. He'd had plenty of names for her singing. *Squealing like a slaughtered hog again? Honkin' louder'n the goose, you are!* But she'd give it a try, and then Mamie would see.

"Back to work, now. And no more telling jokes, not until you learn some better ones and when to tell 'em. Stick to smiling and flattering. And of course, act like they're the best lover you've had all year."

Were any of the customers fool enough to believe it when a whore said that? Well, she should know by now how big a man's ego could get.

Mamie hadn't insisted Jenny go to any particular girl to smooth her rough edges, so Jenny could think about who she liked who'd also help her satisfy Mamie and the more stuck-up customers. There was Aileen, whose Scottish accent Jenny loved to listen to, but Aileen hadn't been at Mamie's much longer than Jenny, and Jenny didn't know as she was popular enough with that kind of customer. Mamie had mentioned Lucette and Penny. Penny was English and pretty stuck up herself. She might not say no to something that was Mamie's idea, but she'd probably find a way to make Jenny feel lower'n a snake while "helping" her. Lucette, now, was friendlier, as well as dainty and pretty. If she taught Jenny some of her French words, Jenny could try some out next time she had the kind of customer who'd got Mamie sore at her.

So at the slow time of morning, she went up to where Lucette was embroidering a lacy handkerchief and explained what Mamie wanted. Lucette's eyes went bright. "But of course! I would be happy to help. Come up to my room, and we can talk about it."

That was for sure better than talking where the other girls might hear and make fun. She followed Lucette to her room, which Mamie had decorated to remind everyone that Lucette came from somewhere fancier than Cowbird Creek. The curtains had more lace on them than in the other rooms, the blanket was embroidered with fancy blue and white and red designs, and a thick close-shaved blue and white area rug stretched under the bed on all sides. Even the easy chair was less, well, easy, less comfy-looking but more elegant-like, though it was big enough for most customers to fit in.

Lucette hopped onto her bed and crossed her legs

under her petticoats and skirt. "Please, take the chair! We will talk."

Jenny sat, glad she had enough of her own padding that she didn't need much from a chair.

"Let us start with what Madame Mamie did not like, what you did or said that made her send you to me."

Jenny didn't see the need to tell Lucette that Mamie hadn't done exactly that. As best she could recall, she told Lucette what joke and what slang had got Mamie's back up. Lucette listened with her plucked eyebrows up into her forehead. "Ah, *oui*, I see why that joke might displease Madame. Let me think. Why did you decide to tell the gentleman a joke in the first place?"

Jenny shrugged. "He just seemed stiff, is all. He didn't unbutton his waistcoat or nothing when he came in the room. And he didn't look right at me. Not until I told that joke, and then he looked at me like I was some sort of bug."

"You may well have been correct that he was ill at ease. It is good that you noticed this. But it is less risky to relax a gentleman in some other way, unless you know you share a sense of humor — and so many people do not, don't you think? You could instead tell him how glad you are that he came in, that he chose you, and how flattered you are that such a handsome —"

Jenny let out a guffaw.

" — Well, then, so distinguished a gentleman would be spending time with you. You could offer to have some refreshment brought for him, and ask what he would like. Not only may this allow him to compose himself if he is nervous — and no matter how well regarded he is, or how well he regards himself, he may be nervous — but it will ensure that your encounter takes longer, which will mean that he pays for more time. A man such as we are discussing can afford it."

Jenny wished she could be sure she'd remember all this, and whatever was coming next. It wasn't the first time she'd thought how handy it'd be to know her letters better, though it was hard to imagine writing quick enough to keep up with Lucette's way of talking.

"As for your comment on the weather, rather than describing the rainstorm as a *toad strangler*, you could have expressed your hope that the excess of rain had not inconvenienced him. I do not think Madame, or — which gentleman was it?"

Jenny told her. Lucette tittered. "I can imagine his face! No, I do not think he would have objected if you had expressed such a wish. As for jokes, you must wait and see if he tells any of his own accord, and if he does, laugh as if you never heard anything better — but not too loud, and without slapping the furniture. Only if he has told you perhaps five or six jokes might you venture to tell your own — perhaps something similar you have heard from another gentleman. And apologize beforehand in case he has heard it already."

Jenny couldn't help but sulk. "I don't see why that old coot and his sort are so picky. I made him feel good enough! And they ain't coming here for a manners lesson, are they, now?"

Lucette frowned and wagged a finger. "No, but neither are they coming here only to relieve a physical need. A man seeks more than that release. He seeks companionship, and to feel welcome, and admired, and special. Think of what he may have left behind at home — a wife with at least as many pretensions as he has, and not always inclined to be easily pleased. She may have the habit of scolding him, or ignoring him, or paying attention only to what luxuries he provides her. While he can come to a parlor house such as this and find a woman not only willing and handsome, but eager to see him and listen to whatever he has to say, and appreciative of what physical prowess he displays, however it may compare to that of other, perhaps younger men."

Jenny couldn't keep from imagining those younger men Lucette was talking about. They'd surely be a welcome change. "Sounds like I've got to turn myself into some sort of actress."

"*Exactement!* We must be actresses, and hostesses, and confidantes, all together. But the rewards may be great. It is not only that by pleasing these men, we will please Madame, who decides whether we remain employed and what our wages will be. It can happen that a wealthy gentleman will be so taken with our charms, will so much enjoy how we make him feel and how we help him to see himself, that he will wish to have us available only to him. Girls have left places like this to have their own establishments, their own houses with as many luxuries as any wife — or even to become wives themselves!"

Lucette's face fairly glowed as she talked. But Jenny couldn't see what was so much to fancy in the picture Lucette was painting. Having to spend hours every day with some flabby or skinny old man, one as full of himself as the blowhard who had got her into this fix? Having to pretend he was fine as cream gravy?

Maybe she could learn just enough to keep Mamie from kicking her out, but not enough to please that kind of customer *too* much.

What else had Mamie been going on about?

"Do you think you could teach me to sing something pretty, maybe in French?"

Jenny had three old men as customers the next two days, and she tried to do the things Lucette had talked about. She even sang to the banker, soft-like, when he came in looking like he was carrying half the world on his back. Not in French, but it seemed to soothe him some.

When she finally got to go to sleep, in the early hours of the morning, she thought she'd fall asleep the second her head hit the pillow. But she ended up lying awake for near a quarter of an hour, thinking about how much more she liked it when a young man came in, a cowboy or a farmer's son, and how much she'd rather have only such customers as she could be Jenny with, and even tell a joke to, instead of trying to be somebody else without knowing how.

Chapter 3

THIS FIRST day, Tom didn't like to stop much to stretch. His back was aching plenty when he finally got a good excuse. The door opened, giving Tom a glance at sunshine, and there stood Mrs. Finch, as used to be Mrs. Arden, and who knew what before that. Her flowery dress and her pink and white bonnet looked like spring walking in, for all she couldn't make the shop smell any better. She wrinkled her nose just a little, but by the time Finch looked up, she had a pretty smile to show him as she held out a basket. "Here's your dinner, darling."

Finch, who had been stitching what looked like a lady's pair of shoes, came to meet her and take the basket. Tom thought he might give her a kiss, but no. Would Finch have kissed her if Tom wasn't there? He'd hate to be the reason a lady didn't get her kiss.

She turned to Tom. "I'm so sorry — I didn't know you'd be here, so I've nothing to give you."

"Don't fret, please, ma'am. I've got something I brought." It was nothing but jerky, but it'd have to hold him until supper.

"Tomorrow I'll be sure to bring you some dinner as well."

Finch gave his missus a kind of sharp look, like he hadn't been intending to feed Tom along with employing him. It'd sure be interesting to see how much was in that basket tomorrow.

She moved back toward Finch and patted his cheek.

"I'll see you at home, darling. Shall I bring Hope with me tomorrow? She wanted to come today, but she hadn't finished stitching her sampler."

Tom held back a shudder. At least he hadn't had such fiddling work to do as a boy.

Finch headed back toward his workbench. "Bring her, then, if the lass is done with her chores."

Finch's missus left, a sweet breeze blowing in as she went out the door. Finch looked at Tom and cleared his throat. Tom stretched one more time and sat back down to his work.

The shadows were long behind Tom as he finally trudged toward home, his stump aching something fierce, with a few burning throbs thrown in. It had got a fair bit colder since morning, the wind picking up and jabbing at him. Not to mention that he was starving.

He wasn't sparing much attention for looking right and left, but as he drew near Doc Gibbs' house, he saw the front step was occupied again. Not Mrs. Gibbs this time — Doc himself was setting out there. He might have been watching for Tom to come by. Tom thought about not noticing. He didn't need Doc, or his missus, looking after him.

Doc must have guessed what Tom had in mind. He came down the steps and stood almost in Tom's path, to where it'd be downright rude for Tom to go around him. Tom stopped, resting his weight on his good leg, and waited for Doc to speak his piece.

Doc looked a little embarrassed, which probably meant Tom was glaring at him. He owed Doc better'n that. Doc most probably saved his life. And even crippled, he'd rather be alive, most days.

But as good sense as that was, it was hard, sometimes, to feel friendly around the man who'd cut off his leg.

Meanwhile, Doc had got over being embarrassed and started talking. "Won't you come in for a minute and warm up? Besides, I've been meaning to get out to the farm and check on how you were doing, and here you are. I'd take it as a favor if you'd save me the trip."

Tom could see through that easy enough. However he'd be doing at the farm, he was doing considerable worse just now after walking to town, and getting up and down a fair number of times during the day, and now walking partway home. But he had to admit getting off his feet, just for a minute, sounded like a borrowed bit of heaven. "Yessir, I'll do that."

He wasn't even through the door when he smelled something baking. He'd never figured Clara Brook for much of a cook, but his nose said she'd learned how to bake at least. He looked around for her, but Doc, seeing him do it, said, "She's off taking some corn muffins to the barber. She left enough for us. Maybe a muffin will take your mind off my poking around."

Tom sat where Doc told him to, rolled up his trouser leg, took a muffin, and paid as much attention to it as he could while Doc took off the wooden leg and moved the stump this way and that. He snuck a look at Doc's face, from which he could've figured what he already knew, that he'd been overdoing things. If Doc's handling made his leg smart, well, he had that coming.

What with just jerky for dinner, the muffin didn't last long. He didn't like to ask for another. But then he had quite an idea for how to stay distracted. With Doc here, and his missus not here, and none of Tom's family around, it was the perfect time to ask a question he'd been wondering on.

"Doc? If you don't mind saying — you doctor the girls at Madam Mamie's, don't you?"

Doc got a little smile, and his face turned kinda pinkish. "Yes, I do. Did you have questions about that establishment, or about the ladies who work there?"

Tom opened his mouth to answer, but a yelp came out instead. Doc paused in his poking. Before Doc could apologize, Tom said, "I've had questions for a while now. Like, what sort of girls work there? How are they different from other girls?"

Doc chewed his lip for a minute and then said, "They're not so different from the girls you know. They have their various reasons for getting into their line of work, and some of those reasons aren't happy ones. A few may act hardened, but it's usually a fairly superficial pose." While Tom tried to remember what "superficial" meant, Doc smiled again and said, "Come to think of it, I recall one lively young woman there who might be your very type. . . . Are you considering patronizing Mamie's establishment?" When Tom looked blank, he rephrased. "Thinking of going there as a customer?"

It was Tom's turn to blush. His first try at answering came out more of a stammer. On the second try, he managed to say, "Not exactly thinking of it. But it's crossed my mind a time or two, as a someday thing."

Meanwhile, Doc had been smearing some sort of ointment on Tom's stump. Now he wiped off the extra, fetched the wooden leg, and put it back in place, moving careful so's he wouldn't hurt Tom more than needful. Once he'd done that, he went over to his doctor's bag and fished around in it, bringing out a small thin box. "Here. For whenever you go from thinking to doing, you should use these. They're called French letters. Have you heard of them before?"

Tom shook his head, trying to figure why he would want to hand a painted lady something in French. Doc opened the box and pulled out something like a sack, except a lot smaller and almost see-through. He held it up and said, "I keep the ladies as healthy as I can, but they have plenty of chances to catch diseases they could spread to customers. If you should become one of those customers, even just once, you should put this over your member before it has a chance to touch the lady's personal parts. It could save you a lot of trouble."

Tom stared at the little sack. He was supposed to sit there in front of the girl with his tallywag hanging out and put that thing on? What if he made a mess of it, and she laughed at him?

Doc seemed to guess what he was worrying on. Putting the French letter back in the box, he said, "Back when I was a customer as well as the ladies' doctor, I used these every time." He paused, his face wrinkling like he'd tasted something sour, before going on, "They've gotten harder to obtain lately, due to a wrongheaded federal law I won't bore you with describing, but I had plenty of them when I stopped needing them. In any event, most of Mamie's ladies are used to them, and could even help you put one on. Which is more pleasant, in my experience, than doing it for oneself."

If Tom had imagined as hard as he could all the day long, he'd never have imagined this conversation. But he took the box when Doc held it out to him.

"Now let's get you on your feet and see how your stump is feeling." Doc stood up and waited for Tom to do the same. The stump still pained him some, but a sight less than earlier.

"Thanks, Doc. I'd best be getting on my way."

Doc patted his shoulder. "Take another muffin with you. Clara will be pleased to know you enjoyed them."

Tom was more than happy to oblige. It'd help take his mind off the rest of the road.

Chapter 4

BEFORE Finch set himself up as a cordwainer and started making shoes, he'd made himself a reputation for good solid saddles. Folks still came to him to fix their saddles or make new ones. The cowboy who came in whistling this morning had come by two weeks earlier, about a week after Tom started work, with a saddle that'd had the hell beat out of it over some years. Finch showed Tom how to measure it, and then set to making the replacement.

Tom had always known saddles came expensive, but now he could see why. They needed a deal of work. Finch had Tom do much of it, what didn't need fine handling — cleaning the hides, rough cutting the wood for the saddle tree, brushing on glue, crimping the edges of the horn top, pounding tacks, sanding. He almost got to shave some edges, but Finch got nervous at the last minute and did it all himself.

Then there was warming up water, hauling the saddle seat into it and back out again, draping the seat around the saddle tree, strapping it down, and sewing through four layers of leather.

Much of the work had to be done standing at or bending over the stand the saddle tree stood on. Much as Tom liked helping them as rode for a living, he paid pretty dear for it in pain. Not that he was going to tell Finch as much.

The cowboy came in as Tom was doing the last part of the job, rubbing oil into the leather to protect it and give it more color. Tom polished over where Finch had carved the cowboy's initials and the brand of the ranch he rode for and then, finally, stood back. He wouldn't sit down until the cowboy left.

The cowboy gave Tom a friendly slap on the shoulder. Then, a grin stretching his face, he made for Finch and shook his hand. "Now that's a fine saddle. They were right as sent me to you."

The cowboy pulled coins out of his vest pocket and gave them to Finch, who looked mighty gratified to get them. Finch tucked the coins away in his own vest and asked the cowboy, "Are you taking this fine saddle with you now, or spending some time in town first?"

The cowboy guffawed. "Oh, I'm not leavin' town without a meal Cookie didn't make and a visit to that fancy parlor house! But I'd best go to the barber first and clean up some, or they won't let me in the door." He turned back to Tom. "Just look at you, eyes wide as dinner plates! Ain't you been to Mamie's, a big fellow like you? You come along with me, why don't you?"

Finch sidled up to the cowboy and muttered in his ear. It didn't take hearing it to know what Finch was saying. Tom clenched his fists and his teeth, and walked a few steps away to make sure he didn't punch out his boss. But the cowboy laughed again and said, "Naah, he don't need two whole legs for it! Hell, there used to be a fellow on our crew that lost a leg to a wild bronc, and he spent himself broke on calico queens every payday."

Finch snorted. "That's as may be. But Tom here has work to do. You go on and have your fun. I'll have your saddle for you when you're through."

As the cowboy headed for the door, Tom managed to work up the nerve to ask, "Mister, how much does it cost to go to Mamie's?"

The cowboy winked at him and said a number that Tom could manage — if he didn't turn over all his wages to Pa like he'd been doing. Pa did say, when Tom started working for Finch, that Tom was a man now and should have some money of his own. This might be the time to act like it.

Once the cowboy left, Finch didn't turn out to have all that much for Tom to do. He'd probably been trying to "protect" Tom from the cowboy, as if Tom had asked for such. He'd about made up his mind to ask if he should go on and leave, for all it was just midday, when Dolly Finch walked in, her little girl Hope bouncing along behind her with the dinner basket.

Tom couldn't help but notice how pretty and curvy Mrs. Finch was, for all she was so much older than him. When she took the basket from Hope and put it down on a bench, her chest swayed, and Tom could feel himself start to sweat. He backed into a corner, but he couldn't get away that easy — Mrs. Finch smiled sweet at him as she unpacked the basket and set aside Tom's share. He nodded back, feeling stiff and stupid and six kinds of fool.

If he couldn't even keep his head clear and his thoughts clean when the boss's wife walked in, maybe he'd better make his way to Mamie's pretty soon. It was high time he became a man, as much as he still could. And it wasn't as if he had much chance with decent girls. The one or two he'd seen noticing him, the last year or so that he was whole, didn't look at him the same way, after.

He might not know what he was about, but the girls there would know how to show him. They probably wouldn't laugh at him much, not if Mamie ran the place as tight as he'd heard.

Doc Gibbs seemed to think it'd be all right. He'd even said there was a girl there Tom might like. And now he thought about it, that made Tom plenty curious.

How many times had Tom walked by the tall building with the bright red trim and the red lanterns, wondering what it was like inside? The first time must have been before he learned just what went on in there, when all he noted was how fancy it looked. But over the years, he went from a confused "something naughty" notion, to puzzlement over why anyone would want to see half-naked ladies, to understanding and feeling the same.

It was growing dusk, and the lanterns glowed. His heart beat pretty fast as he finally, finally touched the doorknob and pulled it open.

The first thing he noticed was the piano music coming from the bar. But next second, he saw the women, sitting and standing all around, in fancy dresses with short sleeves and cut low to show bosoms, and lacy petticoats underneath.

His head could've been mounted on a swivel as he looked from one to another. But it stopped short when he saw a girl he thought he'd seen before, on the street that day he'd come to town with Pa. But hadn't that girl had yellow hair? This girl's hair was red, a pretty bright-copper color that made him think of firelight.

No, it was the same girl, he could swear it, however she'd managed to change her hair. The same pretty face and fetching shape, and a sort of freshness to her. She caught him looking and smiled at him, friendly but kind of bold — no wonder, given where she was. What she was. No wonder he'd never seen her at a church social.

Then movement caught his eye from the wide staircase with the shiny banister. A woman was sweeping downstairs, graceful but quick. He didn't know as he'd ever seen Madam Mamie before, but it had to be her. She was older than the other women, and her dress wasn't cut so low or so bright-colored, but more than that, you could tell just looking at her that she was in charge and wouldn't take no guff from nobody.

Sure enough, she held out a dainty hand with painted nails and said smiling, "I'm Mamie. Welcome to my place. Your first time here, isn't it?"

Her eyes scanned him from head to foot, just barely slowing down when she got to where the wooden leg peeked out of his trousers, and then up again. "I have just the girl for you — Amanda Jane over there. Mandy! Come meet this fine young fellow."

A woman who might be in her middle twenties stood up. She had a lot of paint on her cheeks and eyes and lips — well, they all did, but more than some — and thin eyebrows with kind of a funny shape to them. She came toward Tom with a business-like kind of walk and a smile he had the notion she'd smiled hundreds of times before, exactly the same every time.

Tom took a step back before he could stop himself. His cheeks hot, he stammered, "Thank you kindly, ma'am. But . . . I wonder if I might . . . spend my time with that other girl instead? The red-headed one?"

Mamie blinked, but she held her hand out toward the painted-up woman. "Never mind, Mandy. Young man — what's your name?"

"Tom." He hoped a first name was enough, here.

"Well, Tom, we aim to please! You have a seat at the

bar and ask for whatever you'd like to drink. I'll just talk to Jenny for a minute."

Jenny — the name suited her — had started talking to another girl by then, but she heard her name and looked over. She tilted her head, quizzical-like, as Mamie moved off in her direction. Tom hustled to the bar and asked for a tall glass of whatever beer was most handy. When it came, he took such a big gulp that he like to choked.

* * * * *

Mamie took Jenny by the elbow and tugged her over to the corner furthest from the bar. "That young man should've gone with Amanda Jane, but he wants you. Makes sense — he's got farm boy written all over him, and you're as close to a farm girl as I have just now, not to mention near his age. But he's got a wooden leg, and you need to learn what to do."

He might have *farm boy* written all over him, but poor as she was at reading, she'd have added *fine-looking*. And maybe *nice fella* along with it.

Mamie was talking so fast and quiet it was hard for Jenny to follow. "This may be his first time with a woman, which'd be good so he won't be comparing things to how they were when he was whole. From how he looked walking in, I'd guess he still has his knee. That'd make things a lot easier. He could lie atop you, but he might not balance real well. You'd best hold him tight enough that he can't topple. He won't think anything of it. If I'm wrong and he has less leg than that, you'll need him lying on his side or on his back. You can make lying on his back sound good by saying you're dying to play cowgirl and ride him."

Mamie looked over at the bar, probably to make sure

the boy hadn't run off. "Leave it up to him whether to leave the wooden leg on. Either way, make sure you don't bump up against the leg or the stump, whichever, or it could hurt him and shut everything down."

Jenny took a deep breath. This was going to be different, but not all in a bad way. At least she wouldn't have to remember all the not-to-dos she had to keep in mind for the older, richer, snootier customers.

And she probably shouldn't sing to him. Young as he was, he might take it as singing him a lullaby.

She'd seen plenty of men leer at her, or stare at her chest, as she went to take them upstairs, but she couldn't recall seeing a fellow's face light up like Christmas morning and a brand new sled.

When she grabbed his hand to lead him, he gripped it almost tight enough to hurt. Excited and nervous both, she figured. It made her feel kind of excited and nervous herself. A nice change from bored or worse. But also strange. It was almost like she was at home and entertaining a gentleman caller in the ordinary way. Except she'd never lived anywhere with two stories and a staircase between them, not to mention rugs and chandeliers and fancy wallpaper and such.

Speaking of which, Tom — Mamie had introduced them downstairs — kept looking around like he'd never seen the like. Growing up nearby, he'd probably been wondering about this place for years. She took her time on the stairs to let him get his fill of gawking.

At least, gawking at the place. When she led him into her room and let go of his hand, he did his looking straight at her, his face saying he couldn't hardly believe his eyes.

She gave him a big smile. He was easy to smile at —

young and good-looking, and he seemed a friendly sort. And not drooling or eying her like a big thick steak.

She was about ready to invite him to sit on the bed when he talked first. "You're so pretty."

Was that a blush heating up her cheeks? She hadn't blushed since she couldn't remember when. Maybe the day Mamie interviewed her and went through all the things she'd best be prepared to do. "Why, thank you!"

"And, and you've got such nice teeth."

She hadn't heard that one before. He probably wasn't used to being around folks who cleaned their teeth regular, like Mamie insisted on.

Time to move things along. Mamie had her notions of how long the girls took with any one customer, unless she knew they'd pay extra for longer. "How about you sit down and get comfy? And I'll do the same, all right?"

She could see his breathing speed up as soon as she sat on the little chair and took off her shoes. She got up and turned her back to him, standing right up against his knees. She could feel two of them — Mamie'd been right about that. And somehow she'd managed to forget about the fellow's wooden leg for a minute. She'd better keep it in mind. "How about you undo my laces?" She had ways of shedding the dress without such help, but it'd get him started touching her, which he seemed a little shy of.

His fingers weren't as clumsy as she'd thought they might be, nor soft like some of the customers who spent their days at some desk, nor yet as rough as cowboys'. As soon as he'd unlaced her far enough, she turned back toward him and shimmied out of the dress, making sure to bend over and give him a nice view. His jaw actually fell down, which she wanted to chuckle at but didn't. Seeing as he liked the front of her so well, she reached around and undid her corset herself, then did the same to unfasten her petticoats. That left her standing there in nothing but stockings and garters and a smile.

Tom probably didn't know he was panting. He opened and closed his mouth a couple of times before he managed to ask, "Do I need to take off . . . ." That was as far as he got.

From his not wanting to say more, he probably meant his wooden leg, but to cover all points, she just said, "You don't *have* to take off anything, cowboy."

When he flinched and glowered, she realized she'd took a wrong step. It didn't need him growling at her, "I'm no cowboy." Maybe he'd thought of being, before.

She took his hand and said, "I'm sorry, Tom. I didn't mean that. Cowboys don't clean up as good as you."

That took him off stride enough to lighten up a little. She kept going. "Anyhow, you take off just what you want to. I'll admit, though, I'd surely like to see more of you."

He studied her face like he was trying to read lie or truth, and stood up slow. He tugged his shirt out of his trousers, fumbled at the buttons, and got it off, tossing it onto the floor. He might like the look of Jenny's chest, but she liked his better — some light-colored hair but not bear-thick, and plenty of muscle. She let her face show him how she was admiring him, and waited to see if he'd keep going. It wasn't any big surprise that he didn't, much — just unbuttoned his fly and let his maypole jump out, all ready to get to work.

Now for the tricky part. Except she couldn't let him know it was tricky. She'd best decide, right now, which of those positions Mamie listed would be least likely to go wrong. Him on his back would be easiest on the both of them. And of the two conditions, being shy part of a leg and being grass green, her guess was he was more prickly about the first. So — "Now, then. There's different things we can do, but seeing as I've done this a lot, and you, I'd guess, not so often, I can show you something you maybe hadn't thought of, that'd also make things easy. How about you lie back on my nice big bed, and —" Mamie notwithstanding, she'd better not mention cowgirls, not after that misstep before. "— And I'll give you a fine old time while having plenty of fun myself. Let's get started, can we?"

By the time she'd made him happy, and he'd got his pants buttoned up and his shirt back on, she was feeling pretty pleased with herself. Which didn't exactly explain why, as he was set to leave, she pulled him back toward her and gave him a soft warm kiss. She couldn't recall having done that before, ever, not once she was a lady of the line.

And he tasted sweet.

Chapter 5

TOM MIGHT just as well have floated home on a cloud, fine as he was feeling. It did bring him some way back down, just for a minute, when he went to bounce on his toes and almost fell over, but he shook it off. That sort of thing happened often enough, and an evening like this one surely didn't. And the stars were shining bright above, like they were celebrating along with him.

Jenny had managed things so well that his stump didn't hurt more'n usual. And what pain he was used to didn't seem to matter tonight.

Only thing was, he could've turned right around and laid with Jenny one more time and been that much the happier.

How soon could he manage another visit? He'd a deal of thinking to do about what he was going to do with his wages from now on. How often they'd go into Madam Mamie's pocket rather'n Pa's, and whether he should be saving up for something, though he'd no clue for what.

Remembering and wanting kept him restless overnight, but he still couldn't help grinning now and again over his breakfast. Ma and Pa kept sneaking looks at each other when they thought he wasn't watching. Pa, at least, must have known something was up when Tom didn't turn in his wages. He'd just as soon not know if Pa guessed why.

Walking to town went easier when he had more to think of than his leg and his day of work to come. First he pictured Jenny's pretty face, and then her hair laying on her shoulders, and then her round squeezable bosom and even rounder backside, and every minute he could remember of what they'd done together. It seemed to take considerable shorter'n usual before he made it to the door of the shop.

Finch, now, after everything that cowboy had said, would be sure to figure things out if Tom came in all cheerful. He could act extra glum, but then Finch might think he'd gone to Mamie's and made a mess of it. So he kept things businesslike, not chatting but not sulking neither, and Finch didn't make any show of drawing conclusions.

Speaking of drawing. That's just what Tom would've liked to do, draw a picture of Jenny, head and shoulders and just a little of what came below. It'd been a while since he got a hankering to draw. He used to do a lot of it, with a stick in the dirt or on his slate at school. Got a licking one of those times, drawing when he was supposed to do arithmetic. And then when he was maybe ten, he'd used his pocket knife to draw on a bit of leather he didn't think anyone cared about. Turned out he was wrong, and he got a licking from Pa that time.

Wasn't the lickings that stopped him, so much as not having the time once he got big enough to do more farm work. And since that plowshare took some of his leg and more of his use on the farm, he hadn't thought about it, or about much else that he might do just from wanting to. Today, though . . . when Finch finished cutting out a pair of boots, Tom asked, as casual as he could, "You have any use for what's left of that piece? Because I might if you don't."

Finch looked at him kind of sideways, but he shrugged and tossed it Tom's way. Mrs. Finch came in not long after, and that gave Tom his chance. Finch cared a deal about his dinner and never paid attention to much else while he was eating it. As soon as Mrs. Finch left and Finch dug in, Tom moved off to the farthest corner of the shop and laid the scrap of leather on the edge of a table Finch used for storage of this and that.

The biggest piece was about a foot by eight inches. Tom trimmed away the rest and looked at his knife, considering. It was just fine for cutting through leather, but not so good for just scraping away one thin line at a time. What he needed for that was . . . Where was that tool Finch had used for the cowboy's initials on the saddle, the one Finch called a swivel knife?

But Finch had gobbled his dinner already, and Tom hadn't taken but a bite or two. He quickly tore away at the chicken leg and wiped his hands on his trousers.

He'd hardly be able to get at that tool without Finch knowing, even if it were right to do it. He'd have to fess up.

"Mr. Finch, when you close up for the day, could I borrow what you used to carve that cowboy's initials? I'd treat it real careful and have it back in the morning. And I wouldn't touch nothing but leather with it, the leather you let me have earlier."

Finch wrinkled his forehead to make his eyebrows stick out even more than they did by nature. "What've you got to be carving? You wouldn't be making one of them pictures that make fun of folks, carry-whatsits, of me, would you?" Clearly, that'd be as much as Tom's job was worth.

"Oh, no, sir, I've no such intention. Just — just a drawing I've been wanting to do, on something that won't wash away or rub out."

Finch stroked his scraggly beard. "Well, all right then. You take good care of it, and if you lose it, you'll be working to pay it back and not for whatever else you use your pay on. And you clean it like I showed you." He fetched the tool and handed it over.

Finch might be grumpy and suspicious, and he watched his coin, but he wasn't that bad. Not altogether. Or at least, not always.

By the time Tom made the walk home, ate supper, and did what chores he still could, it was full dark and he'd have been about ready for bed, but for the scrap of leather calling to him. He filled a lamp, lit it, and laid the leather out on the kitchen table. Pa, wandering out in his nightshirt and cap, saw what Tom was doing and hoisted an eyebrow. "Hope you came by that leather some way that won't get you in trouble."

"Mr. Finch gave it to me when I asked for it." What a memory Pa had! He'd hardly've thought being on the other end of that strap would stick in the memory as well as Tom's end of it. Was that part of what being a father meant? He'd have to ponder that some time.

Seeing as he'd never used the swivel knife before, he should've kept another scrap to practice on. Thinking ahead maybe wasn't his strong suit. With a sigh, he cut a long thin strip off his piece of leather and started teaching himself. At first even his straight lines wouldn't stay straight, let alone an even thickness, but it didn't take too long for him to get that right. Next came curves — he'd need plenty of curvy lines for Jenny! That thought got him remembering, which heated him up to where it got distracting. He went out to the pump and splashed cool water on his face, then got back to work.

When he'd used up most of the strip and figured he was as good at this as he'd be getting, he smoothed out his main piece of leather again. He maybe shouldn't draw lower'n her shoulders after all, seeing as her dress had showed more than a regular girl's would. Or he could draw the dress different, but that'd be a sort of lying.

He drew her face first, heart-shaped even to the bit of a point to her chin, with the dimple he'd noticed every time she smiled. He puzzled over how to show her nose with its tilted-up end, all too aware that once he set tool to leather for it, there'd be no rubbing out any wrong moves. But it was getting late, and him getting tired, so he finally made a few thin lines suggesting it and moved on to her eyes. There was no chance of drawing them pretty enough, but he showed them big and wide open, with the long lashes that might get help from some sort of paint. He tried to use a light touch on the eyebrows — better to have them a little thinner'n life than to make them too thick and frowny.

Jenny's smile was another tricky task. Better to give her upper lip more of a Cupid's bow than make it too flat. Then shape the lower lip to match, kind of plump, like she was ready to kiss someone.

He had the most fun drawing her hair, which didn't have to be exactly the way she wore it so long as it was long and full and wavy. That left only her neck and the top line of her shoulders. And then, finally, he was done and could fall into bed.

He slid the drawing under his bed where no one would happen on it, and fell asleep before he could notice how long it took.

Tom made a point of showing up early the next morning, so's he could clean the swivel knife and leave it where Finch would be sure to see it. He'd hoped Finch would forget about his suspicions of caricatures or whatever else, but no such luck. When Finch turned up, he first took the tool out into sunlight so's he could check it every which way and make sure it wasn't dirty or somehow damaged, and then put out his hand toward Tom. "And now let's see what you used it for."

Tom pulled the piece of leather out and showed it to Finch, keeping a grip on one edge. Finch leaned over it and laughed. "Well, that's sure no picture of me! Pretty thing, ain't she? Who is she?" Then his grin twisted toward a leer. "I'd bet my boots you went to Mamie's, like that cowboy wanted you to. So she's one of the shakes there? I could use me some o' that, sure enough."

Tom tugged the leather back away from Finch and turned away to hide the look he could feel on his face. Finch laughed again. "Don't be getting sweet on her, now! If it ain't me next, it'll be someone else, and another after that."

Tom stomped over to the hide bucket without looking back. "I'd better get to work."

On his way home, Tom stopped at Doc Gibbs' office. He didn't recall which days Doc saw patients there, but if today wasn't one, he'd try the house next. Doc was there, in fact, and looked up as Tom came in, his forehead wrinkled up in concern. "Well, good evening, Tom. Is your stump giving you trouble, with all that walking to and from Finch's shop?"

"Nossir, it's fine." That might be overstating the case, but he wasn't here to get his leg looked at. "I was just wondering . . . ." It came more awkward than he'd figured on, but he kept going. "When might you next be going to Mamie's? To treat the ladies there, I mean."

Doc's eyebrows went up, but he brought them back down as quick as he likely could. "Next week, probably Tuesday not long after their dinnertime. I would hazard a guess that you've been there yourself since we last spoke about it. I hope you used my little present."

Tom cleared his throat. "Yessir, I did, thankee." Though he'd almost forgot to.

"Is there a girl there that you have some . . . concerns about? That might need my assistance?"

How many wrong guesses could one man make? "No, Doc, nothing like that. I was just hoping . . . as it may be quite a while before I make another visit, and I have something I'd like to give to one of the girls, I was hoping you could give it to her for me, when you're seeing her anyways."

Doc looked like he might be amused and trying to hide it. Tom did his best not to wriggle about as Doc asked, "Well, then. Which girl will be getting a present?"

About to answer, Tom pulled out the picture instead. "I'm hoping you can tell from looking at this. If not, maybe I should hold off 'til I can do a better one." He held the piece of leather out for Doc, who checked his fingers before taking it, probably to make sure they weren't wet or tainted with something foul. He studied it long enough for Tom to get nervous before he looked up and said, "That's really quite good. I didn't know you had a talent for such things."

Tom relaxed and took the breath he hadn't realized he was holding. "Well, it's my first try, sort of. And no one's seen any of my scribbling before, at least not past being sore about when or how I was doing it, so I didn't know myself."

"Then I'm even more impressed. And I'd venture to say Jenny — I can certainly tell it's Jenny — will be very pleased with it."

So all in all, Tom was feeling pretty pleased with things when he went back to work at the start of the following week, rehearsing how to ask for another piece of leather. He might draw Jenny again, or something altogether different. Cochise, maybe; or Ma — and not tell her he'd thought of a horse before fixing on her! He pictured Ma's face if she found that out and laughed out loud.

And then Finch sauntered in with an oily grin on his face. "Guess we're both starting Monday out feeling fine! I am, for certain. Want to guess where I spent my Saturday night?"

Tom did not want. In fact, he was afraid he didn't need to guess. He stood there glum and stupid, looking at his boots while Finch enjoyed his gloat.

"Mighty fine establishment Mamie's got! And I gotta hand it to you, you know how to pick 'em. That's one fine wag-tail, that gal you drew your picture of."

Tom stalked out of the shop, holding his hands tight against his thighs so's he wouldn't hit Finch as he went. He didn't go far, seeing as he'd have to go back in before long, but stepping out made for his only chance to keep his temper.

Picturing Finch grunting atop Jenny had him ready to puke. Whenever he saw her again, would he be able to pay mind to her without that picture in his head?

Not to mention Mrs. Finch, and what might come of it for her. He'd bet a week's pay Finch hadn't bothered about any French letters. He might've already passed on something catching to that sweet woman, and her not even knowing enough to go to Doc about it, most likely.

Could he tell Doc himself? Wouldn't that be a dandy conversation. But he couldn't trust Finch to do it, so he'd better. Sometime soon.

And as for seeing Jenny again . . . he'd known right along what she was, what she did. And much as he was seeing red just now where Finch was concerned, she probably had slimier sorts to deal with, sometimes. Unless he'd decided never to visit another vaulting-house, he'd best get over being particular.

But all the same, he wished he could meet her somewhere else. He knew she went places — that's how he'd seen her the first time. He'd just have to figure out where and when. Or find somewhere he could invite her, and send a message somehow. Somewhere she wouldn't be too out of place.

Maybe a saloon would do. Customers there wouldn't have much call to be hoity-toity. And what with a bar right there at Mamie's, it seemed likely she took a drink now and again.

*　*　*　*　*

Jenny saw Lucette leave the room where Doc Gibbs was examining the girls and darted in, waving at Lucette, before Mamie could send somebody else. It had been a busy day so far, and she could use the break. Taking off clothes for Doc instead of a customer made a nice change, especially as Doc was better-looking than most of what walked in. She could enjoy his looks even if he didn't give Mamie his custom no more. He'd stopped even before he got married, and why was that? Plenty of married men came in for what they seemingly didn't get at home. What made some men different?

Had she met any, aside from Doc? That fine-looking farm boy, would he marry someone and then come back here for a ride? Not that she'd mind seeing him again, but she'd feel bad for whoever he left at home.

Meanwhile, time to smile pretty at Doc, even if it wouldn't lead to anything. He'd always treated her nice.

Doc seemed pretty tickled about something. All the time he was checking her over, he had this little I've-got-a-secret twinkle in his eye. And when he was all finished and said she was fine except for looking underslept — what else did he expect? — he reached into his vest pocket and pulled out a rolled-up piece of leather. "A young man you met recently asked me to give you this the next time I saw you. He'd have done so himself, but it is not yet feasible for him to return to this establishment."

Jenny felt her eyebrows practically hide up in her hair as she took the little scroll and unrolled it. And her jaw dropped in a way that'd give Mamie fits when she saw the picture cut into the leather.

"Oh, my stars!" Had that come out of her mouth? Mama used to say it, when she was surprised and happy about something. It'd been more years than Jenny liked to think since she'd heard it, let alone said it.

It was a picture of Jenny, and it made her look prettier than she'd ever seen in any mirror. Who had made it? "Was it the farm boy, with the wooden leg?"

Something about that question seemed to bother Doc, which she hadn't intended, but he managed to get his smile back after a second and say, "Yes, Tom. He's working for Silas Finch now, the cordwainer, and I gather he used a scrap of extra leather. It's a fine likeness."

Was it really? It gave Jenny a warm feeling to hear Doc say it.

She wished all of a sudden that she could show the picture to Mama. But would Mama want to see it, any more'n she'd want to see Jenny herself? Jenny pushed the hurt down, like she'd done so many times, just as Doc added, "I believe young Tom would be glad to see you somewhere else, if he could. But am I correct that Madam

Mamie discourages social meetings of that kind?"

Jenny rolled her eyes. "She says if the gents want to see us, they can come here and pay for the privilege, and if we was to meet them elsewhere, they might not bother. But I think really she don't trust us to keep our petticoats down. She's afraid we'll give away what she collects their coin for."

Doc hesitated. "Mamie's a shrewd businesswoman. I wouldn't venture to guess the reasons behind her rules, nor presume to say whether they're justified. Do you have any message for me to give the artist?"

Jenny looked at the picture again. Maybe she could frame it somehow and put it on her wall. Except somehow she didn't fancy the idea of customers seeing it. Other'n Tom, of course, if he should manage to come back.

"Tell him thank you. That I'm much obliged." She ran a finger along the carved lines. "That I never seen nothing finer. And that I hope to see him again, somehow, wherever."

There might be some way to arrange going to meet him, if she was clever, and bold enough to take the chance. But arranging it would have to wait for him to make another visit.

Chapter 6

TOM CAME awake yelling. Sleeping shouldn't work like that, making it so you couldn't keep from hollering and waking folks. And what was the good of dreaming if dreams could be nightmares? If they could make you live your worst times over and over?

Or it was maybe worse, the times he dreamed he'd somehow stopped the plowshare from falling, or got out of its way. Or dreamed about still having two good legs, however, from before or from the accident not happening. Waking up from having two whole legs and remembering he had but one, that might be worse than the dreams where the plowshare fell and he felt every bit of the pain, and saw all the blood, and could've died just from how scared he was even without those. Folks who said you couldn't really hurt in dreams didn't know what the hell they were talking about.

It wasn't just at night and dreaming. Sometimes he got to daydreaming too, about having dodged the blade or Doc somehow stitching him together. He could just about hear Doc saying, "Surely, Tom, I can save the leg. Just you let me give you something for the pain, and I'll take care of it."

But at least he could stop himself daydreaming easier than wake himself up.

Doc and Mrs. Gibbs both were sitting on their front

step when Tom plodded past. Mrs. Gibbs came to meet him. "You don't look well, Tom. Joshua can stop by Mr. Finch's shop at dinnertime to examine you, or if you'd rather not have Finch around, you could stop here on your way home."

Doc joined his missus and stood waiting for Tom's answer. Tom tried to think of how he could look healthier on the spot, gave up, and said, "No, ma'am, he needn't take the trouble. I'm not sick, just short on sleep is all." He'd never thought of asking before, but he blurted out, "Is there any way to stop bad dreams? Anything I could take, or a special way of sleeping, maybe?"

Instead of answering straight off, Doc looked at Mrs. Gibbs. She reached for Doc's hand, squeezed it, and said, "As a matter of fact, we know something of bad dreams. In Joshua's case —" She stopped and looked at Doc, who nodded as if giving permission for something. She went on, "Apart from the passage of time, it seemed to help when he told someone about the dream that had been troubling him." A faint pink color in her face told Tom pretty clear who the someone had been.

Tom pictured telling his dream to someone. He didn't much care for it. Ever after, whoever did the listening would carry that ugliness around in them, at least if they cared about Tom, and why would he tell it to someone as didn't?

He might not've got any advice worth using, but he'd be polite notwithstanding. "Thankee, ma'am, Doc." He turned back to the road, but before he'd gone more than a few steps, he heard someone coming behind him. He wasn't surprised to see it was Doc, though not eager to find out what more Doc couldn't keep from saying to him. He stopped and waited without turning back.

Doc halted alongside Tom and said quietly, "I won't ask any questions about the content of your dreams, but if I figure in any of them . . . I hope you know, Tom, that I wouldn't have taken your leg if I'd had any other way to save your life."

Tom nodded, his jaw locked tight to keep from saying something like *then maybe you should have let me die*. He could feel Doc's eyes on him as they both stood there, not talking.

Finally Doc sighed and said, "Fare you well, then, Tom. Please let me know if there's anything I can do for you, any time."

Tom waited to hear Doc's footsteps behind him before he went on his way.

Tom hadn't found the right time to ask Finch for another piece of leather, nor decided just what he'd want to carve if he got the chance. But what happened instead was maybe better.

A cowboy came in not long after they opened up for the day, carrying a well-worn saddle. He brushed a few rain drops off the leather, not bothering about the ones on his shoulders, and jerked his head toward outside, where his horse must be tied up. "That old scrub of mine, he's acting like the rig rubs him somewheres. I'd like you to check for anyplace that needs smoothing. And while I'm not using it, I've been hankering to get a little something put on to fancy it up. Some pattern or other around the edges."

Finch raised his hairy eyebrows. "Don't see the need for such, myself, but you're the one paying. I can get my assistant to take care of it, once I fix what's bothering your horse. Decorating'll cost you . . . ." He fingered his chin and named what sounded to Tom like an ungodly sum. "Can you leave the saddle here until evening?"

The cowboy shrugged. "Expected that. I'll poke around town, cut the trail dust with a drink or two." He turned to leave.

Tom coughed, managing to get the cowboy's attention and turn him around. "Excuse me, sir. Did you have anything in mind for that decoration?"

The cowboy's mouth twitched at the "sir," but he chewed his lip a few seconds and said, "Always liked seeing those feathered headdresses the Indians wear. Think you could do feathers?"

If he could carve a likeness of Jenny and her hair, he should be able to manage feathers. "Reckon so."

Tom had to wait for Finch to be done fixing the underside of the saddle before he could get started. And Finch didn't leave him any too long for it. He passed some of the wait looking at the shape of the saddle and drawing in his head, figuring out where to put bigger feathers and where little ones, where the cowboy's legs would hide the design so it could be simpler and where he'd need to put more detail in. When Finch still wasn't through, Tom fetched the swivel knife again and found a scrap to practice on. Asking Finch would just mean slowing him down, and there wasn't time to spare.

For all that, he managed to put the tool down before Finch straightened up and dusted off his hands. "All right, boy, you can do your fancying up. Can't see why any cowboy worth his salt would want such stuff."

Old moss-back. Tom kept his face blank, not letting it sneer. He fetched the saddle, picked the swivel knife back up, and got to work.

It was near dusk when the cowboy returned, with Tom

still rubbing the oil into the fresh design. He didn't seem too hurried, though, standing behind Tom and watching as the oil made the feathers stand out more. As Tom wiped off the extra oil, the cowboy said, "Now that's right fine. Natural-looking, and not too fussy. I'm much obliged."

Tom ducked his head in a sitting sort of bow. "Likewise, for your saying so."

Finch bustled up with something between a smile and a smirk on his face. "Well, then, you and your horse'll both be happy. Shouldn't be no more chafing from that saddle." He held out his hand as if the cowboy would likely forget to pay him otherwise.

The cowboy paid Finch, hoisted the saddle, and carried it out, stroking the feather design with his finger. Tom faced the back of the shop so Finch wouldn't see the big ol' smile on his face.

Doc Gibbs stopped by the farm while Tom was still wolfing down breakfast, even though it was out of his way, and he brought Mrs. Gibbs along. Seemed like Doc didn't care to wait until Tom happened by the office or the house to check up on him, and of course Mrs. Gibbs was his nurse, or something like. At least the sun was getting up earlier by now, so they wouldn't need lamp light.

Doc looked the stump over for chafed spots, tested how tough the skin had got, and finally said, "This is looking as good as we can reasonably expect. I was wondering, though, whether you've noticed anything *un*expected."

That would've made no sense at all, if that very thing hadn't been happening. "You'll think I'm soft in the head."

Mrs. Gibbs made a sort of snorting sound. "You're anything but that. Please tell us."

Tom took a deep breath and blew it out. "Well, sometimes — more when I'm sitting or lying down, best I can recall — my foot hurts. The one that ain't there! It kind of burns, or throbs, or aches. And there's no way to ease it."

Doc and his missus nodded at each other, and Doc said, "I thought you might be having that sort of problem. It happens more than you'd think. There's a neurologist who came up with a word for it several years back — he calls it 'phantom pain.'"

Doc didn't seem to have any more to say about it, nor his missus either. "I'm guessing this neur — whatever kind of doctor hasn't found a way to fix it."

"I'm afraid not," Mrs. Gibbs said in her straight-ahead way.

Doc said right after, almost as if it were one person still talking, "But we'll keep reading about it, and do some thinking as well, in the hope of finding one."

There was one more thing been happening, but Tom didn't see the point in mentioning it. Even though it drove him even crazier than pain in a foot that wasn't there. How could a foot he didn't have go to *itch*?

Doc put a foot toward the door and then turned round again. "Oh, I almost forgot! That'd never do. Tom, young Jenny greatly admired your portrait of her. She thanks you, and said she's never seen anything so good. And she hopes to see you again."

That was fine to hear. Especially as sometimes, he almost wished he had that picture back again, so's he could look at it and think about her. Especially when he was thinking about her a certain kind of way, at night when everyone else was sleeping sound.

He kept puzzling how he could scrape up the money

to go back to Mamie's place before he grew a whole beard waiting. He didn't feel right about keeping much of his pay, seeing as he could manage so little work on the farm. And it wasn't like he could do a lot of odd jobs around town, even if he had time for such.

Finch really should have passed on what that cowboy paid for the feathers, seeing as Finch probably couldn't've done it himself. But it was a little late to bring that up. Unless . . . that cowboy seemed plenty pleased with the work. He'd likely showed it off to the other cowboys. Maybe some of them would come in for their own decorations. He could talk to Finch now, just in case.

It took him a couple of days to find what felt like the right moment. Finch tended to be sour much of the time, or else impatient and wanting Tom to look busy even when he wasn't. But finally, one afternoon, Finch finished up his dinner and acted especially pleased with it, patting his belly and saying to Tom, "Durned fine cook, my Dolly. You can't deny it, now can you?"

Tom stood up from where he'd been eating and came a little closer. "I never would! She sure is. I'm grateful she brings me such a fine dinner every day." May as well lay it on thick. Finch would eat that up, almost as eager as dinner.

Waiting wouldn't improve his chances. "Mr. Finch, I was thinking back to that saddle the cowboy had me fancy up. If he shows it around, it could bring in more of the same kind of work. And if I do the decorating, which I gather you wouldn't care to, we could —" The words weren't coming easy. "We could maybe split what you charge for the decorating. Between me and you, that is."

Finch brought down his heavy eyebrows and stared at Tom. Then he sat back and chuckled. "Nice try, boy. But I've got plenty else for you to do, that I'm already paying you for."

Which wasn't always true, but it'd hardly help to point that out. Tom stepped back, almost tripping over a bucket and catching himself on the workbench. Finch, for a wonder, acted like he hadn't noticed. And if that weren't surprise enough, he said, slow, making Tom wait for it, "But I could maybe see my way to raising your wages a mite. I took you on for pretty cheap, not knowing just how much use you'd be, but you work hard and get a lot done. I'll give you twenty cents more a day, starting this week. That make you feel better?"

Not only did it make him feel better, it even made him like Finch a little. Until Finch added with that oily leer of his, "And when you save up enough for Mamie's, you give that little gal a big sloppy kiss from me." And on top of that, he winked.

Tom kept his face as blank as he could manage. "Thankee. I'll be getting back to work, then."

He tried to hang onto being glad about getting a raise. But after that crack, it felt kind of like getting paid to listen to Finch's dirty mouth, and put up with whatever came out of it. And money only paid for so much.

Chapter 7

TOM HAD done plenty of waiting while he saved up for another visit to Mamie's. It hadn't occurred to him he might have to wait again when he got there, at least if he wanted Jenny. But that's what Mamie told him. "All the ladies you see would be delighted with your company. But if it's Jenny you're set on, you can relax in one of those easy chairs, or have something at the bar."

He hadn't even known he'd see Jenny, the first time he showed up here. Why not go with someone else this time?

Because he just didn't want to, that's all. He made his way to the bar and asked for a beer.

* * * * *

When she was a little girl and just wanted to lie abed longer instead of getting up for chores, she'd never've believed you could get tired at a job where you lay in bed most of the time. Not that some of the customers didn't rather you were on your knees or pushed up against a wall or standing bent over the bed. Anyhow, she was tired, and the evening barely started.

It perked her right up, though, when she headed downstairs to be on offer and saw Tom at the bar, sitting sideways so's he could keep an eye on the staircase. She had a moment of nerves that someone else'd pick her first, but he caught her eye right off and fairly jumped to his feet.

She was supposed to make a circuit of the room, but she walked right up to Tom instead, holding out her hand and smiling up at him. "I'm sure glad to see you again!"

Tom grinned all over his face as he grabbed her hand and followed her back up the stairs.

She started peeling down as soon as they got to her room, Tom leaning against the wall and watching, eager as could be. After a minute, though — he didn't exactly wince, but he did make a peculiar sort of face, like a horsefly was buzzing around him. She'd better find some way to ease him, or their joining wouldn't be much of a success. "Does your leg hurt?"

Tom shook his head and came out with a little laugh that wasn't too happy. "It's not exactly my leg, and it don't exactly hurt. Ever heard of phantom pain?"

She surely hadn't. "Does that mean *ghosts* hurting folks?"

Now he really laughed, and at her, she supposed, but at least she was cheering him up. "No, it's something that happens to folk with missing parts. The missing piece, like my foot, can hurt just as if it were still there. That happens to me more'n I like, but what's going on now is almost worse. It *itches*. And there's no earthly way to scratch a foot I don't have no more!"

No wonder he made faces. "That's an awful shame."

He came out with that not-really-laugh again. "Sometimes I get so wild with it that I whack the wooden leg, hoping it'll somehow stop the itch, but all it does is make the leg jitter against the stump. Which sometimes does stop the itch along with hurting, but sometimes I'm left with both at once."

She almost asked whether he'd ever scratched the

bottom of the wooden leg, but he'd have mentioned it if he had. But that was giving her some kind of idea, if it'd only stop tickling the edges of her brain and come on out . . . .

* * * * *

Jenny sure was cute when she was thinking hard. Her pointed little nose pointed up more as her forehead wrinkled, and she tilted her head so her hair fell lower across her bosom. He was about ready to reach out for her and pull her close when her face went bright as a lamp. "Oh, that's the thought I was reaching for!" Then she dimmed again and looked a little anxious. "Do you mind trying something that might be kind of silly, and might not help any?"

He'd try most anything if it'd brighten her up again. And it was sweet that she wanted to help. "Sure. Tell me what to do."

"It'd mean . . . you'd need to take off your wooden leg."

That wasn't his favorite idea. "Would you have to look at it — at what's left?"

She chewed her lower lip, which made him want to set aside all this other business and get to kissing her. "We could maybe manage without. You sit on the bed with your back against the headboard and put your legs straight out." She tossed her extra blanket to him. "Then take off the leg under the blanket and put it somewhere you can't see it. And then I'll reach under the blanket and do something, but not touching you. All right?"

It seemed a lot of trouble — for her, anyway — over nothing, but she was the one wanting to do it. He sat down as she'd told him, fumbled around under the blanket to unfasten the leg, and dropped it carefully over the side of the bed. Jenny had turned her back for good measure, so he said, "Ready for — whatever."

"Now don't look."

He shut his eyes, wondering what in tarnation she was up to. The blanket moved on his lap as she did whatever she was doing, rubbing against his crotch and getting him more'n ready for this distraction to be done with.

"You can open your eyes now."

He did as she bid, to see a sight that took his breath. There was something under the blanket where his left leg ended, something shaped almost like his foot that was gone. His throat got tight, and he turned his face away while he got a grip on his feelings.

"All right, then." Jenny sounded excited and nervous both. "I'm going to scratch your right foot." She did as much, showing him plenty of cleavage as she asked, "If you had an itch there, would what I'm doing ease it?"

"I suppose so, but what —"

"Hush. Now keep watching." She reached down again — and scratched the foot-shaped bump under his left knee, just the same way.

And damned if it didn't feel like she was scratching his missing foot!

She let out a trill of a laugh at his expression. "Did it help? Did it really?"

"You! You are some kind of red-headed, warm-blooded, beauty of an angel of a girl, you are. Come here, you!"

He was going to tug the blanket right off, but she got there first and folded it down so it still covered his knees, unbuttoning his pants and lifting up her skirt as she put herself right where he needed her to be.

After an even better time than on his first visit, and after he'd caught his breath, Tom reached down and fetched up his leg. He didn't bother keeping the blanket over him — he didn't so much care any more whether Jenny saw the stump. Once she'd figured that out, she acted curious, watching how he put the leg back on and asking questions. "How long did it take you to learn how to walk with it?"

"It seemed like forever, but it wasn't more'n a few weeks. And now I've got a question. How'd your hair turn color?"

She'd been fluffing out her petticoats, but that made her whip up straight and stare at him. "You'd seen me before?"

"A few weeks ago. I came to town with my pa and was setting in our wagon near the dry good store, waiting for him. You came along, looking finer'n sunrise, but your hair was yellow then." Seeing her fidget, he hurried to say, "Not that I liked that any better. Your hair looks mighty pretty like this. I just didn't know how it happened."

She shrugged her bare shoulders. "'T'ain't magic. Just dye from a catalog. It cost plenty, though, and I'll be paying it off for months yet, I reckon."

He hoisted himself off the bed, came toward her, and curled a lock of her hair around his finger. "I won't say it was or wasn't worth it, seeing as you looked so nice before and after, but it is something special, and it becomes you right well. I've got another question, though — do you get to places like the dry goods store very often? I might be lucky enough to see you there again sometime."

Her lips tightened up like she remembered something that vexed her. "Not so often as I'd like. Mamie keeps us pretty busy."

Tom tried not to dwell on just what she kept busy

doing. "If I recall, it wasn't long after dinner hour. Is that when you're most likely to have time free?"

"Not as much as morning, but sometimes. You work for Finch, don't you? Don't he keep you working, that time of day?"

Seemed like they were thinking along the same lines. "I could maybe work through dinnertime, tell him I had some errand in town to run afterward."

She pulled her hair slowly through his fingers to get loose, still standing close to him. "You could do that next Tuesday, maybe. I'm about out of tooth powder. I could go out to get some, and then remember I had enough after all." She gave him a wink full of mischief. "But where could we meet?"

"I guess sitting in a park would kind of blow up our stories. Is there anywhere you've been hankering to go, but didn't want to go by yourself?"

"Well . . . I have wondered about the saloon down the street. I've peeked in, and it has pretty stained-glass windows."

He couldn't say as he'd noticed, but he didn't doubt her word. And it fit with what he'd been thinking. "We could both aim to be there around one o'clock. And if the other don't show up, we'll know something didn't work out, and not take it ill."

She gave him a quick kiss and stepped back, beaming. "It's a date!" Then, more softly: "My word, it's been a fair time since I said *that*."

Her face looked soft with whatever she was remembering. He reached out and pulled her back, holding her tight, and said in her ear, "What you did for me before — I can't hardly believe it. You must be as clever as you're pretty. Thank you!"

She clung to him, and for some reason she was trembling. She let go and turned part way away, and she sounded choked up as she said, "Goodbye, Tom. I'll be hoping to see you on Tuesday."

He made his way downstairs, so full of different feelings he didn't even try to sort them out, and headed for home, the moon smiling down like it was happy for him.

Chapter 8

MAMIE didn't drink during the busy time of evening, but she'd have a glass of wine once they'd sent the last man home for the night. She'd relax and tell stories, sometimes, about her life and adventures, while those girls as wasn't too tired sat around to listen. Mostly they were stories from when she was a lot younger and wandering from place to place.

But tonight she walked in different, her head making little jerks this way and that like a bothered hen. And all she wanted to tell about was what it was like when Cowbird Creek was getting started.

"Back then, when this was frontier country, there were hardly any women. Back then, all the men — from the roughest cowboy to the best-dressed dandy to the most pompous banker — respected a woman, whatever her profession." She took a swallow of her wine, almost a gulp. "They'd all take their hats off to me in the street, and ask my opinion about what a new building should look like, or beg my help collecting for charity." Another gulp. "Not to mention valuing what we all do here, seeing as there were no wives around to do it — as much as they manage it."

She tossed down the last of the glass and left the room, calling back over her shoulder, "Go to sleep, all of you!" without the little joke or friendly word that usually came with it. Jenny looked around to see if one of the other girls knew what was eating Mamie. Sure enough, Amanda Jane leaned forward and said in a not-very-quiet whisper, "Some stuck-up lady was rude to her in town. Called her a loose woman and a disgrace, and said she shouldn't show her face in daylight among 'decent' women. Mamie was so angry!"

Jenny had never pictured Madam Mamie at a disadvantage. It wasn't a pretty picture to think on. And if the women in town would treat Mamie like that, how would they treat one of Mamie's girls?

She'd been trying not to get nervous about going to meet Tom, but now she was moving past nervous to downright fretful. At least the kind of lady who'd insult Mamie to her face wouldn't dirty herself setting foot in a saloon.

Oh, *blast*. Didn't the saloon keepers have Mamie's brothel tokens to sell to customers? Mamie hadn't put Jenny's likeness on any of those, had she? The ones Jenny'd seen had what looked like Amanda Jane's profile on one side, and "Madam Mamie's" in fancy script on the other . . . . Too late to pick some other place to meet. Mamie probably hadn't thought Jenny looked special enough for a token, anyhow.

She didn't have much choice of what to wear. The clothes she'd brought to town with her had long since been thrown away, and Mamie allowed the girls just one outfit apiece for trips to town. Even those made pretty clear they weren't farmers' wives or merchants' daughters or the like. Mamie didn't believe in wasting a chance to promote what they had on offer. But Jenny could tuck a shawl around her shoulders and hold it closed, even if tomorrow was as warm as today.

And she should be able to sneak out without painting her face. But on the other hand, she did want to look pretty for Tom. She'd just make her eyelashes longer and put some color on her lips. She was excited enough for her cheeks to pink up on their own.

* * * * *

It would be a day when Tom had the dirtiest, smelliest jobs in the shop. But he'd brought a clean shirt with him, to change into out back, and he managed to wash off some of the mess at the pump and comb his hair.

He made a point of getting to the saloon before the time they'd picked, so Jenny wouldn't be sitting on her own and maybe catching some other fellow's eye. That left him sitting with a beer for a few minutes, trying not to drink it down too quick and end up drunk. But she finally came through the door, afternoon sun lighting her hair from behind so it glowed all around her head and shoulders, fair dazzling him.

Her dress looked like the one she'd worn the first day he saw her, not that he had paid much attention to it. It sure wasn't one she'd had on when he saw her at Mamie's, which would have looked pretty strange anywhere else, come to think on it. But from what he could tell under the shawl she was wearing, it still showed enough of her bosom to get him remembering what it felt like to touch her up close. He took another quick drink of his beer and then shoved it aside as he stood up to greet her.

Jenny's smile was different from the one she had at Mamie's, too — sweeter and shyer. She swished her way to the seat next to Tom, sat down, and asked him, "Is there something I can get here that ain't actually booze?"

Tom hadn't spent that much time in places like this, let alone paid attention to what all the men were drinking. "They've probably got some kind of whiskey punch. You could get that without the whiskey. Or I think they'll have lemonade."

Jenny's eyes brightened up like a kid promised a stick of candy. "I'd love lemonade. Mamie don't let no one but customers drink it. Would you order it for me?" She reached into her pocket and brought out a coin. "I can pay —"

He pushed her hand back toward her pocket. "Think I'd let a lady pay for her own drink?"

Jenny looked down into her lap and then back at him. "That's maybe the first time anyone's called me a lady, except with some other word like *little* or *painted* attached to it."

Tom had nothing to say to that, so he ordered her lemonade, glad they actually had it, and gave in to the barkeep's suggestion of a second beer. They sat not saying anything until their drinks showed up, which was more than long enough to make him twitchy. While Jenny took the first sip of her lemonade, he managed to say, "I'm glad you could make it here like we planned. Did you run into any trouble?"

Jenny bit her full lower lip. "Not yet, anyhow." She smiled again, though it seemed to cost her an effort. "I sure was happy to see you setting there."

Now what?

He should find out more about her. He hadn't asked her one thing about herself or her family up to now. He wet his whistle and asked, "Do you have brothers and sisters?"

She got a faraway look as she said, "Three sisters and a brother. I'm the youngest, and my brother come just before me. Mama was always saying how glad she was she didn't have him first, along of how he might've had to go off to war. How about you?"

"A younger brother and sister. Billy and Martha. It's

different being the oldest, and a boy. At least, it was, before —" He trailed off. She'd know what he meant. It should've been Tom taking care of his folks as they got older, and his sister, and being the one his brother looked up to and tried to be like. But that all changed when the plowshare fell.

Jenny put a hand lightly on his arm, then pulled it away as if he might take it wrong. He wished he had the nerve to tell her how good it felt, and that she could leave it there as long as she liked.

She looked down at her lap again and back up. "At least they're hereabouts. I haven't seen my sisters or brother for years now." She didn't mention her folks. Maybe it hurt too much to think of what it'd be like, them seeing her now and knowing how she was living.

She tilted her head and studied him like his face was a book she was reading. "I'd bet you're wondering how I came to the life."

Tom cleared his throat. "Well, I guess I was. Seeing as you're sweet and pretty enough to have your pick of fellows, without . . . going that way. But you don't have to tell me anything you don't want to."

Jenny looked around as if only now thinking she should've been talking more quiet. She dropped her voice to say, "Well, Papa wasn't the best father a girl ever had, by some ways. To put it straight, he was mean as a snake. Weren't many boys who wanted to deal with him. And he couldn't hang onto a dollar, so by the time I come along, there wasn't much I could expect to start out with. And I was eager to get my distance from him and his belt. So when a city slicker come through town and offered to take me with him, so long as I was obliging about my favors, well, it seemed like better'n how things were, or were likely to get by my staying put."

She didn't have more to say about it, seemingly, and he wasn't about to ask her what had happened to the city slicker, where he'd left her or she'd left him, and how she'd gone from obliging one man to obliging many and for pay. And somehow, he'd made it through half his second beer.

Thank the Lord, Jenny took a turn steering the conversation. "Where'd you learn to draw like that? I've never seen the like of that leather picture."

Tom shrugged. "Never learned, just started doing it. Guess I liked to look at the pictures on posters and catalogs and such, and tried making my own. It's nothing special."

She made a cute little huffing noise at him. "Don't you say that! It's plenty special. I'd bet all sorts of folk wish they could do as much." She paused, wrinkling up her forehead and pursing her pretty lips, and then said, "I've got some paper I don't . . . use much. I could give you some, next time I see you, if you wanted something else to draw on."

Tom thought that over for a minute and shook his head. "Thank you kindly, but paper's awful easy to wrinkle up or lose. I like leather, how it sticks around. And I like the way it feels carving at it, how it don't let you through right at once and you have to work at it a little."

"Well, you keep right on doing it, then. There should be some way you can get folks to pay you for it, wouldn't you think?"

He started to tell her about his idea that Finch had shot down, but just then, a big fellow came swaggering up and sat on the stool on Jenny's other side, looking her up and down and getting his eyes stuck on her chest. "What have we here?" He turned to the barkeep and said, "Whyn't you tell me you'd got your own girls now? Are they just for socializing, or will they get more friendly-like?" He leaned close to Jenny, breathing on her.

Jenny flushed and scooted over toward Tom. "Mister, I'm not here for whatever you're thinking. Just meeting a friend for a drink, if it's any of your business."

"Oh, it's my business I'm wanting to give you, sure enough! What's your *friend* got that I don't?"

The barkeep growled at the big fellow, "None of that. We aren't peddling flesh in here. You can go to Mamie's for that." He jerked his chin toward Jenny. "Where I'm thinking you can see this girl again, whenever." And then, to Jenny: "Meanwhile, you just take yourself on out of here. I don't need trouble, not with customers and not with Mamie neither."

Tom stood up, wishing he'd drunk less of that second beer so he'd be less inclined to wobble. "Now see here —"

Jenny caught his arm. "Let's just go. The more of a fuss you make, the more likely I'll be in trouble with Mamie."

Tom gave the barkeep and the big fellow one glower between them, put his arm around Jenny's shoulders, and took her out the door.

Once they'd put some distance between themselves and the saloon, Tom steered her to an out-of-the-way spot behind the barber shop. "What do you want me to do now? I'd like to walk you partway home, but I don't want to make things worse for you."

She gave him a smile that would've been more convincing without her lip trembling. "I'll be fine. Anyhow, it was worth it to sit and talk for a while, without — without anyone expecting something else to be happening. I'd like to do it again, if we can manage it."

He took her hand in both of his. "I'd like that too. And in the meantime, I'd be most happy to come to Mamie's and see you there, if you're still willing."

She sort of laughed in an unhappy way. "There's a

change, someone coming into Mamie's and wondering if I'm willing. But of course I am, or I wouldn't be there, would I?" Then she reached her free hand up to stroke his cheek. "And I will be, when you come."

He let go and stood there, feeling the warm tingle on his cheek where his hand had been and watching her sweet shape as she walked away.

* * * * *

"I swear, I'd take a strap to you if it wouldn't get in the way of you working tonight." Mamie paced back and forth in her office, too riled to sit still, glaring at Jenny with every pass while Jenny clung to the arms of the chair and tried to keep breathing. "Breaking the rules and near starting a riot to boot!"

"Ma'am, it weren't exactly like that —" She faltered to a halt as Mamie's glare got hotter. "I'm sorry, ma'am. I won't do it again. And it didn't lose you Tom's business, as he's planning to come back."

Mamie finally came to a stop and plopped down in her chair. "A good thing too, or I'd be docking your pay to make up the difference. And you can just do without shopping, or setting your foot outdoors for that matter, for the next two weeks, you hear me?"

"Yes, ma'am. May I go, ma'am?"

"Go on, then. Get dressed for customers and get your tail back downstairs."

Jenny fled, creeping away with her shoulders hunched and hoping no one had been listening. She'd been lucky Mamie was too practical to lick her, even with being so mad.

It was just too bad if that taste of freedom had Jenny hankering for more.

When Jenny got to the second floor, the two newest girls were leaning over the banister waiting for her, together as usual. They'd come to Mamie's as a pair after traveling for something like five years and through maybe seven different towns. There'd been plenty of whispering about just what kind of friends they were and what they got up to together, not that Jenny cared, except she was kind of curious about what two women would do to make each other feel good. Just now, Sophie was grinning and Bessie was smirking, but not in a mean way.

Bessie talked first, as she tended to. "Well, how bad was it? Did she just scold, or did she whip you?"

Jenny headed on into her room, knowing the two of them would follow and not minding the company. "She said she would've if it wouldn't stop me working."

Sophie cackled. "Hell, it wouldn't stop me! Plenty of times I've laid on my back with my rump just warmed. I kind of like it." She winked at Bessie, who tilted her head and wagged her finger. Then the two of them blew kisses at her and sashayed off to Bessie's room, where Sophie seemed to stay whenever she wasn't working.

Jenny trudged on into her room and sat heavy on the bed, wondering. What'd it be like to travel around like that, with a friend who'd have your back and cheer you up when you needed it? The thought appealed, but there wasn't a girl at Mamie's she could picture doing it with. And just thinking about it made her lonely. Which she'd maybe been feeling already, but hadn't known it.

Whatever else they were to each other, Sophie and Bessie acted sort of like sisters. Jenny could remember horsing around with her own sisters, and how she'd taken it for granted, having them around to play with and talk to and just sit with. When she left town, she'd hardly thought about missing them.

But oh, how she missed them now.

Chapter 9

TOM'S OWN groan woke him up. The sticky feel of his sheets woke him the rest of the way.

No surprise that he'd dreamed about Jenny. Who else could he have that kind of dream about? And it wasn't like he'd done her wrong by dreaming about her doing what she'd actually done, with him and who knows how many others. But it felt wrong, all the same. Like taking advantage.

Would it be better if he pictured the two of them somewhere else? Off by themselves on the prairie, maybe, at sunrise. Making love, just because they both wanted to. He could see it all plain . . . and it led to the same ending, but with him awake the whole time and helping things along.

After, he lay in bed panting until his heart slowed down. But his imagination wasn't through with Jenny, seemingly, even though he didn't need to picture any more sex. It wandered off to the sort of place he might have seen her if they'd met, really met, some other way. In the dry goods shop, going through fabrics for a dress, her forehead wrinkled up like it had been before she got that amazing idea to help his itching. Or what she'd look like if she were just another farm girl, churning butter, her chest bouncing as she worked . . . no, he didn't want to go that direction.

He hauled himself out of bed, even though it was early for it. His heart was beating fast again, and he could feel the pulse of it in his stump. He waited, thinking about cold baths, and about staring at a cow rump and milking, until his heart slowed down. When it finally did, he checked the cloth on his stump — still clean enough — and scooted to the side of the bed where he could reach the wooden leg.

Heading to the pump to wash his face, he got to wondering if he could ever find a way for Jenny and his folks to meet each other. Not that it made much sense thinking about that, not unless he was hoping to keep seeing her outside of Mamie's, and he didn't even know how much hell she'd caught about the last time.

Had Pa ever seen her, in town or . . . did Pa ever go to Mamie's? He'd never thought of him doing that. And he didn't much like the taste of the idea. If it was something lots of husbands did, or even most of them, wouldn't Pa have mentioned it? Or maybe he'd been waiting until Tom starting seeing some girl and courting her. Which hadn't happened before everything changed.

Did Pa figure Tom'd never have a girl of his own? Would he be glad or sorry to know what Tom was doing instead?

Doc Gibbs looked mighty serious as he peered at Tom's stump. "Looks like you've been standing and walking too much, or not changing the sock enough, or doing something else to irritate this. Maybe squatting down and standing up? Does Silas make you pick things up and carry them very often?"

Tom looked away. "Not all that often." Probably more often than Doc would approve of, but that wasn't the only reason the stump had got sore. Tom had been volunteering to do jobs like that. And he'd been trying to work standing up, so he wouldn't look lazy.

It maybe didn't make a lot of sense, given that Finch knew his condition and took Tom on anyway. And it wasn't as if it mattered that much what the customers thought. But he kept picturing Jenny watching him, and looking sorry for him when he spent too long sitting down or let Finch do the sort of things an assistant should do. And he didn't want her feeling sorry for him.

Now Doc was studying Tom's face instead of his leg. "I hope you'll understand why I'm asking — has any of what's been irritating your leg, ah, taken place at Mamie's?"

Now *that* might've been more worthwhile. "No, Doc, nothing like that. In fact . . . ." Somehow he found himself spilling the tale about the saloon, and how nice it'd been and then how wrong it'd gone.

When he'd finished, Doc said, "I'll be back there in a week or so for the ladies' usual checkups. I could find out whether Jenny suffered any ill consequences when Madam Mamie found out — as I'm pretty sure Mamie would have, and not long afterward. Would you like me to inquire?"

"Yessir, please. It was my idea as much as hers, and I'd hate to think Mamie came down hard on her."

Doc had got a sort of gleam in his eye. "Your idea as much as hers, was it? That suggests, it seems to me, that it was her idea as much as yours."

He supposed so. And it felt good to remember as much.

The next week somehow lasted twice as long as usual before Joshua finally caught up with Tom on his walk home and brought him up to date. "Mamie wasn't too harsh with the young lady over that escapade of yours, but she's keeping her indoors for a while, and I'd expect she'll continue to watch her closely. I don't think you'd better plan any more sneaking around, not if you want her to remain employed."

Tom had his mixed feelings about that, seeing as what her employment meant, but he could hardly wish her left high and dry. It wasn't as though he could provide for her. He forced out a few words of thanks and headed home in no good humor.

Now he wouldn't even be able to catch sight of her in town.

* * * * *

It might've been the longest two weeks since Jenny was a little girl longing for her birthday. Cooped up all day, whether working or not, and no more fresh air than she could sniff up through the window. Other girls were nice about fetching her things, but then she had to see them come back in smelling of spring and sunshine.

And when she finally could go out again, Mamie still didn't trust her on her own, seemingly. She made a point of sending one of the older girls along with her to keep her out of trouble. And not all of them was exactly patient about it.

Jenny didn't like sulking, and she tried not to do it, but Mamie did catch her at it sometimes, and didn't seem real sure what to do about it. One time she'd lecture, and another time she'd try to cheer Jenny up somehow. The worst was when she made a point of sending Jenny up with a slick sort of fellow Mamie said knew plenty about pleasing a woman. Mamie wasn't to know how much the fellow put Jenny in mind of the bastard from the big city who'd come and coaxed Jenny away from home, and then left her broke and stranded in Des Moines. Not just because they looked kind of alike, but because that fellow had been plenty good in the sheets. He might not have meant to, but he'd tricked her into thinking she could make a living on her back and enjoy it as often as not. She'd sure found out different, when he was long gone.

And anyhow, it didn't take clever and fancy to make a woman feel good. Sometimes all it took was young and strong and eager, and eager to please, and smelling nice.

She didn't know just why Tom smelled so good to her, but he did. Sometimes she woke up and knew she'd dreamed of him, just along of the smell lingering as she shook off sleep.

And what was even stranger and more of a nuisance, sometimes when a customer nothing like Tom did get her to enjoy herself, she still wished he was Tom.

She'd got herself all mixed up and turned around, sure and certain.

Chapter 10

TOM LIKED working with leather, even when he didn't have anything that interesting to do. And he knew he should be grateful to have any kind of job. And he needed to keep saving money, seeing as he couldn't take over the farm when Pa got too old, and he'd be damned if he'd live there as useless as a dried-out cow. But some days, seemed like if he had to look at Finch's face one more time or jump to it when Finch ordered him around, he'd blow up like a pile of gunpowder and take the whole shop with him, leather and all.

At least he'd saved up enough to go see Jenny again, along with what he'd put by for he didn't know what. By this time, Mamie should know not to point any of the other girls his way.

He'd built up such a need that he grabbed Jenny almost the second they got to her room, and didn't slow down enough to be too gentle neither. She didn't seem to mind, though, and they had a fine tumble. And after, she said, "There's no need to go down again right away. Mamie doesn't have to know we finished so quick. I bet you'll be good to go again in a few minutes, and we can talk meanwhile."

He sat up and pretended to take off the hat he'd already hung on the hook near the door. "Thank you most kindly, ma'am."

Not that he knew what to talk about. He couldn't see asking her how her day was going, nor her work. And his own day had been mainly irksome. Which did lead him to think on something he'd had running through his head lately. "I've been wondering whether I maybe could go for a cowboy after all. It don't take a foot to ride, not really. And I'm good with horses. And just about all I want these days is not to stay in one place. I feel like I might go plumb crazy when I think about being in this town all my born days."

A sort of shadow passed over Jenny's face. Before he could ask about it, she glanced at his leg and back up. "Tom . . . do you really think that'd work? I don't know much about what cowboys do every day, but don't the horses have to zig-zag around a lot, real fast? Wouldn't that mean chafing where your stump and the wood come together? And what if you had to jump off the horse sudden, and maybe jar things loose? Or if you rode without the leg, how could you put it on in a hurry? And —"

He was on his feet, and glaring at her. "That's plenty of if and maybe and how! I should've known a girl wouldn't understand. So what if it's maybe tough?" Now she was looking hurt, but not as hurt as he was mad. "What's the last tough thing you did, anyhow?"

Jenny jumped to *her* feet and put her fists on her hips, which he couldn't help but find distracting, full and curvy as they were. "*I* should've known no *man* would have the faintest notion of what's tough for a woman! You want I should tell you every hard or nasty thing I've had to do today already? Or all this week?"

"Hell, no! You picked this life, didn't you? I didn't decide one fine day to have my leg cut off!"

Turned out she could out-glare him, and by quite a margin. "You get on out of here! You've had what you paid for, now get!"

"I'm getting! And I don't know as I'll be coming back, either!" He stomped toward the door and made it through the doorway before realizing he'd forgot his hat. He had to turn back for it, trying not to look at Jenny to see if she was laughing at him. Hat finally in hand, he slammed the door behind him, and then hurried downstairs as fast as he could manage before Mamie could catch him and give him what for.

This sure wasn't how he thought he'd be feeling about now. And on top of all that, he'd paid plenty to feel so chapfallen.

Tom stretched out to stroke Cochise's back with the grooming brush. "I shouldn't've hollered at her like that. And I sure shouldn't've thrown her work up to her. She's got every right to hate me now, and to never want me near her again."

Cochise nudged Tom with his nose and turned his neck so Tom could scratch him in his favorite place. Tom obliged and went back to brushing.

"She didn't say no more'n the truth. And she probably wouldn't've said as much if she didn't care what happens to me."

Cochise blew out softly, sending a little drool Tom's way.

"I can just see me, trying to put my leg on from horseback and falling right off. You'd turn around and laugh at me if you was there, I reckon."

He was about done grooming the horse, but he kept brushing and talking anyhow. Cochise didn't seem to mind.

"How can I tell her I'm sorry, if I can't even go there — or anywhere else — to see her? Think she'd read a note if I wrote one and got someone to take it to her, like Doc?"

Cochise reached down for some hay to snack on.

"If she was a girl down the road somewhere, I could take her some flowers. I remember once when Ma was mad at Pa about something, and he figured she had a right to be, he went and picked some real pretty flowers. Don't recall how much difference they made, but they couldn't've hurt."

Cochise munched his mouthful of hay.

Tom's arm was getting tired. He dropped the brush and leaned against Cochise's warm side, taking some kind of comfort from the horse's breathing. "Even if I wanted to give Doc flowers to take to her, they'd likely wilt by the time she got 'em. And everyone there would see him carry 'em in, and think who knows what. But . . . if I could get ahold of some more leather, I could draw flowers for her. That'd last better, and she'd know I put some time into it. And she liked the picture on leather, before. Maybe it'd remind her of that."

Cochise had had enough of being a leaning post, seemingly. He twitched like he was throwing off a horsefly. Tom scratched his neck one more time and stood up. "Guess I'd better ask Pa if he has any leather to spare, this time. And then ask Doc whether he'd mind, before I take the trouble."

Pa had some old leather leggings — and how he'd come by those, Tom'd love to hear some time — that Ma didn't like him to wear no more. "You'd be giving me a way to give her what she wants without saying so. I'd be obliged."

Tom left early for town the next morning and stopped at Doc's town office, it being one of Doc's days to be there if not called away. The office was still closed when Tom got there, and he was turning away when Doc hustled up. "Sorry, Tom! It's harder to get out the door than it used to be, when I was a bachelor with only Major to stay and talk to."

Tom looked him over. Doc had maybe put on some weight, whether from being married or just getting oldish. He and Mrs. Gibbs seemed to take care of each other pretty well.

Doc opened up the office, still talking. "So how can I help you this morning?" He looked at Tom and must have figured something out, as he said, "Is it doctoring you need, or some other assistance? I'm happy to help with either."

Tom stammered out his problem. Doc listened and nodded and looked serious, except once in a while his mouth twitched a little. "I'd be happy to be your courier once again, and I think it's as good a plan as any."

As he opened his mouth to thank Doc yet again, Doc added, "My friend Robert told me once that different flowers mean different things. If you like, I can try to find out what sort of flowers convey an apology. Though that might just complicate things for you as an artist. And I doubt the young lady will care greatly about the point."

Which was a kind way of saying Jenny wouldn't know the difference. "I reckon not. Thank you anyway. For the thought, and for helping."

Now he just had to find the swivel knife, or something else he could carve with on leather.

He spent the hours at Finch's puzzling on what to do, all the while he did his usual work — soaked and scraped hides, and traced the shape of one half of a shoe onto another piece of leather and then cut it to match. What he needed, really, was for Finch to do him a favor. And unless you were Mrs. Finch or little Hope, it wasn't real likely that Finch would do anything of the kind.

It was getting on for late afternoon, and even Mrs. Finch's generous-sized dinner felt like a long-ago memory, when he realized he'd got it wrong. Finch looked at most things in terms of money. How could he make it worth Finch's while to let Tom use the swivel knife once in a while?

Of course, he'd have to pay him, or owe him, or (he winced) take less in pay.

That'd mean longer stretches between visits to Mamie's. But the way things stood, he'd got no reason to go there anyhow. At least if he could make the flower picture and if Jenny liked it, that might change. And if he kept on using his head, he might be able to come up with ways of making money he hadn't thought of yet.

When Tom headed home that day, he did so with a sight less coin in his pocket than he'd planned on the day before. And with the swivel knife, its sharp edges wrapped in a scrap of waste leather, in the other.

Finch had listened to Tom's proposal with a particularly satisfied smirk on his plump face. "Happens I ordered a new one of those a few weeks ago, and it just came yesterday. Maybe I didn't mention. It never hurts to have two of something, even if I don't use it all that often. But I suppose I could let you borrow it sometimes, if you'll take less pay in exchange. Or for a little more, you could have it outright, so long as I can borrow it back if need be."

It was powerful tempting, the idea of having the swivel knife to take home and use whenever he wanted. Without Finch looking over his shoulder and tossing out his opinions, or interrupting him, or maybe jostling him so his hand slipped. "All right, then. That last thing you said."

And now, if he didn't mind staying awake and working by lamplight, he could get started on making Jenny some flowers pretty enough to change her mind.

Chapter 11

"COME ON in, Jenny! You're the last girl Mamie's sent up, so we'll have a while to chat."

Jenny remembered when Doc might have done more than chat when his work with the girls was done. Not that he'd ever picked her. If she was guessing, she'd guess she was a mite too young for him to've felt right about it.

He was looking her up and down now, but not with any desire behind it. "You seem more tired than usual. And I haven't seen that pretty smile yet."

She did her best to conjure one up, little as she felt like it. He was right about her being tired. She'd been sleeping more restless than usual, and the daily grind (now that made her want to giggle after all, for just a second) like to wore her out these days (there she went again!).

She'd made a point of not wondering why, not that it'd take much wondering. For some damn reason, she'd been missing that thickheaded dolt of a farm boy. Where had she got the notion he could cheer her up, when he'd riled her so much the last time he'd been?

Doc went on with her checkup, listening to her heart and her breathing with that funny snaky earpiece of his, along with taking a good close look at her lady parts. He finally straightened up and said, "You're just fine, and I'll tell Mamie so."

She thought he'd leave, but instead he stood there with

his eyes twinkling. Before she could ask why, he pulled out a leather scroll that looked a whole lot like when he'd given her Tom's picture. Had Tom done another one? Maybe one where she didn't look so pretty, or had her mouth open hollering at him?

She took it kind of cautious, studying Doc's face to see if he already knew what was in it. He didn't give her any more clues, though, so she went ahead and unrolled it.

It wasn't a picture of her. To her mind, it was prettier — a bouquet of all sorts of flowers, flowers you'd never see all together given they bloomed at different times. Black-eyed Susans, coneflowers, Lenten roses, bluebells, asters, all tied together with a big carved bow. She could almost see the colors and smell the scents.

Jenny's jaw dropped open in a way that'd make Mamie scold something fierce, if any customer was to see it. Doc came as close as he ever did to grinning. "It's a nice picture, isn't it?"

Jenny closed her mouth. "Yessir, it surely is."

"And it must have taken him quite a while to make it, I should think."

Jenny tried to imagine making anything of the kind. "I guess it must've." Remembering the way she'd railed at Tom, she had to add, "I wouldn't've expected him to take so much trouble."

Doc sat on the bed like he figured he was going to stay a while. "Tom told me you quarreled the last time he was here. That you were quite angry with him. Are you still?"

Jenny looked inside, trying to answer him. "I don't rightly know. I was, before you gave me this. But truth to tell, I guess I was trying to stay mad. Because — what good does it do me to think kindly of him? He don't come here often."

"Well, Mamie's fees are something of an extravagance for a young man like Tom. And I gather he took a pay cut in order to obtain the swivel knife to make this carving, not considering it feasible to keep using one of Finch's."

She thought she might cry, and bit her lip to stop it. Which might not be such a good idea if her next customer felt like kissing. "And I can't go nowheres else to see him, not after the last time. Mamie'd toss me out for sure."

Doc's lips went tight. For a second, Jenny thought she'd said something to bother him, but then she realized he was probably annoyed he couldn't fix everything wrong in her life. He was that sort of man. He got over it, for now anyway, and asked, "Do you have any message for me to give to Tom?"

Jenny tried to think of something fitting, and to hurry up about it before Doc had to get going. "Please tell him — that this is a right pretty picture, and I thank him for it, and I'll be looking at it often. And that I'll be glad to see him again, whenever." She gave Doc a smile as close to her usual as she could manage. "And thank you, Doc, for bringing this, and for taking messages and things back and forth like you've been doing."

Doc patted her hand this time as he headed out the door. "You're most welcome, my dear. Now I hope you'll be getting some sleep to put the roses back in your cheeks."

"Yessir, I'll try."

Doc closed her door behind him. She should go downstairs. Mamie would be expecting Jenny to get right back to work. But she stole herself a couple of minutes looking at the flowers, tracing the lines Tom had carved. When she got too nervous stalling, she kissed the biggest flower and then squeezed the leather to her chest before she tucked it under her pillow, heaved a big sigh, and walked slowly to the stairs.

Mamie's didn't close on Sundays, but not too many customers came in, so Mamie let the girls take turns taking the day off. Most of the lucky ones would get together in the small lounge, the one Mamie only used for customers when things got specially busy, with a bottle of whatever wine Mamie let them have. They'd tell tales or, if someone was feeling generous, share a few tricks they'd picked up. It was the sort of thing she'd never seen at the other houses she'd had to work at, where the girls treated each other like competition and sniped at each other every chance they got. Not long after she arrived, Jenny had got up the nerve to ask Mandy about it, and Mandy had told her it was Mamie's doing. "She says life's too short to put up with any more squabbling than necessary, and if a girl looks to be a troublemaker, out she goes." Jenny hadn't exactly needed the warning, but she'd appreciated it all the same.

Tonight, Lucette had something new to share, a book of smutty limericks a friend had sent her from wherever home was. She read a few, her accent making an odd fit with the words so they was even funnier.

"There was a young man of Peru
who had nothing whatever to do
so he took out his carrot
and buggered his parrot
and sent the result to the zoo!"

Jenny had heard tell of zoos. She'd surely love to see one, sometime, somehow. And wherever Peru was, that'd be worth seeing too. Not that she ever would. She pushed down the pain that came with knowing as much, while the other girls begged Lucette for another.

After a few more, most mentioning more far-off places

and some using words Jenny couldn't make head or tail of, Lucette tossed the book aside and the talk turned to each girl's worst and best customers. Amanda Jane tended to have the best of the best and the worst of the worst, 'cause Mamie knew she could satisfy the uppity and also handle the ornery. Mandy could do impressions, and the way she strutted around with her belly pushed forward and her chin doubled up brought the mayor's brother to life just as if he'd walked in and interrupted them. When they'd done laughing and clapping, Mandy pointed to Jenny. "How about you, young 'un?"

Jenny never much liked having her nose rubbed in how young she was, and Amanda Jane wasn't the only girl who did it, but it wasn't a time to be quarrelsome. She plucked at her chin, thinking, and said, "The worst lately would be that fellow on his way east, who struck it rich mining for gold. All that gold, and he can't buy hisself a new suit of clothes, or a shave, or a bath! And not that I was hankering to see all of him, but it would've been better than those clothes stiff and stinking with sweat rubbing on me, and his breath that could kill a mule 'til I thought I'd die right there under him."

The girls let loose with their cusses and other reactions. Sophie and Bessie, who somehow always managed to be off on the same nights, leaned forward together, Bessie saying, "And the best?"

Jenny opened her mouth and closed it again, holding back the name that wanted to pop out. She chewed her lip and said, "Oh, that'd prob'ly be the lawyer who just come through town. Now *he'd* troubled to buy a new suit not long since, and smelled of something I'd fair like to try for myself. And he spoke purty, all polite."

They went round the circle from her, and when they'd

all had their say, they straggled on out and upstairs. Jenny wasn't sure what to expect when Sophie and Bessie caught up to her on the stairs, one on each side, and stuck with her all the way to her room. She'd no special wish to be on her own, though, so she let them come in and close the door.

They tugged her onto the bed with them and made themselves comfy, Bessie sitting tailor fashion and Sophie lying down with her arms and legs sprawled out and her head on the pillows. Jenny sat up next to where Sophie was lying, leaning against the headboard, and waited for whatever they had in mind. It didn't take long. Bessie waggled a finger at her and said, "Jenny Hayes, I do believe you *lied* downstairs. And on the Lord's Day, too!"

Jenny turned away and hugged her knees. She might just as well have confessed outright. Sophie rolled over to her and poked her in the ribs. "All right, then, talk!"

Bessie piped up, "It's that big blond farm boy, isn't it? The one with the wooden leg —" Jenny turned back to face both girls, her face getting hot, but Bessie held up her hand to stop Jenny interrupting. " — and all them lovely muscles in his arms and . . . where else, Jenny?"

Jenny let a grin take over her face and started counting on her fingers. "Lessee now, there's his shoulders . . . and his back . . . and his legs . . . and his backside . . . ."

Both girls squealed, and Sophie said, "You sure you ain't paying him, instead of the other way round?"

Not that Tom was exactly paying her. Mamie was the one taking in the money. Though Jenny would have felt pretty bad taking money right from Tom's hand, at that.

Bessie leaned across to pat Jenny's hand. "Well, you have all the fun you can with that young stud. Just don't you go taking it serious. You're young, but not too young to know that much, I hope."

Jenny started to sigh and managed to turn it into a yawn. "I'm ready for bed." Sophie snickered. Jenny gave her a light slap on the arm and said, "To *sleep*, you! I'll see you both in the morning."

Bessie cocked her head and looked at her in a way that made plain she'd noticed Jenny not answering her question. But she slid on off the bed, crooking her finger for Sophie to follow, and the two of them left Jenny's room and went down the hall. She could hear them whispering to each other as she closed the door.

Chapter 12

IT WASN'T nothing but some fruit. Nothing special, really. And nothing Mamie's cook hadn't served before. Just stewed plums.

Jenny must be feeling specially tender-hearted this morning, was all she could figure. Else she wouldn't be eating the plums with tears trickling down her face. Or maybe she was getting her monthly, which'd make her get worked up easier. It was just about time.

It would've been worth crying over nothing, if only her monthly meant a vacation. But Mamie always said, "Every single girl in this place has her bleeding time every single month, and I don't plan to go broke over it. There's plenty the gentlemen'll like without needing to spread your legs." So if someone asked for a girl during that time, Mamie would offer the choice of that girl using just her mouth or her hands and showing off whatever part of her body they'd like to see, or some other girl ready for more. . . .

It wasn't as if Mama's stewed plums would've won prizes. The cook's were as good or better.

But when they didn't have much of it, Mama always used to share it with Jenny, who liked it best of all the children, even though she figured out as she got older that Mama liked it even better.

Jenny finished her breakfast as fast as she could and hurried upstairs. It was time to get herself dressed and prettied up. But maybe she could squeeze out a few minutes to do something she hardly ever tried to do.

She closed her door, wishing it had a lock on it, and tried to remember where she'd put pen and paper. In the little drawer in her dressing table? Nope. How about under her unmentionables? Not there, neither. Finally she found them on the closet shelf. But all that looking had left her even less time to spare.

She sat at the dressing table with the paper in front of her, chewing on her pen, for a precious half a minute before writing out, slow and careful, *Dear Mama and* —

Which of her sibs would still be at home, and which would've married and set up housekeeping somewhere else? No way of knowing.

Would Papa even let Mama have the letter? She could hope so. And if he didn't like it, she was way away out of his reach.

Dear Mama and all of you —
I hope you are well. I am fine.
I hope the grasshoppers didn't eat up everything on the farm, like happened some places, though not here.

Should she tell where here was?

I am in Nebraska, in a town some bigger'n any near you. I get to meet lots of folks.

And she'd be trampled by horses before she said how. Not that Mama wouldn't have written her off as a tramp long since, most like.

There she went crying again. And leaving teardrops on the paper. Maybe they'd tell her tale more than she could ever stand to do.

I'm sorry I left so sudden.

She shoved herself back from the chair before the tears, coming fast now, could smudge what she'd worked so hard to put on the paper.

Amanda Jane called from outside the room, knocking heavy on the door, "Jenny! Aren't you ready yet?" Jenny startled and jumped out of the chair, almost knocking it over, and opened her mouth to say not yet — but glory be, there was that heavy feeling below her belly, just when she needed it. She opened the door, glad now for the tears on her cheeks. "My monthly's coming on. I'll get dressed real quick, but would you tell Mamie for me?"

Amanda Jane gave her an up-and-down inspection and seemed satisfied. "I'll do that, but don't you keep her waiting." She closed the door, not quite slamming it but making it bounce a little. Jenny picked up the paper by its edges, slid it into the drawer, dropped the pen in, and fair ran to her closet, grabbing the dress easiest to put on in a hurry.

She made it downstairs to see Mamie tapping her foot and holding her pocket watch. "About time, girl!" She shoved Jenny towards a fellow as thin as a rail with a balding head and a sallow complexion, saying in her smooth way, "Here's the girl I was mentioning. If you like her, she'll make you happy in any of the ways I told you about."

The fellow looked her over in a way that reminded her of Amanda Jane just now, except for the leer twisting his mouth up toward his long skinny nose. He didn't waste words on her, just grabbed her hand, *sniffed* it, and tugged her toward the stairs.

* * * * *

Tom had been resigned to a longish dry spell as far as getting to Mamie's was concerned. It was harder to think of than it would've been before he learned what he'd been missing. So it came as a real nice surprise when the bank manager's wife picked up the shoes he'd helped make, not that he'd done that much to them, and gave him a tip before she left. The size of it made Tom's eyes bug out and Finch's go narrow. The old skinflint was probably wondering how he could make Tom turn it over. Tom closed his hand tight around the coins, making a fist all the while he kept his expression casual, and Finch gave a snort and turned away.

Tom had taken to carrying some jerky every day, so he wouldn't forget and find himself with nothing to hold him if he had a reason — well, it was only one reason, so far — to stay in town. He tore at it with his teeth as he quick-stepped to Mamie's the minute Finch locked up the shop. But when Mamie saw him, she looked somehow like she had news he mightn't welcome. "Oh, Tom! How lovely to see you again. If it Jenny you're here for, she's, ah, not quite as usual just now. You know, don't you, about how ladies have a certain time of month when they're somewhat . . . indisposed?"

Tom hoped he wasn't blushing. "Yes'm, I do." He'd picked up that info from having a sister. He supposed it was the same for Ma, not that he cared to think on that. The whole business didn't make a lot of sense to him, not in people. When a mare or a dog bitch came into season, you'd want some sign of it so you could breed them or keep them from breeding, whichever suited, but a woman could breed any time, so what exactly did it signify?

"You can still spend time with her, of course. There's plenty she can do to make you feel good. You can ask about what you'd like and see if she can oblige, or she can explain to you what services she can provide. Of course, you may see one of the other girls if you'd prefer."

Tom cast his eyes around the room, just in case there

was someone who somehow outshined Jenny. Nope. "I'll go with Jenny, ma'am."

Mamie smiled brightly at him. "Lovely! Jenny, come here and say good evening to Tom. You'll take good care of him, won't you?"

Jenny'd already been on her way over. She reached them and said, "Of course, ma'am." She looked a mite pale. Well, if he'd been bleeding for maybe days, he'd look plenty pale himself. He sent a quick prayer up to Heaven thanking the Lord for sparing him such.

Jenny moved a little slow as she led Tom up the stairs and to her room. When she'd closed the door, she took his hand and said, kind of shy, "That was a beautiful picture you made. You're a real artist."

That was a label he'd want to take out later and look at. But he had something he'd better say right off. "I'm sorry I shot off my mouth last time I was here. I — I was hateful, and I'd no call for it."

She looked down at her feet. "I said too much, at that. I'm sorry too. Can we let bygones be bygones, then?"

Tom felt a load most as heavy as Cochise lift off him. "We sure can."

Jenny looked happier too. "I'm glad. So now, what would you like? There's lots we haven't done yet that I can still do. Show you some things you might like later, even after I'm done with . . . you know."

Tom felt his eager part getting more so at the idea, but he'd decided something on the way upstairs and meant to stick to it. "That sounds a real treat, but you could show me those things any time, I reckon. I was thinking that today, you could take it easy, and we could just talk for a spell, like we did at the saloon before things got out of hand."

Jenny stared at him like he'd started speaking Chinese.

"You'd *pay* Mamie? Just to sit and talk?"

Something about how startled she was made him want to put an arm around her, but she'd likely take it as his changing his mind. "I'll pay to sit and talk to *you*. Seeing as that's the only way to do it, the way things are."

Jenny got tears in her eyes, as Tom gulped and wondered what he'd done wrong and how he could fix it. She must have read his face, because she laughed through her tears and said, "Don't be worrying! Girls cry easy when they've got their monthlies, at least plenty of us. Now you just sit yourself down right there." She pointed to the chair in the corner. He sat, expecting her to perch on the bed, but she startled him considerable by plopping herself down on his lap. She laughed again at his expression. "You don't mind, do you? It's cozier this way."

Sure it was, but he was trying to be a gentleman, and her warm round rump on his lap wasn't helping any. What did help a little, in a weird kind of way, was . . . up close like this he could tell she smelled different from usual, probably blood and whatever she used to soak it up. Still, he'd better get to talking, if he could think of even one thing to talk about.

How about her sibs? "You said you had three sisters and a brother? What're their names?"

That was the wrong question, seemingly. Jenny sighed, her bosom pressing into his chest. "My little brother's called Joey, after our pa. And the other girls —" Her lip started trembling, and she bit it.

He put his arm around her, trying for just enough of a squeeze to give some comfort. "Never mind that. I'm sorry I made you homesick. How about — Mamie's pleasant to folks who come here. How is she with you girls? Is she nice or mean?"

Jenny managed a smile, though kind of a shaky one. "Oh, she's all right. I've seen — that is, she could be a lot meaner. Though I've seen her not so much mean as cold, cold as a blizzard." Jenny huddled up in his lap like she was taking shelter there. "That's if one of the girls steals something from a customer. That's the worst. Other'n that, well, she's got her rules, and she can get riled if you break any. Like I did, going out to meet you. She locked me up good and proper for a while."

"I'm sorry I helped get you in trouble. What other rules has she got?"

Jenny pursed her lips, looking so cute he'd have grinned if it wouldn't interrupt her. "Well, you noticed one thing right off, about my teeth. She makes sure we keep our teeth clean, even though —" She made a face — " — it means we smell and taste the customers' breath more, and some of 'em, the older ones and the lazy ones, have breath that'd drop a goat."

He laughed at that, which had the effect of pressing her backside against him more, so he stopped. "What else?"

"Well, you might think our dresses show a lot of us, but there's plenty of girls here who'd show more if Mamie didn't say no to it. She says she aims to run a classy place, and skirts up to the hip or bubbies hanging all the way out ain't classy. And we have to eat everything on our plates, because men don't come here for no skinny girls with bony ribs."

Tom was plumb out of questions. Jenny waited for one and then, he guessed, gave up, asking, "How about Mr. Finch? What's he like to work for?"

He'd better tread careful, even though Jenny might not be one to gossip. "What do you know of him? He comes here, don't he?"

She wrinkled her nose. "He used to. Not lately, though, not since he got married."

That was decent of Finch, Tom supposed. And good news for Mrs. Finch. But — wait just a damn minute! "Are you saying he never came in a few weeks back? And — spent time with you?"

Jenny shook her head, red curls flying. "I'd've remembered. He *sweats*, more'n most. I had to send what I was wearing to the laundry ahead of usual." She wrinkled her nose even harder. "If he'd paid for me to strip naked, I'd've had to have a bath right after, in the middle of the busiest time, and explain it to Mamie. Don't know which of us she'd've been madder at."

Those words put such different pictures in Tom's head that he didn't know how to corral them. Finch, sweating and probably grunting like a hog on top of Jenny. Jenny, naked, all her warm soft curves there for him to look at as well as touch. That last was almost enough to make him forget —

Finch had *lied* to him, or at least squeezed the truth all out of shape, just to bedevil him.

Tom's fists clenched so tight his hands started shaking. "You want to know what kind of man Finch is to work for? Well, he's a snake, is what he is — a lying, black-tongued skinflint of a snake." And how Tom was to go to work tomorrow and not strangle the son of a bitch, he couldn't hardly think on.

Jenny put a hand on Tom's cheek. "I'm right sorry to hear that. Isn't there any other work you could do, to get shut of him?"

Tom just barely managed not to snap at her. "You recall I'm not a whole man, don't you? Can't even stand up for long without my stump hurting like thunder. Can't move quick without taking a chance on sprawling on the floor." He looked around the room. "Hell, couldn't even be a bouncer at this place, along of any man with two good legs could flatten me in no time. And I don't read and write well enough for a clerk, even if I could stand to sit at some desk all day and peer at paper. What else am I supposed to do?"

Jenny didn't have an answer for that, or so he thought. But after sitting quiet for a couple of minutes, she sat up straighter and said with some energy behind it, "What about the way you make pictures on leather? Those flowers were so pretty, any girl'd be glad to have something like. And didn't you tell me you put some fancy design on a cowboy's saddle?"

He could still see that saddle as clear as if it were lying on Jenny's bed. "I sure did. Feathers. And he was right pleased with it. But Finch don't want me trying to get more of that work. I asked." And anyway, he'd still be working for Finch, having to listen to his oily voice and dirty jokes, and maybe to more lies about what he and Jenny had been up to.

Still, Jenny had tried to help, and she was looking worried about how glum Tom had got. To please her, he said, "I'll think about it, and maybe come up with some way, all right?"

Jenny got off his lap and shook out her skirts. "You do that! I take it as a promise. But now I'd better get back to really working, or Mamie'll be after me."

Tom stood up and stretched his back, hanging onto the chair as he did it. He hated to just walk out. Which gave him an idea.

"Would you see it as me going back on my word, if I was to kiss you? Just that?"

Jenny came close again, her eyes kind of shiny. "I wouldn't see it that way at all. And I'd like it fine."

She was almost up against him already, but he reached out and pulled her in the rest of the way. He'd kissed her before, but that was in bed, or just after, and all mixed up with what else they were up to. This was more like the couple of kisses he'd had with neighbor girls, except not much like those, really. Those girls hadn't known much more'n he did. And there'd been awkward feelings on both sides, part of trying to be something different with each other from what they'd been all their lives. This was — was more like what he'd dreamed a kiss could be, before he tried it and found it not so sweet as all that.

Kissing Jenny was sweet as molasses candy. And it somehow made him want to get teary-eyed. And he didn't want to stop.

But Jenny had to go back to her work, much as he hated the work she did. And he'd rather be the one to pull back first. So he did, but gently, sliding his hands from her back to her shoulders and giving her a little squeeze before letting go.

There didn't seem more worth saying, after that. He stood looking at her just a little longer, and then made his way out.

Chapter 13

TOM LOOKED down the road for maybe the tenth time that morning, saw no buggy coming, and chided himself for being so impatient. "Doc'll get here when he gets here. He's got his breakfast to eat, and the missus to visit with, and maybe even church. Right, Cochise?"

Cochise blew out a snort as if to give his opinion on how likely Doc was to bother with church. Tom laughed, in spite of how nervous he'd got, and scratched behind Cochise's left ear. "Well, maybe not. But I won't hurry him by fretting, will I?"

Cochise cocked his head as if unsure whether fretting might not do some good, after all, seeing as he didn't know much about how things worked for people.

"Sorry I can't take you with me. A fair fool I'd look, riding in a buggy with you trotting alongside or following after. But I'll tell you all about it later."

Horses couldn't shrug, but the way Cochise looked at Tom and away from him and put his head down to graze seemed like it had much the same intention.

Movement caught Tom's eye. The buggy! Doc had finally shown up, his mare Nellie-girl pulling the buggy at a pace that could've been quicker. Tom tried to slow his hearbeat down to match, meeting the buggy as it swung into the yard, the wheels kicking up dust.

Doc watched close as Tom hoisted himself into the

buggy, good leg first, and then relaxed against the driver seat as Tom made it without either himself or the wooden leg falling back on the ground. Clapping Tom once on the shoulder, he said, "All ready to speechify?"

"I guess we'll find out. Don't know how to get readier, anyhow."

Doc turned his attention back to driving, maybe to give Tom time to settle down. It didn't work so well. He got more nervous, not less, with every clip-clop of hooves and rumble of the wheels. And he could tell himself he was sweating due to the day being so warm and close, but he'd've been sweating anyway.

He'd better find something to say to Doc. "Thanks again for the ride."

"Glad to do it! I'd have passed pretty close to your place in any event. And I don't mind an excuse to sit back and relax instead of riding Nellie-girl."

Excuse or no, Doc had spent money to hire the buggy. And he'd brushed off Tom's offer to pay him back. Which didn't mean Tom wouldn't do it, if his scheme actually led somewhere.

As they pulled up to the bunk house of the Two Rivers Ranch, he had to take hold of his breathing to keep from panting. Doc swung down from the buggy, big doctor's bag in one hand, while Tom made his own clumsy way to the ground. Meanwhile, a couple of cowboys had come up, one hailing Doc. "Come on in! We've got a broke thumb and a maybe-broke ankle waiting, and a big ol' cut needs stitching."

The other one eyed Tom and said, "You got yourself a new assistant? Sorry to say, he ain't near as pretty as your missus." The cowboy gave a horselaugh at his own wit.

Doc smiled and waved Tom forward. "This here's Tom

Barlow, and he did a service for one of the hands over at the Double T that you'll want to hear about. He can tell you all about it while I tend to those who need tending."

The second cowboy nodded amiably to Tom and headed into the bunk house, beckoning Tom to follow. "We can gather in the mess hall where there's room for everybody, and you can tell us what Doc's talking about. Jim, get everyone there who ain't busy." The first cowboy grunted and headed off to corral some others.

It would've been easier if Tom had the saddle to show. Instead, he'd had to scrounge up some more leather and make the feathers over again, along with a few other patterns he thought likely to appeal — wildflowers, lassos linked together, horseshoes, mountains. As cowboys filed into the bunk house and filled maybe half the tables, Tom's guide led him to one end of the big room. "You can stand there, if you can holler loud enough to reach the other end."

He hadn't done much hollering lately, at least on purpose, but he reckoned he could manage. He used his sleeve to wipe sweat off his forehead, then took his place and pulled the leather sample out of his vest, waiting for the cowboys to quiet down. They didn't, altogether, but it didn't seem waiting any longer would help. He cleared his throat and fairly shouted, "A good morning to all of you!"

A few of the cowboys called back greetings of one kind or the other. The rest just looked at him. Was it hotter'n outside, for all he was out of the sun?

"My name's Tom Barlow. I live some ways from here on my family's farm, but these days I spend most of my working time at Finch's — he's the cordwainer what also makes and fixes saddles. And one thing I do that Finch won't is engrave decoration on saddles. Haven't done any for you folks, but this here shows what I can do."

He held up the leather. Those closest to him leaned forward to squint at it, but the rest were too far away to see much. Tom, his chest tight, handed it over to a cowboy at the nearest end of the nearest table. "I'll pass it around for you all to take a look."

The cowboy peered at it and ran a finger over the lasso pattern before handing it to the fellow next to him. Slowly, as Tom watched and tried not to fidget, the piece of leather made its way from one cowboy to the next, some of them just handing it along without looking, others studying it with their eyes or fingers or both. When it finally made its way back to Tom, he took it, tucked it away, and looked around the room. "Who's got questions?"

A cowboy in the middle of the mess hall called out, "What'll you charge for that kind of work?"

This much he'd thought out ahead of time. "The one time Finch had me do this kind of work, he charged the customer five dollars for it. I'll take three. More if you want something that'd take much longer, and we could talk that over when you come tell me about it."

Another stood up and almost glared at him. "How long'd it take? How long'd I be stuck with no saddle?"

Tom tried for a look somewhere between glaring back and seeming cowed. "If you're getting a new saddle, you'd have your old one in the meantime. If you're wanting something added to the saddle you've already got, I'd put that job first to keep the wait as short as I can. I did that other job in a bit less'n a day. Anyone else?"

The first cowboy who'd looked the sample over asked, "What if I have my own idea of what I want, something you didn't show us?"

Tom could feel his face brighten up. "I'd like that fine. Always looking to do something new. I could make you a bit of it right then, and you tell me if it's what you're looking for." He'd have to make sure he had scraps of leather on hand, not knowing ahead of time when someone'd show up.

Doc came through the door and joined Tom, calling out across the room, "Anyone else here need my attention before my friend and I head out?" No one spoke up, and a few cowboys shook their heads.

Tom looked around and said, "If anybody has more questions, you can stop by the farm of an evening or on Sunday, and I'll do my best to answer." And then, not knowing what else to say, he added, "Hope to be seeing you!"

Doc gave a general wave to the room and headed out again, Tom following. When they reached the buggy, caught up with Nellie-girl, and harnessed her again, Doc lingered beside the buggy while Tom climbed in, doubtless in case Tom needed a hoist or maybe rescuing. Tom made it on the first try, thankful not to look too much a fool in front of any cowboys who might be watching, and they headed back toward the farm, a breeze picking up the dust of the road and swirling it like tiny twisters.

Doc waited just long enough to be out of earshot before asking, "How do you think it went? Will you have any takers?"

"Hard to tell. A fair number of 'em looked at the samples. I expect maybe one or two'll turn up sooner or later. But if they want new trim on the saddle they've already got, I'll have to work fast."

Doc took that in. "And new saddles are a major expenditure. Still, once word gets around, I suspect any cowboy investing in a saddle won't be satisfied with a plain one. They'll want your artistry."

That was a pretty fancy word for what Tom could

manage, even if Jenny'd said it first, but he could hardly argue the point. Besides, there was one thing troubling him that Doc must've already done some thinking on. "You work Sundays sometimes, don't you?"

Doc started to smile and then went real sober instead. "I do, when a patient needs me. You may recall I came to you on a Sunday morning."

It was plumb foolish to think, all of a sudden, that if he'd told Doc to wait and take care of him on the Monday, maybe Doc could've saved his leg. . . .

But Doc had more to say. "There's plenty of folks who can't put aside work on the Sabbath altogether. Farmers, for instance. You can't tell a cow she'll have to hold her milk until next morning. And I don't know as I've seen a farm leave eggs in the coop that could've been sold or used for breakfast. Not to mention many farmers that harvest on Sundays, especially if rain or snow threatens."

Many, maybe, but not all. Some would rather keep the Lord's day than make sure of their crops. Ma and Pa, now, they'd always done what couldn't keep and nothing more.

Nellie-girl clopped along. Doc kept talking. "I'm not one to tell any man how to practice his religion. We all make our choices and have our reasons. Just as an example, you go to Madam Mamie's and see Jenny now and then." He paused, maybe to see just how hot Tom was flushing. "The Bible calls that fornication. You might call it any number of other things, and I won't go saying you'd be wrong." Then, quieter: "When I used to go there, I might have called it keeping my body healthy, or lifting spirits that had sunk very low. The preacher might not care what I called it, but I never troubled to ask him."

Nor did Tom plan to tell the preacher about Jenny, not for all the coin in Cowbird Creek. But he might just talk to him about Sabbath-keeping.

The first step in talking to the preacher was actually going to church. He'd gone with the family all his life, before he lost his leg. Afterwards, he'd had plenty of reasons not, what with how he felt about God letting it happen, and not wanting everyone staring when he walked in. After a while Pa had made Ma stop asking.

He felt kind of bad about how Ma's face lit up when he came down to breakfast in his Sunday clothes, knowing as he wouldn't've gone without a particular reason. Martha and Billy sat there goggling at him, which he barely managed to pretend he didn't notice. Pa just stroked his beard for a minute and then attended to his breakfast.

Once they all climbed into the wagon and headed for town, it seemed like everyone on the road, almost, took a good look as they rode past. The womenfolk seemed most interested, mothers smiling at him like he'd finally done his chores or read from the Bible without stumbling on the words. Had every soul in Cowbird Creek noticed that Tom didn't come to church no more?

He was less surprised to see the preacher raise his eyebrows when they walked in. After a service that hadn't got any shorter since Tom had been there last, he hung back to let everyone else leave first. Pa gave Tom one of his long looks and then shepherded Ma and Martha and Billy out toward the wagon.

The preacher hovered like a hawk, and then fair dove at Tom once no one was in the way. "What a pleasure to see you joining us, young man! I have continued to hope your misfortunes might turn your heart toward the Lord."

All right, he had *not* come today with the design of punching a preacher. He supposed he couldn't fault the fellow for taking that view of it. Though he'd mightily like to know whether the preacher'd feel the same if it was his own leg cut off and thrown away.

Now he had to fess up to what he'd come to ask. The preacher's face never had far to go for a frown, and it went there quick and kept going. By the time Tom finished, he'd call it a scowl. "I am disappointed, truly disappointed, to hear you contemplate such a course. From what I hear, you've managed, by Mr. Finch's good grace, to obtain gainful employment despite your limitations. You should be thanking your Savior for His mercy instead of indulging in the fatal sins of ingratitude and discontent. Your needs are provided for, and yet you seek to amass more wealth, and gratify your ego, by taking on work you can only perform on the Lord's Day? I must hope — and I will pray — that you think better of it, and repent the impulses to which you have yielded."

Tom could think of absolutely nothing to say that wasn't cussing or worse. And the preacher might even tattle to Finch! He turned on his heel, almost losing his balance — and wouldn't that have made a pretty picture for the preacher to be smug about — and stalked out. He almost slammed the door.

Chapter 14

TODAY it was Sophie who got the job of going to town along with Jenny. It was Jenny's good luck, or maybe Mamie doing a little favor along with still insisting on a chaperone, that Sophie was so easygoing and didn't fuss about it. What's more, she let Jenny pick where they went first and next. And when Jenny asked her opinion on what fabric would look best for Jenny's next new dress, she read Jenny's face and picked the one Jenny was lingering at already.

Then, when they passed the ice cream shop on their way back to Mamie's, Sophie even let Jenny go inside on her own. "Bessie'd be less'n pleased if I ate ice cream without her. You go on, and I'll wait for you on a bench in the square. I can work on my bird calls. Bessie likes it when I do bird calls."

That suited Jenny more'n fine. She liked Sophie's company, usually, but by now, doing something by herself would be as much of a treat as ice cream.

The owner undressed her with his eyes the way most men did, but he didn't say nothing rude and handed over her ice cream without making her wait longer'n anyone else. And it was a pretty day, still warm enough that the owner'd propped the door open for breezes, but not humid like a couple of weeks before.

To put the cherry on the sundae, so to speak, a lady just a little older'n Jenny came in with a baby, a cute little boy with a sweet round face, his plump arms and legs all waving around. Jenny loved babies. She'd tended neighbor babies often enough as a girl, all the way up until she left home.

Bringing her plate of chocolate ice cream with fudge syrup, she came toward mother and baby, smiling. "He's so precious! How old —"

The woman snatched the baby out of his basket and clutched him to her breast, starting him howling. Over the noise, she said, voice colder'n any ice cream, "How dare you approach us, a hussy like you!" Turning her shoulder to Jenny, she crooned to the crying baby, "Don't worry, sweetheart, I won't let the nasty lady hurt you."

The woman stood up as if to hurry her baby out of reach of whatever poison it might breathe in, just from being near Jenny. But Jenny ran out first. Only outside did she realize she was still holding her plate and spoon. She crouched to leave them at the door, took a deep if shaky breath, and walked as quick as she could to find Sophie. It wasn't until Sophie looked at her with big eyes and wrinkled forehead that she realized she was crying.

Mamie saw them come in and marched downstairs to stand at the bottom with hands on hips, looking like a hanging judge. Jenny still hadn't managed to stop crying, so Sophie had to do the talking, as much as she could from whatever Jenny had blurted out on the way. Then, for a wonder, Mamie made things better, opening her arms for a hug. Jenny couldn't remember Mamie giving her a real hug before, nor her wanting such, but now she rushed into Mamie's arms and fair snuggled up against Mamie's big bosom. Mamie stroked her hair. "There, there, girl. Bitches will be bitches, and we can't hardly stop 'em."

Jenny had to laugh, which stopped her crying. She pulled back enough to wipe her face on her arm — or would've, if Mamie hadn't pulled a handkerchief from somewhere like a magician with a hat. By now Sophie had gone off somewhere, probably to tell Bessie all about it.

Jenny wiped her face and followed Mamie to the empty small lounge. Mamie gave her a little push toward an easy chair, one usually reserved for the men, and went behind the bar, pulling out a bottle and pouring two glasses. She handed one to Jenny and sat down next to her. "Join me, why don't you, in a little sherry. It'll relax you and maybe help you get some perspective on this afternoon's events."

Relax her, sure. Perspective, not likely, but getting to drink sherry instead of colored water, the customers paying liquor prices for it, was treat enough. That word in her head made her think of her ice cream, not finished and melting by the door, and she burst into tears again. Mamie looked vexed. "What am I going to do about you, girl? You're over your monthlies, aren't you?"

Jenny tried to stop and finally did. She didn't want to waste the easy chair and the sherry on sniffing and blowing. Mamie, reassured, sat back and sipped her drink. "That's better. Young or old, we've got to be tough in this business."

Jenny poured half her sherry down her throat in two big gulps. Mamie sat up and plucked Jenny's glass out of her fingers with half an inch left in it. "That's enough lazing around. You go on up and wash your face. Plenty of customers'll be here before you know it."

Jenny handed Mamie back the handkerchief. "Thanks for the borrow. Oh, you want I should wash it?"

Mamie's face had gone all business, but now it went softer. "Never you mind, child. I'll give it to the laundry. Run along."

Chapter 15

TOM WAS sitting on the front steps reading his Bible, to sort of make up for the Sabbath-breaking he hoped to be doing sooner or later, when a cowboy rode up on a tall bay mare, sitting on one saddle with another slung along the side. Tom put the Bible down, carefully and with respect, on the porch near the steps and hoisted himself up to go meet the cowboy in the yard. Close up, both the cowboy and the saddle, the newer-looking one, looked familiar. He'd been doing the simpler cutting and shaping on one just like it — the saddle, that is — a few days before. As best he recalled, the saddle's owner rode for the Two Rivers Ranch.

The cowboy dismounted, pulled the newer saddle down and held it out for Tom to see. "Could've asked ol' Finch about getting this fancied up, but I figured I'd save some coin and do you a favor both, just as long as you can work quick enough that my old saddle don't fall to pieces first."

Tom tried to smile easy, like this'd happened plenty of times. "I should be able to oblige you. Why don't we go to the barn, and you can set that saddle on the work bench and tell me what you'd like to see on it."

All of a sudden, the cowboy looked bashful. "Well, now. You see, I've a liking for a particular kind of bird. A bird someone around here must've liked plenty, seeing as they named a creek after it."

There might be another creek with a bird's name on it, but Tom guessed the one everyone knew about. "Cowbird?"

"Yup. Now I know they're kind of plain and fat when they're just sitting, on a cow or a fence post. But I have a sort of fondness for a bird that likes hanging around cattle, like I do. And when they take off and fly overhead, with the light coming through the wing feathers, I'd call that purty, and — " (this with a defiance that gave the lie to the words) " — I don't care who knows it."

Seeing as the cowboy did care, Tom looked for a way to ease his mind. "I could maybe not trouble too much over it having exactly the shape of a cowbird flying, so long as the wings are out and the feathers look about right. Small as the design'll have to be, it shouldn't stand out as a cowbird unless you tell folks."

He thought he could picture what the cowboy had in mind. What he couldn't quite see was him doing it, not with the swivel knife he'd used before. He'd have to come up with something thinner. And it wouldn't help that the saddle'd already been oiled. He'd need to oil some scrap leather and figure out how to work on it. All of which would take some time.

Tom settled himself on the seat by the workbench and said in as casual a tone as he could muster, "This'll be a job with a lot of finicky work in it. And of course, once I set tool to leather, there's no undoing it. So I'll be practicing on other leather first, practicing plenty.

"Here's what I'll do. I'll charge you less'n I would normally, even though it's more work, to make up for you having to wait a little longer for your saddle."

The cowboy stayed standing, and his hand twitched toward the saddle like he was planning to pick it up again. "What if you can't do what I want, after all your practicing?"

Tom stood up and looked him in the eye. "Here's how I see it. I won't start on the actual saddle unless I'm sure I can do it right, nor charge nothing. You ain't gambling the saddle, nor any money. But you'd have to gamble a little time. Are you up for that wager?"

Like he'd hoped, the cowboy didn't want to back down from a bet. "Sure, I'll do that. I've already seen you do nice work. And you think you can do it, right?"

Did he? 'Think' didn't mean knowing for sure and certain. "That's right. Do we have a deal?"

"Yup, we do." The cowboy stuck out his hand. Tom shook it, feeling the callouses from rope and reins.

Tom nodded toward the saddle. "Well, then, I'd best get started. How about you come back and check on things in three days' time?"

Good thing he'd already gathered plenty of scrap leather. It was going to take most of it, Tom figured, to get these birds right.

He figured wrong. It took more. He had to scrounge at home, and at work the next day, and he still had to give up some chaps with plenty of wear left in 'em. Not that he'd be riding, but it still hurt.

Lamp oil did well enough in place of what he used at Finch's, so at least he didn't have to sneak some home or ask Finch for the favor. Finding a way to carve wings with sun shining through 'em, or as close as he could come on leather, had him stumped for longer. But by the time he'd got his leather close enough to a finished saddle and could carve on it with the swivel knife, he hit on using a nail, tapping the head with a hammer to poke lots of little holes in a row. It took nigh on forever, and by the time he had it right, his eyes were blurring from working by lamplight and not sleeping more'n four hours at night.

Then, when he finally got started on the saddle itself, he had such a scare when he made a wrong cut that he almost pissed himself. But he managed to fix it so's it looked all right and like he'd meant to do it.

Ma had been fussing at him almost the whole time, along of his using up lamp oil and not sleeping and getting big dark circles under his eyes. But when she got to hovering around and nagging, Pa took her arm and gave a gentle tug away from where Tom was working, saying, "You let him be, hon. He's got this to do, and he'll have to find the best way, which he won't do quicker for your jawing at him."

It was his sister who first saw the finished saddle, wandering into the barn after she washed up before morning chores. The light slanted in, just reaching the work bench and hitting the leather so the design fair jumped out. He'd have pulled something over the saddle to hide it if he'd seen her coming, but she was good at creeping up behind. He first knew she was there when she said right behind his shoulder, "Is that what you've been doing these three days?"

The way he jumped, if he'd had a tool in his hand near the leather he might have wrecked everything. He spun around on the seat and yelled, "Don't you sneak up on me like that!"

She blew her hair out of her eyes and rolled them at him. "Oh, pooh, you scaredy cat." She sidled closer and took a long look.

He didn't mean to ask, but somehow it came out. "Well, what do you think?"

He could see her think about teasing him and then decide agin it. "I think it's right fine. I wish I could do something like that."

He relaxed and gave her shoulder a little squeeze. "Why, you stitch pictures better'n just about anybody, 'most as good as Ma. You just keep on with that, and you'll get even better. You and Ma can have a contest, even."

She laughed at that notion, but she looked pretty chipper as she trotted off to her chores.

The cowboy showed up right when Tom was heading off to work. Tom turned right around. Finch could wait for once. He walked as quick as he could back to the barn, the cowboy falling into step beside him. Tom fetched the saddle and hauled it outside into the sunlight, putting it down on a stump. "There you are, and I sure hope it's what you had in mind, because I don't mind saying I'm pretty pleased with it."

The cowboy hoisted the saddle and turned it this way and that. When he looked back at Tom, his eyes were wide and his mouth a little open before he said, "And I don't mind saying I'm pleased. And paying you what I owe."

The cowboy put the saddle back down to fish out coins and count them before handing them over. As the coins hit Tom's hand, warm from the cowboy's trousers, he mumbled, "Thankee," and watched as the cowboy carried the saddle to his horse. The cowboy took off the saddle he'd rode in on and strapped the new one in place, muttering to the horse to keep him from fidgeting. Then he stood there for a second before holding the old saddle out to Tom. "Don't reckon I'll be needing this one. Even if something happened to the new one, this one's so wore out I'd be a fool to ride it. Maybe you could use it for your practicing, next time you've a need."

Tom swallowed hard and took the old saddle. "Reckon I could."

The cowboy swung up onto his horse, took the reins, and said, "I'll be showing this all round the ranch. Happen you'll see some of the other hands here, wanting something of their own. But I'd take it kindly if you don't make the same birds for any of 'em. I want my saddle to stay special."

Tom had a moment of regret that all that practice went for only one saddle. But he should be able to use what he'd learned on some other kind of picture. "I can do that, sure."

The cowboy nodded, tipped his hat, and rode away. Tom stood watching until his first customer had gone quite a piece down the road before heading off to Finch's.

Tom walked in the door ten minutes late, which made it ten minutes later'n he'd ever shown up. Finch was sitting down smoking a pipe, and shook his head like a preacher at the funeral of someone heading to Hell. "What's this, then?"

Tom had no intention of telling him. "Sorry, Mr. Finch. I'll try not to let it happen again."

Finch frowned at him saying *try*, but took another puff on his pipe instead of saying anything. Tom looked around for whatever Finch would be wanting him to do. He didn't see any job waiting, which made him feel better at having been late and more sour at Finch complaining of it.

Finch put his pipe aside and stood up. "We're off to pick up some hides from the Two Rivers Ranch. You can bring my wagon around to the front."

Tom near choked on his own spit. "Two Rivers Ranch. Yessir."

Finch could've picked up the hides without a helper, but this way he got to sit back on the seat next to Tom while Tom drove, blathering on about everything from next week's weather to Nebraska politics to when the grasshoppers would be coming back (any minute, seemingly). Tom did as little listening as he could manage, trying to pick out different bird calls instead. This time, he listened special for the cluck-and-squeak of a brown-headed cowbird, and smiled to himself when he heard a couple. It almost kept his mind off of worrying whether they'd see this morning's satisfied customer, and what the fellow might take it into his head to say.

It was an older, colored cowboy who stood by the big pile of hides when they pulled up, chewing tobacco and kindly spitting away from the hides. At a nod from Finch, Tom climbed down and started tossing armfuls of hides into the back of the wagon, while Finch got his pipe back out and lounged on the wagon seat.

Tom was close to heaving a sigh of relief when the cowboy who'd ordered the cowbirds strolled on up, whistling. He walked by Tom and winked before he tipped his hat to Finch up on the wagon and called up, "A fine morning, Mister! Picking up more hides to make more saddles like mine? I declare I couldn't be happier with it."

Tom didn't know whether to cuss or laugh, and knew better than to do either. He kept pitching hides while Finch thanked the cowboy for the compliment and then, kind of grudging, added, "Tom here helped a bit, with the glue and oil and such."

The cowboy looked like he was two seconds from a belly laugh, but he held it in. "Did he now? Well, then, thank you, Tom here. Much obliged to you."

Tom tossed in the last armful of hides and strapped the tarp over them just as a light rain was starting, while Finch finally climbed down and walked over to the main house to pay the rancher. He was barely, maybe, out of earshot when the cowboy said in a loud whisper, "All the fellas think the world of that work you done."

Tom let himself grin, his back turned to the house. "Well, you know how good I am at rubbing in oil."

The cowboy guffawed, slapped him on the back, and loped off toward the bunkhouse while Tom pulled himself back up into the driver seat. He hadn't thought to bring a slicker, so he had no choice but to get wet and wait for Finch, who took long enough that he might've been having a tipple with the owner. When he showed up again, he was wiping his mouth on his sleeve. He did a bit of grumbling about the rain and then pulled an extra tarp Tom hadn't known about out from under the wagon, draping it over himself while Tom just got wetter.

They were halfway back to town when Finch, who'd been dozing, sat up and said, "What was that cowboy going on about? Seemed like he was sitting on some joke or other."

Tom shrugged, maybe too hard, as he like to fell off the wagon. "He must've been making fun of me some way, but I'm not sure exactly how. I don't know a lot about cowboys and what they laugh at."

Finch snorted. "Any fool thing, seems like." Then he switched to talking about how much he wanted his dinner and what he hoped his missus would bring, and Tom was safe, at least for now.

Chapter 16

THE MILLER hailed Tom, grinning, as Tom trudged homeward after the longest Monday since the world was made. "Well, young feller! I guess you wouldn't be a proper farm lad without sowing some wild oats, now would you!"

Tom thought about playing deaf, but reluctantly stopped and faced him. "Good evening, Mr. Burgess. I hope your day's going well."

"Aw, then, don't be shy! Why shouldn't you blow off some steam at Mamie's place? I don't mind saying I do the same, which is how I come to see you there." Burgess winked and twitched his elbow, like he'd have nudged Tom in the ribs had Tom been any closer. "You sampled much of the merchandise yet? I just saw you the one time, with that pretty red-haired girl. She's got curves you can hang onto, don't she?"

Tom gritted his teeth and reminded himself that anyone looking at Jenny could say as much. It didn't mean the miller had actually done the hanging on.

When Tom didn't answer right away, the miller just got louder. "C'mon, tell me how many of 'em you've tried! It ain't just the one girl, is it?"

If Tom wasn't embarrassed about going to Mamie's in the first place — and if he were, he wouldn't tell the miller so — he was hardly going to act embarrassed about sticking to one favorite girl there. "Sure it is. What of it?"

The miller gaped. "Why, son, that's like going to a picnic supper and having nothin' but chicken, no potato salad or buttered corn or cherry pie!" He stopped to leer. "I guess that little gal is some kind of cook all by her lonesome, then!"

It was time and past time to get walking. Tom did, but the miller just trotted alongside him. "Don't go getting too stuck on that gal! Mamie's'd be a real odd place to pick up a sweetheart." He chortled at what he must think was his wit. Tom speeded up as much as he could, in the hope Burgess would get winded and shut up.

Burgess did go to puffing, but he still kept talking. "You ain't thinking like *that*, now, are you, boy?"

Tom stopped and whirled around to face the miller. "You can just stop calling me boy, mister. And I could go elsewhere and do worse for a sweetheart. Not that I see as how you're such an expert." Everyone knew the miller had never married, that he'd kept company with a couple of girls who'd found someone they liked better.

The miller clenched his fists and stuck out his chin, then relaxed. "I might call those fighting words, but you ain't exactly fit for fighting, now are you? Which you might keep in mind, if you was thinking of sparking a shake like her. It'd be bad enough if you was whole, and ended up spending all your time fighting folks to defend her reputation. Way things are, you'd just have to take it." He shook his big square head. "I wouldn't hanker for a life like that, not one bit."

Tom wanted to punch the miller's head, or find something to say that'd catch him flatfooted and make him take back everything he'd said. But Tom'd be no good in a fight, just as Burgess said. The miller could just kick Tom's wooden leg out from under him and send him sprawling.

And whatever the clever thing to say might be, Tom hadn't the first notion of it.

He looked down the road, pretended the miller was nothing but a carved cigar store Indian, and headed home, doing his level best to ignore the miller's call behind him. "You try out some of the others, see what you've been missin'!"

What he thought on, as the miller's voice finally faded behind him, was that he might be better off forgetting about women altogether. Jenny, who seemed to like him notwithstanding him being a cripple, would be all the trouble the miller prophesied, and what other girl would take him, even if he could get Jenny out of his head enough to look at one?

When Tom got home, having walked off most of his mad, Pa had a message for him. "There's a cowboy came by wants saddle work." Pa's face was a picture as he added, "With women on it. All the way around, head to foot, fancy as you can make 'em. Said he'll be back in the morning to see if you can do it."

If that didn't beat all! If he said yes, he'd be seeing women in his head every spare minute for days. And thinking of Jenny with every line he carved.

* * * * *

The small lounge where some of the girls gathered on slow nights had its own stove, but Mamie wouldn't pay for burning coal unless it was customers using the room instead. Still summer as it was, they didn't miss it, and sometimes, like tonight, one of the girls would put a bunch of flowers on the stove to brighten things up. Tonight it was coneflowers, red ones like Jenny hadn't hardly seen.

Somewhere along her path, Amanda Jane had picked up lace making, and she had a long strip going, colored red like the flowers. As Jenny leaned over to admire it, Amanda Jane inspected it and picked out some little mistake Jenny wouldn't never have seen.

Watching her work, wondering how she'd learned to do such a thing and where she'd lived before Cowbird Creek, Jenny suddenly remembered the first night Tom had come in, and how Mamie had intended him to go with the older woman. When Amanda Jane leaned back and closed her eyes to rest them, Jenny made bold to ask, "Mamie said once that you know all about men with missing parts to them. How'd you learn?"

Amanda Jane opened her eyes and gave Jenny a knowing look. "I spent a year or so in a city with a big hospital for soldiers. Lots of those boys had an arm or leg missing or only half left. When they got well enough to walk, and kitted out with crutches or wooden legs or whatever as needed, they'd make their way to the vaulting house where I'd settled at the time. Girls as had been there longer would train the rest of us. And some of the soldiers who'd been in the hospital longest had figured out what worked best and what they most liked a girl to do." She smiled, her wide mouth curling up pretty. "Whatever Mamie told you, I'd bet I can tell you more, if that good-looking farm boy is likely to come back again."

"I never know if or when. He doesn't come here but once in a while. Still, I'd be glad of whatever you could tell me." It felt good to have someone saying how fine-looking Tom was, even if at the same time it made her a little jealous. As smart as Amanda Jane was, and as good at making the most of her figure and her features, she could probably get

Tom's attention if she wanted it. It was silly to care, as if Jenny was some girl in town and Tom was sparking her.

Amanda Jane examined her lace some more. "There was one, he wrote me and said how he'd never thanked me properly for being so kind to him. A handsome fellow too, and he had some sort of store, and people working for him. A man like that, he could take care of a woman."

Jenny'd never seen that look on the older woman's face, kind of mournful. Like maybe she was wishing that man had stayed around and offered to take care of her.

Whether or no, Amanda Jane shook her head a little and went on, "Yes, and better than a farm boy."

Jenny bristled. "I bet Tom can do plenty, on a farm or off it. He's plenty strong. And stubborn enough to find a way to do things, specially if folk think he can't."

"Now, now, child, settle down. I'm not claiming to read the boy's future." She went back to her stitching.

Jenny gazed at the stove, imagining a fireplace instead, where you could watch the flames on a winter evening. Would she ever sit at her own fireside of an evening, talking quiet with someone and watching flames burn low?

Or maybe a campfire, traveling from town to town with another girl, like Sophie and Bessie did between bedhouses? More likely it'd be on a train, sitting side by side piled under with blankets, the clatter and grumble of the train making a sort of lullaby . . . . She'd have to talk to one of 'em sometime, Sophie maybe, and find out how they liked it. Whether it felt good, choosing where to go, no one telling them what to do until the next time they allowed someone like Mamie to boss 'em for a while, 'til they got tired of it and moved on again.

"Girls!" Mamie's voice startled Jenny out of her wondering. "You go on up and get your rest. Tomorrow and all the gentlemen it brings will be here before you know it."

Amanda Jane didn't move right away, and when she did, she acted like she'd got heavier since she first sat down. Jenny wondered at it, but not for long. She had a deal to think about once she got up to bed.

Chapter 17

"THAT FELLER must be on a cattle drive. Can't get that dirty on a ranch." Finch was peering out the door at a cowboy down the street, heading toward the shop. Tom might have gone to look if he hadn't had his arms full of smelly, dripping hides. He put them down as quick as he could, not much liking the picture of a cowboy seeing him doing that kind of job.

The cowboy who ambled in was coated head to foot, and not just in dust, but something (or maybe somethings) heavier. And cowboys didn't usually smell like fine ladies fresh from a bath, but this one was further from it than most. Tom could believe, easy, that he'd been on the road for weeks, getting up close to cattle and everything they put out.

Tom's stomach went tight to see that the cowboy was carrying a saddle.

Maybe something was broke, or loose, and just needed fixing. But he had a feeling otherwise. He felt a lot of things, but no surprise, when the cowboy said, "I heard from some cowpoke coming back from another drive that your place could put pictures on a saddle, along the edges. He had some, and they looked right fine. I've got my pay in my pocket, and willing to pay handsome for work like that."

Business hadn't been at its best, and Finch didn't act inclined to turn any away. Tom waited, his heart jumping around somewhere near his throat, to hear what pictures the cowboy had seen. If they was birds or ladies or his latest job, the pairs of bull horns tip to tip, he was sunk, unless Finch would credit they came from someone else. But wouldn't the cowboys who ordered that work straight from Tom have sent this fellow to the farm instead of here?

The cowboy kept him in suspense by not saying what the pictures on that other fellow's saddle had been. He just plunked his saddle down on the table and looked at Finch, his face eager enough to give Tom a warm feeling along with his nerves.

Finch twitched like he was going to look Tom's way, but stopped himself. "Yep, we can do that. How long you stopping for?"

We. At least he hadn't had the nerve to say *I.*

The cowboy stretched and yawned. "Today, tonight, and one day more, along of tomorrow being Sunday. Not that the boss usually bothers about Sabbath-keeping, but I guess he figured one time might do him more credit'n none."

Finch stuck his chest out, and his face twisted into what might be Finch's best try at looking pious. "Well, we can't do the work on the Lord's Day, so it depends what you're wanting, whether it'll be ready in time."

Tom managed not to snort. Finch wouldn't know near as well as Tom how long different designs would take, and Finch, it was plain, didn't want to ask him or let the cowboy know who'd be doing the work. Finch was in a bind, and serve him right.

The cowboy looked confused. "Didn't I say? I want what that other feller had. Feathers. 'Cept I'd like 'em bigger and not so close together."

Of course Tom was relieved not to be found out, but he

also found he was disappointed not to have something new and maybe harder to try. Finch, meanwhile, was nodding and looking like he could just about feel those coins in his hand. "Sure, we can get that done. You just leave the saddle here, and we'll get right to work."

Finch didn't say another word until the cowboy was out the door and halfway down the street, heading toward the nearest saloon. Then he muttered, "So can you do it? Today or tonight? Or will you have to work on it tomorrow to get it done?"

Tom clenched his fists behind him. So it was just fine for Tom to work on Sunday, for all Finch's playacting. He couldn't let on that he'd had practice since the last time, and got quicker at carving leather, so he made himself take a minute as if to think and then mumbled, "Should be able to do it by tonight sometime." He could work slower while Finch was still around, and then finish up quicker once Finch wasn't there to see.

Tom made his way to town after as good a Sunday as he could expect. He'd spent some time sleeping and a lot more finishing his latest job, cresting waves for a cowboy from New England of all places, who missed the ocean. He was putting by some real money, at least compared to what he could save from what Finch paid him. What he'd find to do with it, well, he hadn't got much forwarder on that. But at least he could use some on seeing Jenny again. The thought carried him along the road like he could float on it.

As he got near Doc Gibbs' place, he saw Mrs. Gibbs sitting on their front steps, reading a letter. You could tell at first glance, now, that she was expecting. She waved to him and said as he got closer, "You've got some spring in your step this morning. I'm glad to see it." She didn't ask why, for which he was grateful even though he figured he could trust her about his side business.

"Thank you, ma'am. You look cheerful yourself." In fact, she looked like she'd been laughing. He didn't recall seeing her laugh before.

Mrs. Gibbs held up the paper. "Reading a letter from Freida Blum is almost as good as talking to her to bring a smile to your face. There's nobody like our Freida. Here, for example, she says, *How are you feeling, are you as big as a house yet or just a little barn? Are you eating enough, Joshua had better make sure, you've always been so thin! Remember you're eating for two now, I wish I could bring you some of my beef stew, it's just right for making big strong babies!*"

Tom could just about hear Mrs. Blum, with her accent and her way of stressing different parts of words from other folks. Mrs. Gibbs wasn't copying her, exactly, but she'd picked up a little of the rhythm. It made Tom smile along with Mrs. Gibbs. She glanced over at him and kept going.

"*If Jedidiah and I can make our way there, we'll stop by and visit, I'll see how you're doing, not that Joshua won't be doing his doctor best, but sometimes what you need is an old Jewish lady making sure you're taking care of yourself. Don't you go having that baby before I get there, except if we can't come after all, then you have it whenever it's ready, babies make up their own little minds, don't they? And get plenty of rest, you should probably have your feet up right this minute . . . .*" Mrs. Gibbs laughed out loud and folded up the letter, tucking it in her dress pocket and giving the pocket a fond little pat.

Tom glanced down the road, where he should be taking himself before much longer. "Guess you and Mrs. Blum are pretty good friends."

Mrs. Gibbs got a thoughtful look on her face. "Indeed we are. But you know, Tom, we didn't start out so. Freida

Blum took rather a dislike to me when we first met."

Tom made some sort of surprised noise. It wasn't that hard, in fact, to imagine someone finding Mrs. Gibbs — or rather, Clara Brook, as she used to be — an odd sort. She hadn't been one to smile at all comers, or flirt, or agree with everything a body said. He'd been enough younger to be just a boy in her sight, but he could tell that much.

But Mrs. Gibbs had more to say. "You don't always know what people are like at first, and they don't always know about you. Give them time, and sometimes they can learn, or you can."

If she had a special point to make, he'd no more time for thinking about it, much as he'd rather listen to Mrs. Gibbs than Finch. "I'd best be going. Enjoy your letter, and I hope Mrs. Blum, or rather Mrs. —" What was her married name? Oh, yes. " — Mrs. Kennedy and Mr. Kennedy will be able to come through town."

Mrs. Gibbs gave a little sigh. "I do hope so. And that they come soon. Well, take care, Tom." She looked straight at him, almost like through him. "I hope you and Mr. Finch get along today."

Tom just tipped his hat and went on his way. Mrs. Gibbs didn't know Finch as well as he did, or she wouldn't bother hoping.

Chapter 18

IF MAMA or someone didn't write back, this would be the last letter Jenny sent home.

So she should try to make sure and spell the words right.

She'd heard about a book that helped folks spell, and she'd guessed right that Amanda Jane would know about it. Amanda Jane said the book was called something like a dick-shun-ery. At first she thought the older girl must be making fun, but Amanda Jane swore that was the real, actual name.

Then it was just a matter of getting up a little early and going into the lounge before breakfast when no one was about. Of course, the bookcase might not have had that book, but she found a thick one with a long name that ended in *Dictionary*. That looked about two-thirds right, and the book had nothing inside but words and what they meant. She stuck it under her skirts and hustled upstairs with it, hiding it under her bed.

Now she had it open on her dressing table, next to a sheet of paper with nothing but *Dear Mama* on it. And a fat lot of good the *Dictionary* did. She'd wanted to know how to spell *friends*, having a vague notion it wasn't just like it sounded, but she couldn't find it in the book, along of not knowing how to spell it! What good was a book about how to spell if you needed to know already before you could find anything?

She cussed out loud and crumpled up the paper, then grabbed the *Dictionary* and threw it across the room. It hit the wall and fell down into the corner between the wall and her bed.

Well, that was a bad idea! If the book got damaged, pages bent or cover dented, she'd be in real hot water. She went and picked up the book, which looked all right at a glance — but a glint of something in the corner caught her eye. She bent over to see better, and there was a cuff link on the floor. A cuff link with a diamond set in silver.

She jumped back like she'd seen a rattler. This was so much worse than the *Dictionary*. Whoever'd lost the cuff link — and it might be that fancy lawyer passing through town, or worse, someone who lived right in Cowbird Creek, maybe the banker — he was bound to miss it, and to figure just where it might be.

Like she'd told Tom, she'd seen what happened to girls who stole from customers, just a few weeks after she came to Mamie's and another time since. It didn't matter how much they cried or begged or promised never to do it again. They got thrown out in the street with just the clothes on their backs, and the threat of the sheriff to send them out of town. Mamie'd prob'ly be happy to turn them over to the law, except word would get around that her girls were thieving. But she might even do that if what was took cost enough.

And here Jenny stood, holding a book she'd took without asking.

The first step, then, was to put the book back. And then find Mamie, and tell her about the cuff link. Should she take it with her, or leave it on the floor? Maybe leave it, so Mamie could see just where it'd ended up.

She tucked the book under her skirts again and headed downstairs. But she was so shook up she wasn't watching where she walked, and she bumped right into Amanda Jane. Who said "Oh!" pretty loud, and then looked right where the book stuck out like Jenny'd grown an extra hip bone. "What in the world is that?"

And wouldn't you know it, Mamie was right at the bottom of the stairs and heard the whole thing, and came whooshing up to them. "What, indeed?"

Jenny, her stomach sinking down toward her toes, pulled up her skirts and took out the book. "I was just putting this back, ma'am."

"And you thought it might catch cold, unless you sheltered it under your skirts?"

She could feel she was blushing, and might start crying any minute. "I — I didn't want the other girls to see it, for thinking they'd make fun of me. And I was wanting to talk to you about something, right after I put it back."

Mamie raked her with a look sharp as a kitchen knife. "I do believe I have something to talk to you about as well. Come to my office. Mandy, put the book where it belongs."

Jenny followed Mamie, starting to sniffle and trying to do it quiet-like. Mamie closed the door and sat at her desk, leaving Jenny to stand and fidget. After what felt like long enough for Jenny to get old and gray, Mamie said, "I just got a letter from one of our gentlemen. You might remember the lawyer who passed through Cowbird Creek recently. It appears his letter was delayed somewhere along the way, or I'd have had it sooner. He says he's missing a valuable cuff link, and wonders if I might know anything about what happened to it."

She'd better speak up, or look even guiltier. "That's what I was coming to tell you, ma'am. I found it, or what I figure is the same one, in the corner of my room just now."

Mamie leaned on her elbows and looked in Jenny's eyes like she was reading what was behind them. "And you were just coming to tell me this, as soon as you'd put back the book you took without asking."

Jenny finally starting crying for real. Mamie could make whatever she wanted of it — Jenny couldn't hold it back a second longer. But she managed to say, "I never took that cuff link, ma'am! I never! And I was so scared when I found it, along of you maybe thinking I did, but what would I do with it?" She fought to stop crying and mostly did. "I'm not some magpie to go collecting shiny things!"

Mamie almost smiled before she set her face back to stern. "You could have tried to sell it, perhaps to a customer."

"You can ask any of 'em, ma'am, whether I done any such thing. If I had, they'd prob'ly tell you, since they'd've said no, or it wouldn't have been in that corner for me to find, or anywhere here, would it?"

Mamie stood up. "Show me the cuff link and where you say you found it."

Jenny opened the door to find three of the girls standing around nearby. For one blessed second, Mamie was madder at someone else than at Jenny. She whacked the nearest girl on the backside and pointed down the hall, saying through her teeth, "You take yourselves back downstairs and make yourselves useful! If there's no gentlemen waiting, you can just go help Cook in the kitchen. Get!"

The girls scattered, and Jenny led Mamie to her bedroom. She climbed onto her bed to where she could point at the cuff link without going near it. "Right there, ma'am."

Mamie looked at Jenny instead of the cuff link. "And how did you happen to find it in the corner?"

Jenny hung her head. "I got mad at the *Dictionary*, ma'am, and threw it against the wall. Along of I couldn't find a word without knowing how to spell it, which was what I wanted the book for in the first place."

This time Mamie did smile, which let about a quarter of the load on Jenny's heart drop off. "Yes, that is the problem with dictionaries, isn't it? At least if you try to use them for spelling. They're really meant to tell you what a word means."

Could that be true? "If I didn't know what a word meant, I'd hardly be using it, now would I?"

Mamie's look shifted toward almost gentle. "Dictionaries are intended for those who read a good deal, and come upon words they don't know."

Well, that left Jenny out. But Mamie added, "Reading more is likely to help your spelling, if you care about that."

While Jenny thought that over, Mamie went over to the corner and crouched by the cuff link, looking at it close and finally picking it up. She stood up and suddenly thrust her hand with the cuff link in Jenny's face. Jenny fell backward on the bed. Mamie bent over her, studying her face some more, and finally nodded. "All right, girl, I believe you. If I can't read a face by now, I should retire and knit booties for somebody's grandbabies."

Jenny just managed not to start crying again. She scrambled off the bed and stood with her hands clasped in front of her. "Thankee, ma'am. I surely do appreciate it. And I'm sorry I took the book without asking."

Mamie patted her on the shoulder. "If you want to do some reading, you may take one book at a time without bothering me about it." Her eyes went narrow again. "And

I will be watching you a little closer than usual, just in case I'm wrong. So you mind all the rules and stay out of trouble."

"Yes'm. I will. I'll do everything right."

Mamie actually laughed. "That'll be a first for any of my girls, or me for that matter. But you go on and try."

Mamie took pity on her that evening and aimed the crankier customers at other girls, sending her upstairs first with a nice old guy who'd come from an even smaller town and was all wide-eyed about what Cowbird Creek had to offer. And after she'd made him happy and let him tell her how sweet and pretty she was, the next fellow was a randy youngster, who'd prob'ly never had a woman before and didn't take much of her time, which she tried to make him think was just how it ought to be. Though if he came back, she might let him know different, or his wife would someday be pretty unhappy about it.

Problem was, that young fellow made her think of Tom. Who'd been better at it right off, leg or no, and by now was a lot of fun to roll around with. Not to mention making his pictures for her and of her. And listening to her when she talked.

Tom'd know she hadn't stolen nothing. Or would he? Maybe he figured all whores was thieves and cheats. How'd she know what he thought?

Even if she hadn't been raised better, it'd be plain stupid to steal here, where she'd be sure to get caught. If a whore was going to do any thieving, it'd make more sense for girls like Sophie and Bessie, who kept on the move. They could take anything small enough to hide and just leave town, as long as it wasn't worth so much that the sheriff'd bother chasing 'em. She'd have to be awful hard up before she'd do a thing like that.

As hard up as she'd've been if Mamie had thrown her out.

It'd be better, some ways, to plan on moving around, and not counting on anyone to trust you or believe what you said.

Jenny came into the lounge after a night of bad dreams, scolding herself for being afeared of wealthy gentlemen. Just because one such had been careless with his cufflinks didn't mean they'd all start leaving their property behind them. It had only happened the once. It wouldn't happen again.

And she'd search her room after, just to be sure.

Still and all, she was gladder'n ever, along with surprised, to see Tom, morning light turning his hair all gold. He walked right up to her, beaming all across his face. "Finch took sick! I thought he'd keep me busier'n ever, but seems he don't want me in his shop without him being there. And I've —" He stopped himself, looked around, and went quieter. "I'll tell you why later, but I ain't so short of money as usual. So I could afford to put my day off to good use."

She couldn't rightly say whether he took her hand or she took his, but she tugged him toward the stairs, and up they went. She thought he'd grab her right off, but he held her by the arms and just looked at her for a minute. "You're always pretty, and tired don't change it, but you do look tired. Is anything the matter?"

She wanted to tell him, even with being afraid he'd think her a thief. She may as well find out whether he saw her as someone likely to do such a thing.

He was looking more worried the longer she didn't say nothing. She opened her mouth and then shut it again, not sure she had the nerve to go through with it. He glanced around like he wanted to be sure no one was watching, and then walked her over to the bed and set her down, sitting down beside her, looking awkward in a sweet kind of way. He took her hand and asked, "Whatever it is, you want to tell me about it? I don't mind listening."

If she didn't, she'd be leaving him wondering and maybe thinking up something worse. And she'd have a hard time getting on with what she was supposed to be doing. She took a deep shaky breath and told him the whole story, about the cuff link and how she'd found it, and what a mess she'd made of telling Mamie. She'd already got started before she realized she couldn't hardly tell the tale without mentioning the *Dictionary*. She wasn't sure what was worse, him knowing she was weak on spelling or knowing how she minded it.

She got through it by hurrying through the telling. At least she had a way right at hand to change the subject as soon as she'd finished. She kissed Tom on the cheek and said as bright as she could, "Now that's over and done with! It's time I cheered up, and you're just the man to do it."

He sat still for a minute and then put an arm around her. "I'd like that fine. Of course. But I'm sorry you had all that happen. I know you must've been scared. You feeling all right now?"

She grabbed his free hand and kissed it before giving him the kind of smile he'd have expected when he come in. "Much better, and ready to do as much for you."

She'd give him as good a time as ever he'd had, to thank him for knowing something was wrong and caring that it was.

* * * * *

Lying on his back, trying to catch his breath, Tom thanked the good Lord for the beauty and roundness and warmth of womankind. And for what fireworks a woman and man could set off together.

He'd been afeared that with Jenny upset like she'd been, things wouldn't go so well. It had even crossed his mind to make his excuses and leave. But she'd made plain she didn't want him to, and he couldn't've got his money back anyhow. And in the end, it had all been way better'n all right.

He rolled over to look at Jenny, hoping she was feeling half as much in charity with the world as he was, and saw she was looking up at the ceiling and chewing on her lip a little with her front teeth. Not like she'd started fretting about the rich fellow's cuff link again, but like she was pondering a question. Then she sat up and nodded like she'd figured out the answer. She reached over and ran a finger down his arm. "You know, I've been wishing you'd come in soon. Wishing hard."

That made him sit up, quick enough he almost jostled her hand. She'd never said something like that before. What did she mean by it? Just that he gave her a good time, and wasn't as smelly or homely or wrinkled as some of those she had to put up with? Or that she had some sort of other feelings?

Rather'n try to figure all that out right here and now, he gave the answer that wouldn't change no matter what she meant. "Wish I could. But you know what keeps me from it."

Jenny laid her hand flat on his arm, maybe so he'd know she wasn't trying to get him stirred up again. "I know. Which is what gave me an idea."

She had a different look on her face than what he'd ever seen. In another girl, he'd call it . . . shy? In case that's how she was feeling, he put his free hand on hers and pressed a little to reassure her. "What's your idea?"

She hesitated and then said kind of quiet, "When you come here and spend coin you'll likely miss, I could pay you back some of it. I've saved up a little money. Not a whole lot — and I might need some of it for . . . ." She faltered, took a deep breath, and then went on, " — for something I might be wanting to do. I don't know if what I can spare'll be enough. But it'd help, at least."

She still had that shy look, but hopeful along with it. Could he take her money? It didn't seem right, if she was trying to save up just like he was. "What'd it mean to you, day to day, if you had less coin? Aside from saving up? What do you have to pay for here?"

Jenny scooted closer and leaned her head on his shoulder. "Not so very much. Handkerchiefs and such. New clothes — Mamie has a tailor come through every few months. And little things like ice cream when we go to town."

Tom stroked her hair, fancying he could feel the warmth of its color. "Mamie'd likely have something to say about you not buying clothes when the time came."

And besides that . . . It wouldn't feel right to take her money when he came to be with her. It'd be like — like he was what she was.

Which he had just enough sense not to say out loud.

He felt as well as heard Jenny sigh. "You're right about that. But the tailor won't be coming for months yet. I could help out a time or two before then."

He turned toward her, which made her move her head and look startled for just a moment before he pulled her close and kissed her. It ended up being a few kisses before he could stand to pull away again and say, "It means a lot to me that you'd do what you're offering. But I'll try to come sooner without you having to. And I likely can, along of what I wanted to tell you. I've started working on saddles on my own, outside of Finch's! I've got cowboys coming straight to me now."

Jenny's smile might've been brighter'n ever before. She reached for his hands and squeezed them. "I'm so proud of you, Tom! I couldn't hardly hear better news."

He had a sudden notion to raise up her hands and kiss them. Instead, he squeezed back and waited, awkward, for her to let go. When she did, he took himself out the door before he could say something that made him look a fool. Even something true.

Chapter 19

"MAMIE wants to see you in her office. She's got some fellow there." Bessie looked mighty curious. This wasn't how Mamie introduced the girls to customers. And she didn't have the big 'ol clue Jenny had, so she didn't know Jenny was like to be in bad trouble. Jenny hustled off toward Mamie's office before Bessie could ask any questions, or get a closer look at what Jenny's face must look like.

It had to be that lawyer, come back through town for some reason, maybe just to bedevil Jenny. He didn't believe her about the cuff link, and he'd talked Mamie into not believing her either — and weren't lawyers supposed to be able to talk anybody into anything? Or — she stopped short. What about the other cuff link? She'd never thought to wonder what happened to it. It must have fell out too, and be hiding somewhere in her room, maybe under her bed. And the lawyer had come back to get it . . . .

Jenny could hear Mamie talking to the man as she approached Mamie's closed door. He didn't sound mad, nor Mamie neither. Jenny knocked, louder'n she'd meant to. It was the man who opened the door — and if she'd ever seen him before, she must be worse at remembering than she'd thought. And he wasn't dressed like no lawyer. He wore leather trousers, and he was carrying a set of long poles with some sort of big boxy gadget on one end. Was that a *camera*? She'd never seen one, but what else could it be?

Mamie was sitting at her ease behind her desk, not riled or nervous. "Come in, Jenny. This gentleman came in with a request, and I thought you might be just the girl for what he had in mind."

Jenny couldn't figure why Mamie wanted to tell her the gentleman's tastes up here in her office, instead of in the lounge. Maybe what he liked was so twisted she didn't want other customers to hear about it. And maybe she was handing him Jenny as a punishment for the *Dictionary* and the cuff link and all. Jenny stood there, her hands behind her back, and waited to hear the worst.

Mamie waved toward the man. "Mr. Blixt, why don't you explain who you are and why you've come calling."

The man gave Jenny a big warm smile. "As Madam Mamie says, my name is Blixt, and I'm a photographer. You've seen photographs now and then?"

Jenny nodded, her eyes so wide they ached with it.

"I particularly like taking photographs of comely young women like yourself. I make them — the photographs, you understand — into postcards, that people can write messages on and send in the mail, but mostly just keep and admire."

Jenny wrinkled her forehead. With all the world of girls to choose from, why was he here at Mamie's with his camera and his smooth talk?

Oh. That was it. All those other girls, town girls in fine houses and farmers' daughters with boys ready to marry 'em, might have different ideas about what they'd be willing to wear, or do, with a camera pointed at 'em.

And she could just picture what kind of *admiring* the men would do, once they got hold of these *postcards.*

Well, for all that, it sounded like less work than entertaining those men in person. And she had to feel kind of good that Mamie'd picked her out. From now on, Jenny could hear "pretty as a picture" and know it had meant her, this once.

She dropped a little curtsy, the first one in longer than she could reckon, and said, "Yessir. You just tell me what you'd like me to do." Not so different from what she'd be saying if he were the usual sort of customer. Heck, for all she knew, he'd be that as well, once his picture-taking was over with.

"Jenny, show the gentlemen what you have in your closet. Mr. Blixt, if there's anything lacking for your pictures, you send Jenny to tell me about it, and I'll make sure you get it."

"Yes'm." Jenny put out her hand to Mr. Blixt. "This way, mister."

The photographer's hand was warm and, thank goodness, dry. "Let's go make some art!"

Being ahead of him, Jenny could roll her eyes without him seeing. Art, was it? Well, she'd seen a picture of a sculpture once, some Greek goddess from forever ago, who was curvy enough, and plenty of her showing. Now it was Jenny's turn to be art, seemingly.

She'd figured Mr. Blixt would take one or two pictures. But he had her try on like to half her closet. If she wore a dress, he had her slipping it off her shoulders, or unbuttoned and her looking over her shoulder with a come-over-here smile, or her sitting on the bed with the skirt hiked way up and both limbs showing. And sometimes he had her in just her unmentionables, leaning back on her arms so her bosom stuck out toward the camera. And sometimes smiling, sometimes just looking slutty. And every time, she had to hold still for longer'n she was used to.

And she'd thought this was less work than letting some fellow lie atop her and do what he wanted? Well, now she knew better.

As Jenny was finally taking off her clothes at the end of the night, Mamie tapped on her door and came in. "Well, how did you like being a model?"

Jenny was too tired to worry much about what Mamie wanted her to say. "It was a change, at least. But more work than I'd have figured."

Mamie gave her that look like a customer sizing her up, except cooler and longer. "It's about time I got some more tokens done. If that photographer thinks your looks will make him money, I'm thinking maybe I should put your picture on them. Would you like that?"

She would've surely liked it once, when she was feeling plain and countrified next to girls like Amanda Jane. But now, the notion of her picture being all over town on a brothel token made her feel like the whole town was staring at her.

The postcards might do the same thing. Tom might even see one. But it was too late to worry about that. The tokens might not be any worse, but she couldn't work up a smile to show Mamie about it. "Whatever you think best, ma'am."

Mamie jerked her head back a little, like she hadn't seen that coming and didn't much care for it. But she didn't say any more, just turned and left Jenny be.

*   *   *   *   *

"Hey, young feller! Look what I got!"

Tom turned to see the miller holding up some kind of

card. After a day of putting up with Finch, he had precious little patience left for anyone else, but he stopped and let Burgess catch up with him and wave the card in his face.

What he noticed first was all the flesh showing. This must be one of those penny postcards he'd heard tell of. Photographers got girls to pose wearing not much and then sold the cards at tobacconists and newsstands. But why did Burgess —

Hell! That was Jenny, sitting on a bed in nothing but corset and stockings and a come-hither look on her face.

Burgess saw Tom's shocked expression and laughed. "I've got a couple more! You want one? I'll give you one for free, along of you're a special friend of hers and all."

Tom clenched his fists. "I'll take that."

Burgess raised his eyebrows in fake surprise. "Which one? You ain't even seen the others yet."

Tom pointed to the card in his hand and glared. Burgess pulled his hand back, grinning. "Oh, no, young feller! I'm taking this one home with me tonight. To study special, if you know what I mean."

Tom let out a cuss word he'd never said in public and grabbed for the card, almost toppling over. Burgess chuckled. "You take care, boy. Don't want to fall on your face, do you? That red-headed gal might not think you so pretty if you're all banged up."

Tom took another step forward and took a swing at the miller's grinning face. And fell down, right in the dirt, just like Burgess had said he would.

Burgess laughed a while longer, with Tom laying there grinding his teeth, and then crouched down. "Here, didn't I tell you? Let me help you on up."

Tom spit at the miller's nearest knee. "You get away from me. I can manage without you and your *help*."

Burgess hoisted himself to his feet. "All right, young feller, all right. Sorry I got you stirred up. I shouldn't take advantage of someone in your condition. I'll leave you to it."

Tom waited for Burgess to walk on, cussing again as the man stopped and looked back before finally getting some distance away. It took him a few long minutes to struggle to his feet.

Brooding like he was the next day, it took something special to get Tom's attention, and he was fair glad when it did.

People talked about veterans with missing legs often enough, but Tom hadn't seen one since he lost his own. There the man was, still wearing the torn and beat-up jacket from his uniform, coming in Finch's door and settling himself down in the chair near the door. Finch hustled up to him the way he did for customers dressed a lot finer, and with his best imitation of high-class talk. "Welcome, sir! How may I assist you?"

Tom had to allow that was interesting, not to say plumb surprising, and to Finch's credit.

The man had a boot on his wooden leg and now pulled it off. "I could use a new sole on this here footwear, if you please."

Finch gave a little bow. "Of course, sir. Will you be waiting for it? I can do it right now. There's nothing else as — that can't wait."

The veteran shook his head. "No, I can stump around without it for a bit, so long as I don't go too far. Where's the nearest saloon?"

Finch pointed it out and said, "I should be done with your boot by the end of the day. I'll have the boy bring it to you. And no need to pay anything, sir. It's on the house."

Well, that was a first and no mistake. If Finch hadn't been in the war, he must've managed not to be and felt bad about it. Whichever, it gave Tom a chance to see the veteran again, and maybe talk to him man to man.

Tom had something pretty important to talk about.

An afternoon sure lasted longer when you had a reason to be somewhere else. And then Finch started making grumbling noises, as if the boot was somehow causing him trouble. Would Finch work late for once to finish it, and send Tom along home?

But just when Tom had about given up, Finch started polishing the boot. He took a fair long time over it, which was probably his way of showing respect to the owner, as much as it aggravated Tom to keep waiting. Finally Finch wiped off the extra blacking and plunked the boot down on the work table. "All done. You go on and take it to the customer before you go home." He stopped to bray out a laugh. "And don't you go getting too drunk to find your way!"

Tom wrapped the boot in a clean polishing cloth and left before Finch could annoy him some more. When he got to the saloon, the veteran was sitting at a stool at the counter, an empty glass in front of him, looking like he was daydreaming or maybe remembering. Tom took the stool next to him, nodded to the barkeep, and put the boot on the counter. When the veteran came back from wherever he'd been wandering and reached for the boot, Tom said, "I'd be honored to buy you a drink, Mr. —"

The veteran smiled, which made him look years younger than Tom had been figuring. "My name's Conrad, Miles Conrad. Thank you, son, I could handle one more. Whiskey."

Tom ordered the whiskey and a beer for himself while Conrad put the boot on, as casual as if every other man in the place had one leg of flesh and one of wood. When the drinks came, Tom took a gulp of bottled courage, waited for the veteran to take a sip of whiskey, and forced out the question he'd been stewing on all afternoon. "Sir, unless the folks you've been around since the war are a lot different from folks here, I'd wager some of 'em like to make sport of you one way and another. Or treat you like . . ." He knew what he wanted to say, but couldn't get the words out. The man could easy take it wrong.

"Like I'm not really a man any more, and they're doing me a favor by not expecting me to act like one?" Conrad's mouth twisted in a grimace. "Oh, yes. I encounter folks like that often enough."

Tom took another gulp and blurted out, "What do you *do* about it?"

Conrad drained half his glass. "Mostly I ignore it, act like they've said nothing — or said something else altogether. That can be entertaining, watching them wonder whether they heard wrong or I've gone off my rocker or what."

Tom pictured trying that, next time some fellow in town made a wisecrack or treated him like a halfwit. It didn't sound all that satisfying.

"Of course, sometimes there's nothing for it but to fight. Word of that gets around pretty quick and makes a difference."

Tom put his glass down hard enough for the barkeep to look sharp at him. "*Fight*? How? I tried that —" He remembered yesterday, laying sprawled in the dirt.

Conrad looked at him with a little smile. "I'll bet you stood up as tall as you could and tried to punch the man's head."

Tom stared at him. "That's right."

The veteran shook his head slowly and finished his drink. "That's not how you go about it, not any more. You need to work with what you've got, and in ways they won't expect. Here, I'll show you."

He stood up, looked around the room, and went over to where O'Connor the blacksmith and Davis the tobacconist were sitting at a table, each with a glass almost empty. "Excuse me, gentlemen. I'm looking for a volunteer." The echo of his own words seemed to bother him for a second before he shook it off and went on. "I need to show young —"

"Tom."

" — young Tom here how a cripple fights. Will one of you assist me with a demonstration?"

Just as Tom could've told him, the two men looked at each other with their eyes bugged out in a "did I just hear that?" sort of way. The blacksmith turned to Conrad and said, in a tone Tom had heard plenty times too many, "Sure, and I wouldn't want to be harming someone who fought for our country."

Conrad snorted. "If I was that easy to break, I'd never have made it through the war. I swear I won't hold it against you if I get banged up a little."

The blacksmith shook his head, but the tobacconist, a sight thinner man, stood up. "If you're really wanting to do this, I could oblige you."

From the look on his face, he was thinking something like *and that'll teach the youngster what fool things he shouldn't do*. But Conrad clapped him on the back and said, "Excellent! Let's go out back, shall we?"

By now, a few other men were listening, and as Conrad, Tom, and the tobacconist headed out back, they trailed along after. That got the attention of a few more, and by the time Conrad and the tobacconist faced off, they had a circle of rowdy men around them, calling out encouragement to one or the other, or friendly insults to the tobacconist. Even the barkeep left the counter to come watch, though standing near the door in case someone called for another drink.

Conrad turned to Tom. "Will you do the honors? Give us the word to start. And then watch closely."

Tom cleared his throat, which had somehow got awful dry, and said, "All right then — now!"

The tobacconist looked around as if thinking better of the whole idea, but took a swing at the veteran's head — which suddenly wasn't there to hit. Conrad had dropped to the ground on his hands and his good knee. Next second, he'd lunged at the tobacconist's legs, grabbing one of them and jerking it sideways. Taken by surprise, the tobacconist waved his arms wildly and fell over, dust billowing up where he landed. The veteran scrambled on top of him, sitting on his chest and holding his arms. He said without turning his head, "Now if this were someone who'd done me wrong or meant me ill, I'd be holding his right hand, guessing he was right-handed, and punching his face with my left." He let go. "But seeing as the gentleman has done me no wrong, and means me no harm, and has in fact been most obliging, I'll do nothing of the kind." He rolled off the tobacconist and stood up quicker'n Tom could, dusting off his trousers.

The crowd around them had gone quiet at the unexpected turn of events, but now broke out in cheers and applause. Conrad bowed toward where the thickest cluster of men stood and headed back into the saloon. "Come on, Tom. I've more to say about what I've showed you."

As they sat back down, the barkeep put another whiskey in front of the veteran, with a big smile suggesting it'd be free. But Conrad waved it off. "Thank you kindly, but I've had as much as I think wise. Perhaps my companion would enjoy it?"

Tom didn't drink whiskey that often, and wasn't real sure he could walk straight if he drank it now, but he didn't like to say no. He picked up the glass and took as small a swallow as he thought fitting for a man. Meanwhile, the veteran looked hard at the barkeep, as if suggesting he busy himself elsewhere. When the barkeep had moved on down the counter, Conrad said under his breath, "That audience we collected was less than helpful, as far as your using what I showed you. That trick won't work as well on a man who's expecting it. So you need more." He looked around, and his voice dropped to a whisper. "Here's something they won't expect. It takes practice ahead of time. You need to start standing on your wooden leg — just on that leg — for as long as you can. And when you can do that, start jerking yourself one way and another, and try to stand up notwithstanding. Can you guess why?"

Tom puzzled over it. Why would he want to stand on that leg? Why not . . . oh! "So's I can kick the other fellow with my good leg?"

"Right! Glad to see you're thinking. It's the element of surprise again. You'll need to aim for a spot you're pretty sure you can reach and where the kick'll do enough good, like his ankle or the back of his knee."

Tom could hardly wait to get home and start practicing. "Anything else? Anything that works as well on a man who's seen it before?" After all, some fellows would get boiling mad if a gimp beat 'em in a fight, and come back for more to show it weren't nothing but a fluke.

The veteran got real serious. "Don't kid yourself. You're at a disadvantage in a fight whether or not the man knows what's coming. A bright lad like you might be able to think up some other tricks, but you keep that in mind. That's why you don't fight every time someone riles you. And you never pick a fight to show how tough you are. You fight if you have to."

Tom chewed that over, not liking the taste. "Did you learn those tricks just from fighting when you had to?"

Conrad blinked like he was surprised, and then laughed quietly. "Well, I confess I might have been a little too ready to fight, the year or two after the war." He went sober again. "Like I figure you are. But I was lucky. If there's one thing the both of us should have learned by now, it's not to count on luck."

Well, he couldn't argue that. But still. "I don't know about you, sir, but I figure if I don't keep hoping for some luck now and again, I'll just give up altogether. I need more luck'n the next man, if I'm to have any sort of a life. So I'll hope for it, and try to remember to pray for it. And then see what happens."

Conrad raised his eyebrows. "You might be right at that. And if you're wrong, there's no rush about learning as much. Good luck to you, Tom. And thanks for bringing my boot."

Tom had to swallow before he could talk. "Thank you, sir. For what you showed me and what you told me, both. It won't go to waste."

Tom snuck out early next morning, hoping no one would be awake to watch him. For a few minutes, he thought he'd managed it. But then his sister's voice drowned out the clucking of the chickens.

"What in the world are you doing? You look like a drunk turkey." Martha stared at him like he'd lost his wits, such as they were.

Tom, taken unawares, had to grab the corral fence to keep from falling. He did his best to look dignified notwithstanding. "I'm practicing."

"Practicing what? Being a fence post?"

Tom dearly longed to stick out his tongue at her the way he used to. "I'm improving my balance. You never know when it could come in handy." She'd no need to know just when it might.

Martha shrugged. "Well, you stop practicing or whatever it is you're doing. Pa says finish your morning chores and then come have your breakfast."

Chapter 20

MAMIE stood up from her desk and snapped her fingers in Jenny's face. "Come back here, girl! Where'd you drift off to? I was telling you about that gentleman I'll likely be sending your way, next time he comes in."

Jenny hadn't heard a word of it. "I'm sorry, ma'am. Could you tell me the most important part over again?"

Mamie studied her face and said, in a tone close to a warning, "I hope you're not still fretting about that harpy in town. You've had plenty of time to get over her."

It probably wasn't the time to ask Mamie what a harpy was. "No, ma'am. I mean — I'm not, and yes'm, I've had time enough."

Mamie shook her head, closed the door, and pointed to a chair. As Jenny lowered herself into it, Mamie leaned back against the desk instead of going back behind it. "Set yourself down. Whatever's cluttering up your mind, you'd best spill it so there's room for what I tell you."

She'd been trying to get up the nerve to ask Mamie a question, and here Mamie was ordering her to. "Ma'am, I was just wondering, that is . . . have any of your girls got married? To a customer, or someone in town, or anyone?"

Mamie looked a little smug, like she'd guessed what she was going to hear. "You were just wondering. Curiosity out of nowhere. Not because you've grown fond of a particular customer."

Jenny usually knew better than to answer back to Mamie, but Mamie was poking her in a tender spot. "I don't see how my reason changes the answer none."

Mamie's hand twitched like it might want to give Jenny a slap. Jenny held her breath, trying not to scoot her chair any farther from the desk. But Mamie put her hand back on the desk and even chuckled. "I'd rather a girl have spirit than bore the life out of me. All right, then, we'll start with my answering your question. I've seen it three times in the years I've run this place, and once before then. And now, before you get all starry-eyed, you should ask me how it worked out."

Jenny slumped back in the chair. "Yes, ma'am, please."

"The one who got married when I worked elsewhere, I never did find out about, being as I left not long after. The first one of my girls who married was back here inside of three months. The man'd gone back East and left her. Later she heard he'd gone and got married again, no doubt not bothering to tell his new bride she was the second of two — or maybe more."

Jenny gasped, and right away felt a fool. Mamie kept going. "The second one stayed married, 'til she died in childbed. The third, well, they left town, heading farther west. I got a letter from her a while back. She was still married, but he didn't treat her too well. Kept throwing what she'd been up to her, and spending his evenings at a dirty little hookshop in their dirty little town. She daren't complain, naturally, and he knew as much."

Jenny put her chin down, knowing it probably made her look like a sulky child. "But it doesn't *have* to turn out that way. The one who died, she might've been happy if she'd lived. Not every man would treat a woman like that last fellow."

Mamie slumped a little, which hardly ever happened, and sighed, which happened even less. "Not every man, it may be, but if you were betting — such as betting your heart and your future — that's the way to bet. A man might think he can handle his woman having been a soiled dove, but after a while it eats at him. It'd be a rare kind of man who can live with it. Maybe one who actually thinks that men and women aren't so different deep down, and that if a man can lie with a passel of women and then love and be true to just one, a woman can do the same with a man." Now it was Mamie who had a faraway sort of look. "Don't know as I've ever met a man like that, at least to know he was."

A new thought stung Jenny like a bee. To credit it, she'd have to think she was valuable property in Mamie's eyes, but that stood to reason, really. She let herself sound sarcastic, half expecting that overdue slap. "And you're telling me all this for my own good and nothing else, I guess."

To her relief, Mamie gave a little smile, like she approved of Jenny thinking clear. "Partly. I care about all my girls, whether or not any of you believe it, and I hate to see them making old mistakes. But yes, I'd be sorry to lose you. You're coming along pretty well so far. I can see you making me a lot of money and yourself a pretty little nest egg. Which you could use to go anywhere you like, without some man telling you where and when."

Jenny had traveled alone after the city slicker left her high and dry. She couldn't say whether she'd been more scared or more lonely, but plenty of both. Of course she'd been younger then. Would it be any different if she did it in a few years, and with money in her pocket?

Mamie brushed her hands together like she was brushing away all Jenny's trouble-making questions. "Now then. Mr. Hendershot, as I was saying, saw you on his way out and was quite taken with you — your shape and your hair. Talk to Adeline about his tastes and how to satisfy him most efficiently. I don't know just when we'll see him again, but he'll be in town for a while, so it could be soon. Off you go."

* * * * *

Ma came into the barn where Tom was working on his latest saddle with two lanterns to help him see. Her eyes fair popped when she saw it. "That's real different, isn't it? Where did you learn that?"

Tom looked at his work, still almost as surprised as Ma by what he was doing. "Two cowboys came by, and one of 'em'd been down south into Mexico, got a fancy saddle there. Them Mexicans put silver on saddles, and this saddle had these round engraved silver circle things, with slots for the saddle strings to go through or sometimes just to make the saddle fancy. I told the other feller I couldn't do exactly that, but if he got me some silver, I could maybe get it melted into shapes and put those wherever it'd look nice. It'd cost plenty, but I guess cowboys down south can earn that much somehow." He stopped to push away his old dream of being such. "And that saddle had more carving in the leather that most cowboys around these parts have, which I could do right enough." Though some of it must've been done with tools he didn't have, and had no way to get. Even if he knew where to order them, he could hardly do it without word getting out once they showed up.

Ma reached out to run a finger along the carving and give a light touch to the silver. "How'd you get the silver melted?"

Tom tightened his mouth up. "I had to get O'Connor — the blacksmith — to help. He swore he wouldn't tell Finch. I have to hope he'll keep his word."

He just hoped the cowboy'd be pleased enough for it to be worth the risk Tom was running. Instead of engraving the silver, he'd had O'Connor turn it into thin wavy strips that Tom could put on. He'd had to think up a way to keep the silver in place, ending up with a piece sticking out the back like a pin, but hooked at the end, that stuck partway into the saddle. There'd been enough silver to put it in four different places.

It pleased Ma, anyhow. She admired it a while longer before she fidgeted from foot to foot and said, "I've been meaning to ask you. You haven't been visiting our neighbors much. Nor seeing many other folk your age. Wouldn't it be a nice change from just us here and Mr. Finch in town?"

Tom straightened up and studied her face. She was blushing a little — enough to make him suspicious. "And just why are you all of a sudden thinking I need to get more social?"

Fidget, blush, fidget. "It's just that — well, it'd be good for you, to start thinking about finding a girl. A young man your age, it's none too soon for you to think about courting. Starting a family of your own. Though you could still live here, naturally, if you and she cared to."

He'd been expecting Ma to start singing that song sooner or later. In fact, she had done, right before the plowshare fell on him. Never since. So why now?

He could sort of picture him and Pa building a new room on, him coming home at night to —

But what he saw in his head, coming in that door they hadn't built yet, was a woman with bright eyes, generous curves, and lots of red hair.

That's what Ma must have heard about.

"Ma, is there some kind of talk you've been listening to, that has you so eager to match me up?"

Ma had her apron in her hands and was twisting it like she was washing it. "I did hear, when I went to that quilting bee last week, some of the ladies were saying . . . that you'd been going to that place. The — the house where those women are. Loose women." Her lips went thin. "That you'd been there more than once, even."

Tom stood up and put his fists on his hips. "Well, what if it's true, then? What difference does it make to anybody?"

Ma gasped and seemed to go searching for what to say. "Well — well — you could catch who knows what from those women!"

"Doc showed me how to keep that from happening." Though he maybe shouldn't've mentioned Doc. Too late now.

Meanwhile, Ma had found her next shot to fire. "But women like that, they're not good for a young man, they're — they're hard, like, and bound to take advantage, and lead you away from the good path . . . . Oh, Tom, I'm afraid for you!"

Tom thought back to the months before the first time he went to Mamie's, and almost shivered to remember. "Ma, I love you dearly, and I thank you for caring about me, but you don't know. You just don't. When I first went there, I hated everything I could think of, except you and Pa and Martha and Billy. I hated everyone I saw, on account of what I figured they was thinking when they looked at me. I hated morning when it came, for what the day was like to bring, and I hated the day, and I hated evening when things had gone about like I figured. And then I met Jenny — yeah, she's got a name, and it's Jenny, and she's the purtyiest thing I've ever seen — and she's maybe tougher'n the neighbor girls, 'cause she has to be, but she's not hard — somehow, she ain't got that way. She's nice to me, and maybe I'm just a damn fool —" Ma gasped again at his language, but there was no stopping him now. "Maybe I am, but I think she's nice because she means it, because she likes me. And this — " He whacked his wooden leg hard enough to jar the stump. "This don't scare her or make her feel sick. And she's seen what I can do on leather, and she thinks it's swell, instead of only thinking about all the things I *can't* do, like a farm girl would. . . . It's maybe because of Jenny that I've started thinking about my future, leastwise as something more'n what I've got to put up with until my time runs out. I think it's due to her I'm doing this work you see. Just for that, I owe her more'n I can say. And those who say they love me owe her plenty!"

Ma looked altogether lost. She wrung her hands and then slumped back against the side of the barn. "I just don't know. I don't know what the world's coming to. I don't know how to keep my boy safe, and on the path of righteousness."

"Ma, weren't you just saying how I was a man now, and ready to make my own path?" Well, she hadn't said exactly that, but close enough.

What would it take to get Ma thinking different about Jenny? Was that a trick Jenny could somehow do? "I wish you could meet her, somehow."

He half expected Ma to bolt from the barn at the very idea. But she studied Tom's face as if she could see Jenny's through it. "If this girl has done all you say, I don't know what to think. My thinking's all in a whirl."

Not having her push back hard against the idea took

some of the starch out of him. "Way things are, it's hard enough for me to see her. The one time she snuck out and met me in town, it ended up in a heck of a mess."

Ma seemed to be out of things to say, and Tom too. He stood still for her to come and kiss his cheek, and gave her the hug he'd been keeping. When she left, he looked back down at the saddle. At least that was something he could do, and hope to get right.

Chapter 21

JENNY woke up, saw the slant of the sun through the window, and jumped out of bed in a panic. Somehow she'd managed to oversleep! But how could that happen? Mamie always came through knocking on their doors and calling them to get their bones out of bed — "until you get back in with some company." Why hadn't she done it today?

And there was some kind of commotion in the hall, lots of girls talking, and wasn't that somebody *crying*?

She scrambled out of bed and stuck her head out the door. It was Trudi crying. Trudi was one of the older girls, and one of the tougher, and Jenny'd never seen her cry before nor even imagined it.

Jenny ran up to her, calling out, "What is it? What's happened?"

Trudi turned toward her with red, swollen eyes and wet cheeks. "It's Mandy. She took too much laudanum. Doc Gibbs is with her, but it looks bad."

Amanda Jane? But she always seemed to know just what she was doing. Nothing got under her skin, Jenny'd thought. Was it an accident, or had she meant to —

Jenny started crying herself as she ran to Amanda Jane's room. Most of the girls were clustered there, some talking and some crying like her, blocking not just the doorway but part of the hall. And Mamie wasn't there doing anything about it. She must be in the room with Amanda

Jane and Doc.

Bessie was one of the ones talking, Sophie bawling next to her. Jenny grabbed Bessie by the elbow and interrupted her. "What happened? Who found her, and how did they know?"

Bessie might not be crying, but she looked paler'n Jenny'd ever seen her. "Mamie was waking girls up and wanted to tell Amanda Jane about some customer Mamie expected. From what Trudi says, Mandy was lying there acting half asleep, but scratching herself all over, except real slow. And when Mamie bent over her, she could tell Mandy was breathing awful slow too. So she sent Trudi to fetch Doc, but when he got here, he said she must've taken the laudanum hours ago. I saw him when he came near the door for a moment, and he looked awful sober."

Bessie turned away to take Sophie in her arms, so Jenny looked around for one of the others who might know more. Trudi had joined the group and was standing there real quiet. Jenny tapped her on the shoulder, but nothing happened. When she tried again, Trudi jumped and stared at Jenny like she'd never seen her before.

Jenny mustered up her nerve and asked, "Did you know Amanda Jane was taking laudanum? Did she do it regular?"

Trudi seemed to come back from wherever she'd been. "Not back when I first knew her. She started maybe a year ago, when she got to thinking more about how old she was getting and where her life was likely to head." She stared off at nothing again. "She said something last week about a customer giving her a special kind if she did something extra for him. I didn't think nothing of it."

Just then, Doc and Mamie pushed their way through the crowd of girls enough to stand in the doorway. It seemed to take forever for everyone to hush up. When they finally had, Mamie said, her voice real tight, "Doc says that if any of you want to say goodbye, you'd better do it."

A wild mix of different girls crying welled up. Trudi got hold of herself first and yelled out, "Quiet, all of you!" They mostly quieted down enough for her to ask Mamie, "Why couldn't Doc help her?"

Mamie looked like she was going to tell Trudi off, but Doc put a hand on Mamie's arm and answered, "An overdose of laudanum has to be handled right away. There's a drug I can give to make the person vomit up what they took, but by the time anyone knew what had happened, too much of the drug had been in her too long." He stopped, and Jenny could see his Adam's apple jerk like he was swallowing hard. "I've seen it before, when wounded soldiers take too much laudanum or morphine, by mistake or when their pain became too much for them. The doctors couldn't help if the man was found too late. I couldn't do any better." All of a sudden he looked different, angry, as angry as ever Papa did. "And it seems some scum of a medicine show pitchman gave her something stronger than she was used to." He breathed hard, calming himself, and got to just looking sad again. "I'm sorry."

Mamie grabbed his hand and gripped it hard, pulled him out of the doorway into the room, and faced the girls. "Any of you wanting to go in, you get in a line. Four at a time by her bed. And don't take too long about it."

Jenny stood there frozen. Did she want to say goodbye, if it meant seeing Amanda Jane lying there dying?

By the time she decided to get in line, the group that went in a little ways ahead of her came out, some crying even harder, one screaming. Amanda Jane was gone.

Mamie shooed the girls away from the door. "It's over.

The rest of you can say your goodbyes when we bury her. Now leave us be." As she closed the door, Jenny could see Doc sitting in Amanda Jane's customer chair, bent over, his head in his hands.

Mamie called them all together in the main lounge an hour later. "We're closed, today and the next two days. We'll bury her day after tomorrow. Any of you that don't have something that feels right to wear, you come talk to me."

Sophie piped up, "Where will they be burying her? I heard there's not a lot of room left in the cemetery, that they've talked of starting up a new one."

Mamie clenched her fists tight, another thing Jenny couldn't recall ever seeing before this terrible day. "Didn't you know? They won't put the likes of us in the cemetery, next to *decent* folks. They'll be burying her alongside in that empty field." She looked out over their heads toward where the preacher lived. "But maybe they'll forget and put the new cemetery there, and Mandy'll be in it after all and get the last laugh. She'd like that."

And then, finally, Mamie dropped into a chair and started to cry. Bessie went to her and put an arm around her, and Mamie let her. The rest of them filed out of the room, quiet as the grave.

Jenny went back to her room for lack of any better thought. All she could picture was having someone come hold her, like Bessie was holding Mamie. But she couldn't see any of the girls in that picture.

She lay down on her bed, closing her eyes, wishing hard that she could go back to sleep, knowing it wouldn't happen. But something did drift into her head, like a waking dream. Tom, lying on the bed alongside her, his big strong arm holding her tight.

It'd been a whole day since Amanda Jane died, and Jenny'd hardly been able to think about anything else. She'd been lying in bed, and getting up and pacing around, and lying in bed again, and getting up again, for maybe hours. She hadn't known she could feel drained and restless at the same time. It felt kind of like having a fever, though she hadn't had one since she was little. Remembering that, remembering Mama's hand on her forehead, made her want to start crying again, but she was so sick of crying . . .

When someone knocked on her door, she called out, "Come on in!" and then hoped it wasn't Mamie, who'd be mighty put out at her not getting up to open it. But it was Bessie, and she came in and sat on the bed.

"Doc's here. Mamie called for him, on account of so many of the girls being so upset. She didn't want to give 'em laudanum after what's happened, but she didn't know what else to do. He's in our room now talking to Sophie. Would you like him to come see you next?"

Didn't seem likely Doc could do much to help, but he'd always treated her kindly, and she could use all the kindly she could get today. "I'd like that, and my thanks for thinking of it."

Bessie pressed her hand and left, her feet dragging. Jenny flopped back against the pillow, and rolled around trying to find some way to lie there that felt right. Nothing did.

It wasn't long before she heard the kind of knock that you could tell was a man's. The door cracked a little open, and Doc said, "Jenny, are you ready for me to come in?"

This time she got up and met him at the door. She even called up something like a smile, but it felt so strange on her face that she dropped it. Doc came in, looking almost as sad as she felt, but then he made his own try at a smile, a bit better'n hers. He looked around like he didn't know just what to do with himself, so she sat on the bed and waved toward the chair.

Once he'd sat down, he said, "I've brought something that may help you and the other girls feel better. It's lemon balm tea. Somebody's granny told me once that it was good for soothing people, and it turns out the Indians use it too, though they prepare it differently. I can fetch you some."

"Doc, you shouldn't go fetching and carrying for me —"

He hushed her. "I want to do everything I can, and it's little enough."

He looked even sadder as he said it. She took hold of his shoulder and shook him a little, wondering at where she got the nerve. "Doc, it wasn't your fault. None of us think it was."

He tried for a smile again and didn't manage it. "Thank you for saying that, my dear, but it's what I think that matters more just now. Or rather, what I feel, which is that somehow, I should have been able to save that poor girl." He took a deep breath. "And now, I'll make myself useful and get you that tea."

While he was getting it, Jenny sat at her dressing table and tried to tidy up. Her eyes were still swollen from all the crying she did before, and her hair was such a tangle she could barely get a comb through it. Trying got her feeling so wild, she pulled a clump of hair clean out and threw the comb down just as Doc came back with a steaming cup that smelled good. He acted like he hadn't noticed and put the cup down on the dressing table, saying, "Blow on that a bit and drink it up."

She picked it up and only then noticed that her hand was shaking. She managed not to spill but a couple of drops. Doc patted her shoulder and walked softly away, closing her door behind him.

Something stopped him, though, not far outside her door. Jenny took another drink of the tea, put it down, and crept over on tiptoe to listen. What she heard was Mamie's voice, sounding fretful. "How is she? I don't know whether to worry more about the older ones more like Mandy, who've seen too much, or the young ones who haven't had such a chance to build their defenses up."

Jenny had to press her ear to the door to hear what Doc was saying. "I'm hoping the tea will help. But if I may suggest it, I think it'd do Jenny good to get out of here for a while, get some fresh air and a change of scene." Then, as if Mamie had got ready to object, "Now I know Jenny got into some trouble a while back, but I could go with her, be her escort. Or chaperone, if you want to think of it that way."

Neither of them said anything for a minute. Jenny could just picture the look Mamie was likely giving him. "And does Jenny need this kind of outing more than the others, to make you offer to take her under your wing?"

Jenny'd seen Doc blush a few times, and she couldn't help but wonder if he was blushing now. "Well, she's the one we were discussing, as well as the one you might not trust out on her own, given that bit of history."

Another quiet stretch, until Mamie finally said, "All right, then. I won't ask too many questions. So long as you promise to keep an eye on her, and not let her do anything likely to cause her more grief."

Then Doc's voice, kind of low. "I'm no wiser than any other man, and I can't tell the future. But I'll do my best."

She heard Mamie's footsteps moving down the hall,

and only Mamie's. She jumped back from the door in time to be clear of it when Doc opened it again. He saw how close she was standing, though, and smiled better'n he'd been able to before. "I gather you heard what I proposed. Would you like to get out for a bit?"

Jenny walked over to the corner of the room farthest from the door and crooked her finger to draw him after her. When he'd joined her, or almost, she whispered, "Is there anything you didn't tell Mamie about what we'd be doing?"

He got a funny expression, halfway between a man pleased with himself for being clever and a boy caught in mischief. "Well, I was hoping we could find a way to let you see young Tom."

It felt like he'd lit a sparkler in Jenny's chest. Maybe it looked like that too, because Doc laughed — the first time she'd seen him cheerful since Amanda Jane took the drug that killed her — and added, "I hadn't got as far as figuring out how. I don't imagine you'd want us to go strolling up to Mr. Finch's shop."

Jenny shuddered at the thought. It'd been a long time since she had to lay with Finch, but she remembered his way of looking at a girl like he was stripping her in his mind and then drooling over her. She could just imagine how he'd look if she turned up. "Nossir, you got that right."

Doc fingered his chin. "We could go to my office, and I could ask someone — my friend Robert, perhaps — to take Tom a note. But Tom would have to say something to Mr. Finch before he could come away."

Doc and Jenny walked to Doc's office and drew some stares, but not as many as Jenny had figured. When she asked Doc about it, he chuckled and said, "They probably assume you have some ailment that needs treating at my office, rather than out of my bag. Feel free to look as ill as you can." Then he went sober again. "Though you're looking less than your usual bonny self."

Once they got to the office, he settled her down with another cup of that special tea and stepped out to fetch his friend the pharmacist. Jenny'd seen him a time or two at Mamie's, mostly just drinking at the bar while Doc did his exams upstairs. He took off his hat to her as he walked in and smiled in a regular, friendly way. "Good afternoon! I hear we have some conspiring to do."

The pharmacist sat in a chair, looking real at home, and Doc sat on the edge of his desk, saying, "As Miss Hayes' physician, I've prescribed a meeting with young Tom Barlow to treat her quite understandable melancholy. Isn't that right, Miss Hayes?"

It'd been so long since Jenny'd heard her own last name that it fair startled her. It took a minute for her to get her wits back enough to answer. "Yessir, Mr. — I'm afraid I don't know your name, mister."

He smiled at her again, wider this time, but still like a gentleman. "It's Jones." He leaned back in his chair, quite at ease. "I'm thinking it might be a good sight easier to get Tom over here than the two of you are thinking. Did either of you contemplate just telling Finch the truth? He's not a bad sort, really."

Jenny's mouth dropped open. "That's not how Tom tells it." Too late, she realized she shouldn't tell on Tom that way. "But please don't tell Finch I said that, or Tom neither." Though she'd fess up to Tom sooner or later, maybe when he was feeling good and in a forgiving mood.

* * * * *

People had been drifting in and out of Finch's shop since yesterday morning, with their different ways of gossiping — whispering, or pulling a long face, or practically rubbing their hands over having bad news to share. Finch grumbled between visits about getting no work done, but he seemed happy enough to listen.

None of the folks coming in talked right to Tom, but he heard enough of what they said that he knew what happened. One of the girls at Mamie's, the older one who seemed so sure of herself, had taken so much laudanum it killed her. Jenny must be awful shook by it. He didn't know if she'd been friends with the dead girl, but she might've been, and for sure they knew each other. Maybe she'd even seen the body. . . . Tom had never seen Jenny cry, but somehow he could picture it.

The pharmacist was next to come in. Tom hadn't pictured him for one to enjoy chewing over a scandal, but he didn't know the man to talk to, so he shouldn't be surprised. Seemed like he was one of the whisperers, or almost. He pulled Finch aside and talked to him pretty low. But for some reason, both of them kept looking over at Tom. Was it because Finch knew, and maybe took pleasure in telling the other man, that Tom had been to Mamie's? Well, he'd ignore it. Somebody in this shop would get some work done today.

He was cutting out a boot upper when the two of them walked over. He had to look up then, but he didn't see what he'd expected. Finch wasn't smirking at him, nor winking at the pharmacist, nor looking anything but — was he actually looking sorry about what'd happened?

Of course, he might've laid with the dead girl, back when he used to go to Mamie's. Maybe Finch could have decent feelings about someone he'd known dying, even a soiled dove.

Finch cleared his throat. "Mr. Jones here tells me that your gal from Mamie's is over at Doc's place. Seems she's taken that other girl's death pretty hard, and Doc thinks it'd do her good if you was to go and visit with her." Then, when Tom was wondering if someone had somehow swapped Finch for an imposter, came the leer he'd been expecting. "Just visit, mind. You can go there to cheer her up, if you've a mind to, not to cheer yourself up."

Tom stood up as quick as he was able. "That's mighty good of you, Mr. Finch. I'll go and do that, with your leave."

The pharmacist clapped his hands together. "That's all settled, then! I'll walk with you. And Mr. Finch, thank you kindly for your consideration."

They walked on out the door, Tom blinking at the sunlight and still half believing he'd fallen asleep at the work table and was dreaming the whole thing. Once they got far enough from the shop to be out of earshot, he asked Jones, "How's Jenny doing?"

The man considered before answering. "I don't know the young lady well, but I wouldn't describe her as cheerful. I'd venture to say she'll be very glad to see you."

As they got near Doc's office, Jones said, "You go on in. Doc promised Mamie he'd stay near Jenny, but I'd guess he'll interpret 'near' to mean something less than hovering right over the two of you." He clapped Tom on the shoulder and gave him a little shove toward the door before going on his way.

Tom hadn't thought to look at himself in a shop window on the way over. He combed his fingers through his hair, not knowing whether he was tidying it or making it more of a mess, and wiped his hands on his trousers before slowly opening the door and sticking his head in.

"Doc? Jenny?"

"Come in, Tom!" Doc waved him inside. "I'm glad to see Mr. Finch let you leave the shop. It seems Robert was right." He looked a lot less surprised than Tom felt.

Tom had just started to look around for Jenny when Doc said, "She's waiting for you in back. I'll stay out front, taking care of any patients who stop by." He gave Tom what was, for Doc, a pretty sharp look. "But I may need to pop into the back at any time to get equipment or supplies."

"Thanks, Doc. I appreciate it." Meaning the warning, along with everything Doc was doing for Jenny today.

He headed through the swinging door to the back room where Doc kept all sorts of stuff Tom didn't know the name or use of, and did exams that needed the patient to lie down. That meant there was a sort of raised, padded cot against one wall. Jenny was sitting on it, swinging her feet like a little girl and looking all woman. But sadder'n he'd ever seen her, and so much like what he'd imagined earlier that it spooked him some.

Tom held out his arms, and Jenny slid off the cot and walked into them without saying a word, laying her head on his chest and putting her arms around him. He held her close, then freed up one hand to stroke her hair, and she rested up against him, breathing slower, almost like she was falling asleep.

She finally pulled away, looking almost shy. "I'd hoped you'd come. That you'd be able, and would want to."

"Course I did! Want to, that is. Never would've thought Finch'd let me, but come to think of it, I just might've come anyhow."

Jenny looked up at him with wide eyes for a minute before she moved back to the cot and patted it. "There's no place else to sit." She gave him a weak version of her usual come-here smile. "Course, we could do something else with it, but Doc could come in any time, and he'd prob'ly think he had to tell Mamie on us."

Tom tried to smile back. "Reckon so." He lifted Jenny onto the cot, for the pleasure of feeling her waist, and then hoisted himself up alongside her.

They just sat there for a few minutes. Finally Jenny said, "I've took laudanum before, when I burned my arm one time. I never thought nothing of it. But Mr. Jones says what Amanda Jane took didn't come from him."

That might be the first time he'd actually heard the dead girl's name since it happened, for all the talk about her. "That's good to know. He'd have felt real bad otherwise."

More silence. Tom had just opened his mouth to ask how the other girls were taking it when Jenny said, "Tom, would you please — would you hold me some more?"

He answered by pulling her against his side, her head coming to rest on his shoulder.

With a moment to think, he realized part of why he was so tongue-tied. He had something he really wanted to say, something big. He hadn't known he was quite ready to say it until he walked in and saw Jenny, but now it was pushing everything else out of his head. Would he be taking advantage if he spoke his piece now, while she was feeling low and needed comforting? But if he didn't, when would he get the chance?

"Since I last —" He didn't, right now, want to mention the parlor house. "Since I last saw you, my saddle business is picking up right nicely. I'm learning how to add silver to the trim, and word's getting around." He paused when she distracted him by snuggling up against him. He kissed the top of her head and went on. "I'm making more money from those cowboys than from all my hours at the shop. And with the two together . . ." His tongue felt swole up big enough to trip on. "I reckon I could support a wife, so long as she didn't mind — as long as you wouldn't mind living less fine than you do at Mamie's."

Jenny had gone stiff in his arms when he said "wife." That's why he hurried up to say "you," and waited for her to look at him wide-eyed again, or maybe snuggle closer. But instead, she shoved him away and jumped off the cot, facing him with her hands on her hips and her hair flying all round.

"Tom Barlow, what are you saying? What are you *thinking*? Do you know how folk in town talk about us girls, and how they treat us?" She was just about spluttering. "Do you know where we've got to bury poor Amanda Jane? Not in the cemetery with the almighty virtuous Christian folk, no sir. They're too good for her, even when they're rotting in the ground! No, we've got to bury her *outside* it, so people can walk on her grave and feel proud of how right with the Lord they are." She was so out of breath from shouting — and God knows what Doc, and anyone out there with him, was making of this — that she had to stop and pant. "I don't care a damn about how fine I live, but I won't live among people who think I'm dirt! At least at Mamie's, we look out for each other and care about each other, even if we quarrel sometimes!"

Now that was a fine way to act, when he was offering to give her a decent life, not to mention promising to love, honor, and keep her for the rest of their lives! "Are you telling me you'd rather stay at Mamie's than get married?" *Than marry me?*

For some reason, even though that's what she'd been saying — or wasn't it? — his words got her to stop ranting and speak softer. "That's not it, exactly. And Tom, I'm sorry.

It's a real bad time for me to hear this. It's awful sweet of you to think of me that way. And — and I reckon we could get on together, if it weren't for everything else. I like you real well. I've never liked any man so much."

That was more like it. It was a start, at least —

"But — I've been thinking about something altogether different."

What in blazes could she mean? "Something different like what?"

Now she was acting nervous. "I haven't done nothing about it, not even talked to any of the other girls. But I was thinking I might want to go to traveling with another girl, like Sophie and Bessie who come to Mamie's a few months back. They go from house to house, or set up by themselves, and don't stay nowhere no longer'n they like to."

Tom had been keeping his temper pretty well, he figured, but this was just too much. "So rather'n marry me, you'd rather go be a whore someplace else?"

Jenny flinched like he'd slapped her. She blinked hard, maybe keeping tears back, staring at him. Right away he was sorry. It'd been a true enough word, but it wasn't kind of him to say it to her face. Even if she was talking crazy.

And to top it all, Doc came in, looking all apologetic, and said, "I'm afraid I've got to be getting Jenny back soon. You'd better say your goodbyes for now." He looked from Jenny to Tom, and his voice went low, almost like a preacher might — a preacher less given to shouting than the one they had. "Mamie had a reason for letting Jenny come out like this, and I'll feel I haven't justified her confidence if I take her home lower in spirits than she set out. I'll give you a little more time to put things right."

Doc went out front again, and the two of them looked at each other like kids caught putting horse harness on the cows. Tom slid down from the cot and took both Jenny's hands in his. "How'd this all get so tangled up, when what I came here to do was help you on a hard day — when all I want to do from now on is take care of you?"

Jenny sighed deep enough to make her chest reach halfway across to him, which he felt bad about noticing just now. "Maybe it wouldn't be no better, traveling around and still — doing what I do. But if people I don't hardly know despise me, maybe it'd hurt less than if I've been living down the road from them for years. And maybe we could get folks here to see me different, if we was to marry — but that's not what Mamie says. . . . I just don't know."

Was it Mamie who was spoiling his chances? No time to ask more about it, with Doc coming back any minute. Fair desperate to have Jenny something the better for his coming, he moved closer, slow enough for her to stop him. When she didn't, he put his arms around her one more time. It took a couple of minutes, with Tom all the time waiting to hear Doc at the door, but she finally hugged him back.

Was there anything more he could say or do, to make his coming here less of a mistake?

When an idea came to him, he hadn't time to puzzle over whether it was a good one. "Will you let me come with you to the funeral?"

* * * * *

Of all the things Jenny thought Tom might say just then, he'd hit on one she'd never have dreamed. Tom wanted to be there, standing with Mamie and her girls for all the town to see, honoring a painted lady? She pulled back and stared at him. "What would your folks say?"

Tom looked like he'd be shuffling his feet, if he had two

of them. "Ma knows about you — about how I feel about you. I told her. And I don't care who else knows. If we was to marry like I want, they'd all know soon enough."

How would the other girls feel about a customer being in the middle of them when they were crying and carrying on? And what would Mamie say? "I'll have to ask Mamie, and then the other girls if she says it's all right. The funeral's tomorrow morning, an hour after sunup — I'll try to let you know by then, somehow."

Tom stood up straight with his chin out and his mouth set stubborn. "I'll show up, anyhow, and stand back a ways. If you haven't had a chance to send word, you beckon me closer or wave me off."

As flabbergasted as she was, Jenny hadn't noticed Doc come in. He might've been standing there a while, for all she knew. Now he cleared his throat and said, "I'm sorry, but it's time."

Jenny reached out and grabbed Tom's hands, squeezing them tight. "Thank you. Whatever happens. I — I appreciate it, plenty."

Tom pulled her close one more time and kissed her on the lips, real gentle. "I'll do what Mamie and the other girls say. But I want to be there. I want to be there for you."

Jenny almost started crying, but she was plumb determined not to let folks gawk at her crying in the street. Tom let go, and Doc took her arm and led her out of the office and back toward Mamie's. He didn't say anything the first few steps, but then asked, "Did I hear correctly just now? Has Tom asked to come to poor Amanda Jane's funeral?"

Jenny felt something warm glowing somewhere in her chest. Pride, it was, pride that a man she liked thought enough of her to stand up in front of everyone, showing that what she was didn't matter enough to keep him away. "Yessir, he did. But you may have heard, I'll have to ask Mamie and the others."

"It's a very good thought, and I'm ashamed I didn't have it first. I'd like to be there as well, if I may."

That was too much for her to handle without tears coming. She wiped them away as quick as she could. "That's awful good of you, Doc. Whatever Mamie and the girls say about Tom, I reckon they'd be fine with you coming, and grateful too."

They were almost to Mamie's. Doc said kind of quick, "That's a fine young man. I hope the two of you can work things out somehow."

Jenny stopped and faced Doc head on. "Can you really see some kind of way we could be together, with everyone knowing what I am, and the way folks in town look down on us — to the point where we've got to bury Amanda Jane where we do?"

Doc stuck his lip out like he did when he was thinking. She'd never tell him how it made him look like a boy about seven. "I'll have to ponder that question. If I have any bright ideas, I'll make sure to share them with you."

He wouldn't, of course. Have such ideas, that is. There was no point in her hoping.

So she'd best try not to hope.

Chapter 22

MAMIE sat behind her desk and listened to Jenny with her painted eyebrows halfway to the ceiling. When Jenny finished, she picked up a pen and rolled it around in her fingers, humming a little, before she said, "It's good you came to me first. But you know, I believe I want to see what the girls have to say before I make up my mind."

"Yes'm. Should I go around asking, or do you want to do it?"

Mamie rolled the pen around some more. "I'll call them together and ask. You'd best stay away, in case any of them would be afraid to answer honestly for fear of riling you or hurting your feelings. I'll let you know."

She could only hope Mamie hurried up about it, with Jenny's nerves strung tight with waiting. "If it's all right, how do we let Tom know?"

"I'll find a way to send a message. I've got other business to deal with, as soon as I've talked to the girls." Mamie's face got that tight look that showed she was aggravated. "I'll be seeing the preacher in a while, to talk about the service. Seems he has some concerns about how to hold a funeral with all these *disgraces to womanhood* attending." Jenny'd have bet a silver dollar Mamie was quoting the preacher. "I do believe I'll be ready to strangle that man by the time the funeral is over."

Mamie looked Jenny in the eye. "But one thing I'll be

telling the girls when I meet with them, and I'll tell you right now — you act like ladies, whatever nastiness comes out of his mouth. I'll be keeping my temper, and all of you had better do the same."

Jenny's head was still in a whirl all the rest of the afternoon and through supper. What could she do to settle her mind?

Well, one thing she could do was find out more about whether her own idea — traveling around and working that way — made any sense. She still didn't know who she'd want to, nor be able to, travel with, but at least she could find out more about what it was like. Which meant talking to Bessie or Sophie. Which one, then? Seemed like Bessie was the one who made the decisions and took care of any trouble. But . . . Bessie'd ask more questions, and have more opinions, and be more'n ready to tell them whether or not she was asked.

Jenny had a notion that with the house closed, Mamie might be letting the girls sit in the regular lounge. She peeked in from the doorway and saw she was right, with girls sitting all over, talking quiet or not even that. Bessie was there, one of the talkers, but for a change, Sophie wasn't close by. She might be crying in her room, or trying to take a nap. But it was worth checking whether she might be in the small lounge, not as far from Bessie but not in so much of a crowd.

And there Sophie was, looking lost and pitiful, holding a handkerchief and a needle but not doing nothing with 'em. She looked up when Jenny came in and tried to smile, but didn't come near managing it. As Jenny sat down next to her, she said, her voice shaking, "I couldn't stand no more of everyone jawing about Mandy and why she done it, and if only someone'd found her sooner, and why she didn't talk to nobody about being so low. Talk makes Bessie feel better, so I left her to it. And she knows I don't feel the same, so she didn't stop me."

Now it came to it, Jenny hardly knew how to get started. "I did want to talk, but to you special, and not about Amanda Jane. Would you mind that?"

To her surprise, Sophie brightened up a bit. "That'd maybe help get my mind off things, to talk about something different. And . . . I can't remember when someone other'n Bessie asked what I thought about anything. It's kind of nice."

Did everyone really just write Sophie off? If Jenny stuck around for long, she'd have to make a point of paying more attention to her, instead of just figuring Bessie would do all the talking for the pair. "I had this idea, and you'd know more'n me about how it'd work . . . . I've been thinking a lot about how you and Bessie travel round from place to place, and wondering if it's better'n staying put, and what it's like and all."

When Jenny ran out of words, Sophie sat still like she was gathering up her own thoughts. Jenny was starting to get twitchy when Sophie finally said, "It was Bessie's idea, to start with. That won't surprise you, I reckon. But we didn't much like where we was when we met, and I hadn't knowed Bessie a week before she could talk me into anything she liked."

That didn't surprise Jenny neither. But she pushed down the laugh that wanted to rise up, and waited for the rest.

"Some of the places we stayed for a while was better'n where we'd been. Some wasn't, though. And being the new girls could make it worse."

Jenny hadn't thought of that. She was just getting past being one of the new girls here, after all this time. "But sometimes you set up by yourselves, didn't you?"

Sophie shuddered. "That didn't always work out so good. If there was a house in town, the madam might send her box-herder out to threaten us." She surprised Jenny by chuckling. "One time, the fellow thought he'd knock us around. Bessie kicked him where it hurt and pulled a pistol on him. I hadn't even knowed she carried it before then."

A good idea, that. If she had a way to get hold of one.

Sophie's good cheer didn't last long. "And we was robbed once. We used to take turns sleeping, and it was Bessie's turn." She hung her head. "I didn't hardly know how to stop the feller. I just sat there. I thought about hollering, but by the time Bessie'd wake up, she couldn't hardly have got the drop on him. Bessie'd made sure we hid some of the money in the clothes we slept in, and he didn't look us over, so we didn't lose it all."

And yet they'd kept doing it. Was that all Bessie's doing? "Didn't you like nothing about it?"

Sophie relaxed back against the chair. "Oh, sure, some things. We got to see a few places, and stay longer where we liked what we found. And I wasn't scared too much of the time, along of Bessie being so good at watching over me and getting us out of scrapes."

Which more or less left Jenny where she'd started, except with a sharper picture of what could go wrong. She patted Sophie's hand. "Thanks for talking to me. I sure appreciate it."

Sophie smiled for a second, before it fell off her face. "Like I said, it was good to think about something else for a while." She looked at her sewing like it had got in her hands without her knowing, folded the needle up in the cloth, tucked both into her pocket, and stood up. "I guess I'll go see whether Bessie's got tired of the lounge yet."

Jenny followed her out and headed up to her bedroom. She might do some thinking, or else trying might help her fall asleep.

* * * * *

It was a darkish morning, clouds heavy overhead, though at least it wasn't fixing to rain just yet. Tom took his hat off and looked around.

Folk were supposed to look gloomy at a funeral, and the women all around were mostly crying, but the preacher looked about like his own pa had died and left the land to someone else. It might be having to stand there with fallen women all round him, though he'd found a place to stand as far away from 'em as he could get. Or it might be seeing Tom show up, after everything he'd said to try to keep him from it.

Your soul is in my keeping, young Tom, and I fear for the direction you seem to be headed. I'm not saying some of those women can't yet be saved, but while they live in sin and encourage men to sin, I can't be happy seeing you in their midst — even if it didn't seem you were especially drawn to one of them, to the present peril of your soul should you be taken untimely. And what will your dear mother say?

Well, he'd already talked to Ma again. He couldn't say she was happy about him going and what it likely meant, but she didn't nag him about it. And he'd told Pa as well, knowing Ma would sooner or later, and wanting Pa to hear it from him first.

Pa had been took thoughtful by it, leaning the pitchfork

on the fence in the middle of tossing out the dirty straw. "I look back to when I was your age, and if I hadn't met your ma and fallen so hard for her, I can't swear as to what I would or wouldn't have got up to — especially if Mamie had set up her place by then. Though I can't see me going so far as to make plans about a woman of that kind."

Tom bit his tongue rather'n quarrel about just what kind of woman Jenny was, and made himself be thankful that Pa wasn't lecturing, let alone ordering him to bide at home. He'd gotten more of a fight from Finch, who was awful put out that after letting Tom take time from work yesterday, Tom might be late coming in today and wouldn't take no for an answer. When he left last evening, Finch was grumbling about what things were coming to and what he might do about it.

Meanwhile, Doc had shown up — and not just Doc, but his missus, big as her belly had got, standing real tall and looking at the preacher like she was daring him to make something of it. Seeing the two of them made the preacher look glummer'n ever. Doc came up to Tom and shook his hand before going back to where Mrs. Gibbs was standing.

After doing some more frowning, the preacher started the service, almost drowned out by sobbing women. From what Tom could hear, it was a pity they weren't making a little more noise.

"The day of repentance has *passed* for the woman we inter today, and *woe* to her, and to *all* who follow the *devil's* road . . . .

"Yea, let all the *sinners* among us take *heed*, lest they too be *struck down* in the midst of their *sin* and fall forever into the fiery *pit*, there to suffer the *torments* of *Hell* for all eternity, *writhing* in the *flames*, beyond all hope of salvation . . . .

"*Beware*, all you who *hear* me! For we must *tremble* to think that this fallen woman even *now* suffers those *torments*, for she did not *repent,* as you still have time to do, but for who *knows* how *long*, as death may take *you* without *warning*, may take any one of *you* as it has taken this *sinner*, even while her *sins* blackened her *soul* . . . ."

Mamie and some of the other girls were biting their lips 'til they went white. Jenny was looking awful pale and trembling all over. And Tom, of a sudden, had had just about enough.

"See here, now! Ain't you never heard of 'judge not, lest ye be judged'? And how Jesus came and died so the Lord could show us mercy? And what about the woman taken in adultery? Didn't Jesus talk to those ready to stone her about their own sins? And say he didn't condemn her, and she should go and sin no more? Well, that there woman won't be doing any more sinning, and how do we know where her soul went?"

The preacher's jaw dropped, and his face went red. Mamie turned to Tom with her eyebrows near up to her hair. And Jenny ran right across to him and gave him a big ol' kiss. He kissed her back before moving her alongside him and saying to the preacher, "Well, don't you got a job to do?"

The preacher opened his mouth and shut it again, glaring at Tom as if lightning was about to shoot out his eyes and strike Tom down where he stood. But when Tom stayed standing and no lightning happened, the preacher tugged on his jacket and said, as huffy as could be, "Let us pray."

When Tom got to work after the funeral was finished, he could tell someone had got there quicker with the news. Finch shook his shaggy head at Tom, mumbling, "I don't know. I just don't know about this."

Tom didn't know neither, nor have anything useful to say, so he just waited for Finch to get on with it.

"You've shocked some good folks in this town and no mistake. Bad enough you going to that funeral, but to holler at the preacher!"

To tell truth, Tom was feeling a little sorry about that. Given it to do over again, he wasn't altogether sure he would. But when he remembered Jenny's kiss and the way her eyes shined at him, he figured he probably would, at that.

"I had two people tell me they might not be back here to get their shoes fixed or new ones made. If that's how it turns out, I'll have to let you go."

At least he wasn't firing Tom just in case. Finch might not be exactly good at shoes, but he was all Cowbird Creek had for a cordwainer. Would how Tom acted be enough to make folks take the time and trouble to go out of town? Not many, he'd bet.

He hoped.

A week later, there was no knowing who might've come in and hadn't, though business was slow enough to make Tom nervous. But the butcher did come in, and when he saw Tom, he gave him a grim sort of smile and said, "I've been thinking for years that preacher needed taking down a peg. Good on you for 'tending to it."

Finch, putting the butcher's boot on the mend shelf, acted like he hadn't heard.

Chapter 23

JENNY hadn't seen Doc since the funeral. He'd hadn't cried like the girls, but he'd looked plenty sad all the same. Today, though, when her turn came for her monthly checkup, Doc looked upbeat enough to whistle, not that he actually did. She wished she could manage being that cheerful, but what with Amanda Jane dying and Tom wanting to marry her and her not knowing what to do about that, she'd been dragging around during the day, as much as she could get away with, and then tossing and turning at night.

From the way Doc looked at her, he could see right off that she was poorly. Which she didn't much want to talk about, even with him, so she said right off, "You look happy today, Doc. Something good happen?"

"Lie back, please, and get comfortable. Yes, indeed, something good has happened. Freida Blum — excuse me, Freida Kennedy now — and her husband Jedidiah have come to town."

Jenny'd seen Freida a time or two, bustling down the street or asking sharp questions of the dry goods clerk. "Were you and Mrs. Blum, as she was before, good friends?"

Doc looked a little sad again, which made her sorry to have asked. "Yes, we were. And are. She made quite a difference in my life at one time. Clara and I were sorry to see her go, though glad for her happiness. I hope her new life has not proved too much of a physical strain."

Jenny tried to picture Mrs. Kennedy riding all over creation giving medicine shows. Not that she was likely to do rope tricks or juggle fire . . . or dance with veils and not much underneath! The idea made her giggle. Doc looked at her with an eyebrow up. "Hold still, please. I'm glad to have amused you, though I confess I don't know how I accomplished it."

Well, Jenny sure wasn't going to confess how, not to a good friend of the lady in question. "Was she sick or something?"

He changed the subject instead of answering. "You're looking fine, as far as . . . the area I've been examining is concerned. But I'd rather be seeing you as blooming as usual. And you may have lost a little weight. You must still be in mourning for your friend."

Well, that was sure some of it. Tom turning her world upside down and sideways was in there too. She didn't know what to think, or what to do, and the one thing she wanted was to see Tom again, and she didn't know when it'd happen.

Doc gave her a hand as she got off the bed, just like she was a lady. She squeezed his hand. "Thanks, Doc. For what you do, and for being so good to us."

Doc's eyes went wide for a second, and he squeezed back before he pulled his hand away. "You're more than welcome, Miss Jenny. And I want you to take care of yourself. Get plenty of sleep, when you can, and eat hearty of Mamie's excellent meals."

Excellent? Well, they were good, for sure, a lot finer'n what she could cook herself. If Mamie'd fed Doc sometime, she might have done a mite better by him. But Jenny didn't see a need to say so.

* * * * *

Tom had noticed, since he came to work for Finch, that Doc took good care of his boots, blacking 'em regular and not letting 'em stay dusty if he could help it. So when Doc showed up at Finch's wearing boots considerable more broke-down, he guessed what Doc needed and met him at the door. "Your good boots need some fixing?"

Doc handed the boots to Tom. "I'm afraid so. As many miles as they take me, it stands to reason they need expert attention now and again. I hope you and Mr. Finch can restore them to health." He waited for Tom to chuckle and then went on, "I may have to find a way to invest in new boots before much longer. But please do what you can."

By now Finch had joined them. "We surely will, Doc Gibbs. I can get 'em back to you by Saturday afternoon."

Doc found it easier'n Tom did to smile at Finch, seemingly. "That'll be just right. I'd rather be wearing my good boots when Sunday comes."

Finch took the boots right then and carried them back to his work table. Doc waited for him to get a distance away and said to Tom, quieter, "I also came to give you an invitation. Clara and I would be pleased to have you with us for Sunday dinner. Freida and Jedidiah Kennedy are visiting, and —" He dropped his voice even more. "They'd be most interested in breaking bread with the young man who put our overly self-righteous preacher in his place."

Tom just barely managed not to look over his shoulder at Finch, which would've likely made things look more suspicious. "I'd be most happy to, Doc."

When Mrs. Finch brought their dinners, he took his outside, not troubling to ask Finch's leave, and walked around the square to see what he could see. After all, if Jedidiah Kennedy was in town, wouldn't he be putting on one of his shows? And sure enough, there was the wagon — just down the street from Madam Mamie's. It made Tom's heart pain him standing so close to where Jenny lived without being able to go in, but now he'd come here, he might as well stay and watch. And maybe Jenny was watching from some window.

Professor Kennedy stood on the wagon seat, all in a fancy coat with long tails, and a shiny top hat on his gold-colored hair, hair that reminded him of Jenny's the first day he ever saw her. Kennedy's voice boomed out over the people who'd gathered round. "Give the lady a hand! Wasn't that the finest dancing you've seen in a long, long time? For those of you just straggling up now, don't be too downhearted — you can see her again this time tomorrow, on the other side of the square. And now, a man who's learned his skills everywhere from California to Chicago, from the wild northern reaches to way down in Mexico, here's Cowboy Dan with his fancy roping!"

Tom swallowed the last of his dinner, along with regret that he'd missed the dancing, but at least he hadn't missed the show altogether. A cowboy stepped up onto the seat wearing some sort of spangly jacket, like nothing he'd ever seen a cowboy wear and, he'd wager, nothing a cowboy working a ranch or a cattle drive'd be caught dead in. And the lasso he pulled out had been dyed a bright red. But when he set to whirling that rope around, big ol' circles darting every which way, all so fast the rope was one red blur, Tom had to admit the fellow was good, better'n the cowboys Tom had seen showing off on the ranches hereabouts.

The cowboy stopped to let people cheer, and Kennedy said, "Now that's some fine roping! And now, my friend will come down off the wagon and show you even more, things I won't let him do up here. Everyone back up and make some room! If you can't see, climb up on some steps for a better view."

That was fine for them as were already near steps, but by the time Tom could get there, all the good spots'd be taken. Instead he squirmed up closer, while the cowboy commenced to aim his circles near the ground and then jump in and out of 'em.

Tom could tell Kennedy saw him moving up, and hoped he wouldn't call him out on his manners. But the pitchman bellowed, "What I'm needing now is a volunteer! Young man, how would you like to be part of our show?"

Tom looked around at the townsfolk, who'd started clapping and whistling, and stepped up as Kennedy said, "What's your name, my brave fellow?"

Tom almost rolled his eyes, but at the last second figured it'd be impolite. "My name's Tom Barlow, Professor."

He could see the name register, the pitchman's eyes brightening up as he pointed to a spot in the street. "Well, Mr. Barlow, stand right over there, if you please. Now catch this!" He tossed Tom a broom. "Good! Now hold onto that broom."

Did Tom imagine it, or did the pitchman give him a little wink?

Maybe so, but he decided not to grip the broom handle all that hard. And when the lasso came snaking out at him, fell down over the broom handle, and yanked it away, Tom made a point of looking real surprised.

And all the while, something was nagging at him about the pitchman's joke, the one about Tom being part of the show. Not that he wanted to stand up in front of people in a spangly suit or have them gaping at him, so what thought was trying to shove its way forward like Tom had just done?

The show was over, and Tom had made it back to Finch's shop, before it came clear to him. And then it hit him so hard that he stood stock still in the middle of the doorway until Finch grumbled at him to get on inside and back to work.

Clara Gibbs opened the door when Tom knocked, her belly greeting him way before the rest of her. Wonderful smells surrounded them both as she said, "Come in! I'm so glad you could come. Joshua is just making Freida sit down so he can check her over and make sure she isn't working too hard."

From behind Mrs. Gibbs came a sing-song complaint. "Working too hard, did I somehow get too feeble to cook, how many times did I cook for you? And I should sit down so your wife, so near her time, should do all the work, you want to deliver a baby before we eat? Jedidiah, tell him, he should let me get up, the roast could burn, I still need to put in the biscuits!"

Mrs. Gibbs took Tom's hat and rain slicker and steered him into the sitting room where Professor Kennedy relaxed in an easy chair, seemingly staying out of the battle in the kitchen no matter what his wife said. He sprang to his feet as Tom came in. "Pleased to see you again, my good man! Clara, did I tell you how Tom assisted us with the show the other day? I told him he should join right up, didn't I, Tom?"

Tom might have twitched a bit before he answered, "That's right, Mrs. Gibbs."

Mrs. Gibbs cocked her head. "A man your age might be excused some degree of wanderlust. Were you tempted?"

"Well, now." He'd rather wait a bit before telling the

idea he'd brought with him. "I can't say as I was, exactly. You're right about that wanderlust, though." He paused to listen to the continuing, if one-sided, argument in the kitchen. "When we're all together, I might see what you think of an idea that came to me, owing to that invite. So thank you for that, Professor."

The pitchman waved a big hand at him. "None of that somewhat dubious title among friends! Please, call me Jedidiah. Or Jed, if that's too much of a mouthful."

Doc Gibbs came in from the kitchen, where he'd either won or lost the argument. "Welcome, Tom! Come say hello to Freida. And speaking of mouthfuls, I'm told we'll be ready to eat in just a few minutes."

Tom followed him into the kitchen, where Freida Kennedy, wearing a big frilly apron, seemed to be everywhere at once, looking in the oven, stirring a pot on the stove, reaching in the cupboard for plates. Doc managed to get in front of her there and pull down some plates himself. Mrs. Kennedy picked up the bottom of her apron and whacked him with it. "Out of the kitchen, out! I'll be gone soon enough, you can have it back when we leave."

Doc backed away, grinning. "Before you exile me, may I introduce — or rather, reintroduce — Tom Barlow? I would think you crossed paths in the past, but you may not have actually spoken."

Mrs. Kennedy dusted flour off her hands and used both of them to grab one of Tom's. "I'm so glad to meet you properly, you'd think I'd have met everyone in Cowbird Creek, but somehow I missed people. And to hear what you did at the funeral, I could kiss you, but I'd maybe frighten you right out the door and dinner almost ready . . . ."

Tom bowed as best he could with his hand captured and waited for her to let go of it. Which she did, shooing him and Doc out to the sitting room. "Out, go sit, keep the others company, I'll call you any minute."

True enough, he had just sat down when Freida came in without her apron on. "Come eat, all of you, don't let it get cold, you can talk at the table."

Over the roast beef and boiled potatoes and corn pudding, Doc and his missus took turns reciting lines from what the preacher had said to get Tom — and both of them, seemingly — so riled. They hammed it up to make it sound even worse, maybe to give Tom more of an excuse for losing his temper and his manners. Then they prodded Tom to repeat what he'd said, prompting him when he forgot. Mr. Jed and Mrs. Freida — she'd insisted he use her given name too, and then Doc's missus had done the same — clapped as hard as the watchers at one of Mr. Jed's medicine shows.

Before someone could start a new subject, Tom asked, "Mr. Jed, Mrs. Freida, are medicine shows the only kind of work where folks travel around in a wagon? Have you ever met any other kind?"

The older couple looked at each other and then back at Tom. Mr. Jed did the answering. "Can't say as I have. Though there's no special reason I'd have come across them, if they did."

That wasn't exactly encouraging, but if his idea had a chance, these were the people who could tell him so. "I'd take it as a great kindness if you folks could tell me whether something that's come into my head is pure moonshine, or if it might just work. But it'll take some explaining.

"I've been working at Mr. Finch's cordwainer shop, doing what he'd rather not, and I've found my way back to something I'd forgot about . . . ." He told about his wanting to draw Jenny — not getting into how he'd met her or what she did, though what with all the talk about the funeral, they might guess — and how he'd used leather for it, and how pleased she'd been with it, and everything that came after. It took a lot of telling, and he felt how unmannerly it was to go on so long with no one else getting a turn, but they all listened, even the two who knew it already. Finally he got to what was new even to Doc and his missus. He took a deep breath and pushed out the question. "It's what Mr. Jed said before that got me wondering. Do you think a man as fixed up saddles like I've been doing could travel from place to place doing it?"

Mr. Jed played with his big mustache for a second and asked, "Do you by any chance have a sample of your work with you?"

Tom thanked his stars he'd thought to bring the leather he took to ranches when he made his pitch. Just a few days before, he'd added some bits of silver trim left over from his last job. He pulled it out of his vest pocket, unfolded it, and handed it over, chewing his lip and then making himself quit.

Mrs. Freida and Mrs. Clara got up from their chairs and looked over Mr. Jed's shoulders (Mrs. Clara leaning on his chair), pointing to this design or that, making little noises that sounded like they liked what they saw. Mrs. Freida stroked a finger along the silver. And all the while, Tom waited for Mr. Jed to say something.

Finally he picked up the leather and handed it back to Tom. And said, "Young man, that's some fine work."

Tom breathed out so hard he thought he'd send his chair over backward. "Thankee, sir."

Kind words or no, Mr. Jed looked pretty serious. "So you want to travel around fixing up cowboy's saddles. That's an interesting and ambitious project. But there's something you don't seem to have thought of."

Tom gulped. "What'd that be, sir?"

Mr. Jed played with his mustache some more, until Tom was about ready to pull his own hair out with waiting. And then, real slow, Mr. Jed said, "I don't believe you've thought about . . . footwear."

Tom goggled at him. "About what, now?"

Mr. Jed busted out in a grin. "Footwear. Boots. Made of leather, and every cowboy has at least one pair, even a cowboy so young and broke he uses a borrowed saddle. Why aren't you planning on fixing up boots? You could even do boots to match saddles, for those who can pay for it."

"And let's not forget the ladies," said Mrs. Clara. "I can well imagine that many a wealthy matron or dressy young woman would fancy scrolls or diamond shapes or bits of silver on their shoes."

"Of course they would!" Mrs. Freida put in. "Ladies love something new, I should know, with all the dresses I've made. Just get one pair out where people see it, you could be the new fashion!"

Mr. Jed beamed at his wife. "Right you are, my dear." He turned back to Tom. "And most any town, and anywhere else that has cowboys nearby, will have a blacksmith who can melt silver."

It was all more exciting than anything Tom had felt since — well, since before he lost his leg.

But Doc wasn't joining in. He looked solemn enough that when he finally went to talk, Tom was near certain he'd say that a cripple couldn't go roaming around the country to do any of this. But he could! This wasn't like running off for a cowboy. He could ride and tend a wagon . . . . But he'd let Doc speak his piece, and try to answer back with the respect Doc was owed.

"Tom," Doc was saying, "You know I admire your work. And I entirely agree that your skills could find more scope than what you've already achieved. But this is an uncertain life you think of leading. There could be long stretches where you would earn very little." He looked Tom in the eye. "That risk may not be too much for a young man on his own. But would I be wrong to guess that you have something more in mind?"

Tom couldn't sit still no longer. He got up and paced. "Nossir, Doc, you ain't wrong. I aim to take Jenny with me, if she'll marry me and come along." He looked at all of them, willing them to understand. "She's real tired of living where people look down on her, to where she's about ready to run off on her own, or with another girl of the line, and go plying her trade from one town to the next. Going with me can't hardly put her in more danger'n that. And I'd do whatever I had to do to take care of her. Put aside the leather work, do any work I could find, whatever it took."

Mrs. Freida patted her husband's shoulder. "She must be a woman of spirit, yes? Such a woman, she wouldn't be afraid, I wasn't afraid to go with Jedidiah, was I? Uncertain — you should know, Doctor, we can any of us be struck down without seeing it coming, we have to live anyhow, don't we?"

Mr. Jed covered Mrs. Freida's hand with his much bigger one. "Yes, my wise wife, but I had attained some degree of prosperity before I made so bold as to invite you to share my wanderings." He waited for Tom to pass in front of him in his pacing and said, "Sit back down, Tom, and I'll tell you about an alternative you and our good host might both find acceptable."

"Good, I'll get the pie, everyone wants coffee?" Mrs. Freida bustled off to the kitchen without waiting for an answer, Mrs. Clara following after and slower. Tom hoped he could manage to choke down his pie, tight-strung as he was feeling. Whether it was Mrs. Clara or Mrs. Freida who'd made it, he'd hate to insult either one — nor to waste a good piece of pie.

When Mrs. Freida and Mrs. Clara had put giant pieces of blackberry pie — with custard! — and big mugs of coffee at every place, they sat down and watched Mr. Jed like he was up on his wagon announcing the strangest act yet. He seemed to like it, puffing out his chest some as he got back to talking.

"I am, you may have noticed, a gregarious fellow. And of course, my profession requires me to engage townspeople in conversation, and to put them at ease by encouraging them to talk about their own concerns and interests. So it shouldn't surprise you that I've met many a farmer, many a butcher, many a blacksmith . . . and a fair number of leather workers. There is one such gentleman down in New Mexico Territory who has quite an admiration for the artistry and appeal of Mexican saddles with their elaborate embellishments, including the silver trim that few craftsmen north of Mexico know how to create. He had, when I passed through his area not six months ago, an increasing amount of business, and might well be in need of assistance — particularly if the new arrival had your skills. And while he may not have thought of embellishing boots and shoes, I think it likely he would welcome the idea. I can give you a letter for him, recommending your services."

He held up his hand as Tom started to bristle. "I am by no means saying you must abandon your dream of choosing your own path and maintaining your independence. The journey south would provide a means of testing whether that is a practical way to support yourself and your bride. If your experience on that journey suggests otherwise, my acquaintance could possibly provide at least a temporary refuge from the uncertainty that so troubles our host."

Tom's insides loosened up enough for the pie to start looking — and smelling — plenty tempting. He took a big forkful, Mrs. Freida giving him a nod of approval to see it. Mr. Jed, a man Tom figured enjoyed the sound of his own voice, had more to say. "I suspect he also has a broader selection of tools available to him, which you might enjoy using."

Tom forced the mouthful of pie down. So much for Mr. Jed's praising Tom's work, if he'd looked at it and seen what Tom couldn't do. And Tom already hankered after more tools. Which might be easier to get hold of, once he didn't need to keep his work a secret no more . . . .

Mrs. Clara took a good-sized bite of her own pie, chewed it up pretty quick, and said, "I have my own concerns, as to which I hope any of you might have possible solutions. What is Jenny to do to contribute to the success of this enterprise? What skills does she have, other than those you would not want her using?"

No one spoke up. Tom tried to come up with something Jenny could do that would help them on the road. She might be able to patch their clothes, but not to sew for other folks. Aside from what she'd be keeping for him, she was mainly good at looking pretty and charming folks . . . .

He slammed his fork down as the thought finished coming. "Mr. Jed! Don't you think a pretty girl could make a cowboy sit up and take notice? And if she's used to getting strangers to like her, couldn't she get 'em interested in buying *whatever* she was selling?"

Mr. Jed sat up even straighter'n usual. "By gum, Tom,

that's a good thought! A girl like Jenny could wrap those cowboys round her little finger."

Mrs. Clara, her breath a little short and her hand on her belly, added, "I'd venture to say the same would be true of men in town, so long as her dress and manner were proper enough not to upset their wives." She stopped to breathe. "Which would be quite handy if you were selling footwear to men other than cowboys. And with a little more polish — which a bright girl like Jenny could pick up by observation — and a suitably deferential attitude, she could be helpful in selling shoes to women as well."

Doc looked a good bit more cheerful at the way things were heading. But when he spoke up, it was to say, "I believe we've gone as far as we can in this discussion without including a missing participant. As the one man who can enter Madam Mamie's establishment without onlookers universally assuming I come as a customer, I volunteer to go ask if I may bring Jenny to join us. Does anyone here have any objection?"

Chapter 24

JENNY sat curled up in an easy chair in the small lounge, trying to read a book. She'd maybe have understood more of it if she used the *Dictionary*, but after all the fuss about it, she hadn't had the nerve to touch it again. She sighed and looked up when footsteps came near, knowing it was most likely Mamie coming to fetch her for one of the few Sunday customers.

She was partway right. Mamie stood there looking at her, but there was no fellow behind her, and she wasn't wearing either her impatient where-were-you frown or the smile she used when customers might be about to see her. Instead, she looked kind of serious and kind of puzzled, like she didn't know which look belonged to the occasion. What was going on?

Then Jenny saw Doc behind Mamie, and her heart jumped in her breast. Something must've happened to Tom, and Doc was here to break the news, along with her heart.

After a century or so, Mamie said, "It seems Doc Gibbs is here to convey an invitation."

That didn't mean an invite upstairs, did it? Doc had sworn off such things when he got married. Jenny looked at Doc. "What's she mean?"

Doc had been looking kind of serious too, but now he smiled. "She means, Miss Jenny, that Tom is at Clara's and my home for Sunday dinner, as are Jedidiah and Freida

Kennedy, and that a subject has come up on which we would like to hear your opinion."

Jenny looked at Mamie, who said, a little exasperated, "I suppose you'd better go along, if you care to. And tell me what it's all about when you get back!" She turned toward Doc. "Unless you're planning to swear her to secrecy."

Doc didn't answer right away. And when he did, he said, "I don't expect to do so. But if it should happen that Jenny would prefer not to confide the subject of the discussion, I would ask you to allow her that privacy."

Mamie tossed her head and then puffed at a lock of hair that had somehow come loose. "This day is not making a whole lot of sense. But go on, the pair of you. Jenny, you'd best be back here before evening."

Jenny didn't look at Doc before answering. "Yes'm. I'll make sure of it."

As they stepped into the street, Doc asked, kind of quiet, "Is it true that Tom has asked you to marry him?"

"Um, not exactly asked. He just talked about it. But I told him I couldn't possibly marry him and live in this town with everyone knowing about me." She hated having to say it again. Things sounded so hopeless, said out loud.

"I'd like you to join me in a daydream, if you will. If you knew that no one in town would treat you rudely or criticize you because of your past — if you can imagine such a thing — would you want to marry Tom?"

She'd hardly thought about it, given how things really were. Just once or twice, she'd let herself think *if only I could*. She'd stopped because of how much it hurt. "Doc Gibbs, you've always been kind to me. Please don't say things like that."

He twitched his hand like he would've liked to take hers but didn't think it was a good idea. "It's important,

Jenny. Please try to answer."

Jenny bit her lip and tried to do what Doc wanted. To imagine waking up in a Cowbird Creek made magically different, where she had as much right to get married as ever Clara Brook or Dolly Arden had. Would she marry Tom then, if he wanted?

She thought about the way he'd looked at her when they first met, like she was the best present he'd ever got. And the things he'd said when she helped him with his missing leg itching. And how it tasted to kiss him. And how happy he always looked to see her. And how happy it made her to see him. And how he hadn't let losing a leg stop him from living — at least not since they'd met.

He'd called her a lady. And sweet. And he'd listened to her talk — even paid to talk to her. And he'd made her those beautiful pictures. And he'd apologized when he hurt her feelings.

And he'd showed up for Amanda Jane's funeral no matter what folk said or what it cost him. And talked back to the preacher, even, defending Mamie's girls. Defending her.

And how she'd love to have a baby of her own, some day, some way.

Here they'd almost got to Doc's house, and she hadn't hardly said a word, nor answered his question that he said was important, though she couldn't see how. She'd spit it out, and then not think about it no more. She said, her heart pounding, "I guess I'd want to marry Tom if I could, if things was different like you say. I'm — I'm awful fond of him, if you want to know. A woman'd be lucky to marry a man such as him."

Doc got this big happy smile on him. "In that case, come on in and have some of my friend Freida's blackberry pie, and listen to the plan that Tom and Clara and my guests have come up with. It may surprise you. But I hope the surprise is a good one."

They weren't even at the house yet when Tom came out on the front step, looking down the street. His eyes lit up the second he saw them, even while he looked nervous, like someone was giving him a peek at Paradise and he didn't know if he'd make it inside. He came down the steps a little too fast, tripping and having to catch the rail to keep from falling, and it didn't even faze him. He met them in the street and grabbed both Jenny's hands. "It's going to happen, Jenny. We can be together. And we can both get out of this town. There's a way."

When they'd sat Jenny down and explained, and she'd listened to it all, and asked all the questions she could think of and got answers to just about every one, Tom pulled her out of her chair and took her hands again. She could tell he'd have got on one knee if it wasn't so hard for him. Instead, he gripped her hands almost tight enough to hurt, and said, "Please, Jenny. Please marry me and come away with me. It's all I want. Please want it too."

She felt like she could just about float off the floor, if it weren't for Tom holding her hands. But she'd rather he kept holding them, all the same. She could hardly talk for how big she was smiling, but she managed to say, "I will, Tom. I'll marry you, and come away with you, and travel wherever we need to."

Tom looked over his shoulder for just a minute, and then pulled her close, her hands still in his, and kissed her, soft and sweet. She started when she heard people clapping — she'd almost forgot where they were, and who else was. She let go of one of Tom's hands so's she could turn and look at the others, all happy, happy for her and Tom.

And then, Mrs. Freida made her sit back down and have some pie, with custard.

She and Tom walked back to Mamie's holding hands again, Doc trailing a few steps behind. And when Mamie came to the door, ready to scold over how long she'd been, the three of them explained it together.

When they'd run down, Mamie just stood and looked at them for the longest time. Finally, she stuck out her hand toward Tom. "This might be the strangest thing I've heard in a while, and I hear plenty. But I'd be worrying more if it were any young man but you, Mr. Barlow. You're a good man. And you're getting a girl with the makings of a good woman."

Tom shook her hand, let go, and pulled Jenny to him, holding her tight against his side. Mamie turned to Doc. "Joshua, this isn't the first time you've surprised me, and it probably won't be the last. Now you and Mr. Barlow had better be going."

Doc tipped his hat to Mamie and looked at Tom. But Tom kept hold of Jenny a little longer. He looked like he was fixing to say something and didn't know just how. Jenny pulled to get loose before Mamie could lose patience, and maybe think better of the whole idea. Tom let her go, swallowed, and said to Mamie, "Ma'am, I don't know what you're thinking about these next days, but I'm asking you to let Jenny stay here without — without earning her keep in the way she has been. Just until I can do a few things that need doing before we can marry and leave town."

Mamie sniffed. "Well, we'll work something out. Now off you go. Jenny, take a moment to say goodbye to your — intended, and then come to my office." She nodded to the men and swished away.

Doc cleared his throat. "I'll be just outside. Please don't be long, Tom." He headed out the door, humming a cheerful little tune.

Tom pulled Jenny into a long, warm hug, saying real low, "I can't believe it. I'm really going to have you as my wife."

She pulled back to look in his face. "Oh, I sure hope you won't be sorry. I'll work hard as I can to be everything you need me to be."

He cupped her face in his hand and kissed her. When he pulled away, he said, "You *are* everything I need you to be. And I'll work as hard as *I* can to give you everything you need."

It was time he left, and she didn't even know when or how she'd be seeing him next. But somehow, they'd make sure it was soon.

When Jenny made it up to Mamie's office, Mamie was sitting up straight and looking her most businesslike. "While you've been seeing your young man out, I've been thinking. You'll need to stay out of the customers' way, to avoid any misunderstandings. And I won't have you lying about idle. You're going to use this time to prepare for what you're undertaking. When you leave here, go to the kitchen and get the mending basket. You'll need practice at sewing and darning, and you can start with that. Tomorrow, you'll help Cook with the meals. Who knows, maybe she can even tell you something about cooking over campfires."

Jenny bowed her head. "Thank you, ma'am. For letting me stay, and letting me use the time to learn something." She almost stopped there, but there was more to say. "And thank you for letting me go."

Mamie just looked at her and shook her head. "I hope you'll have cause to thank me down the road, and not wish I'd done different. You know you don't have much idea of what you're getting into? What sort of hardships you'll face?"

There wasn't a lot of room in her for worrying about that, but she owed Mamie some sort of answer. "You're right, ma'am. That's how it's been for me since I left home. And so far, I've made it through the hard times, and mostly on my own. Not to say you didn't help me when I needed it! But being with Tom, that's a whole new kind of not being alone, and I can't help being happy about it."

Mamie waited to make sure Jenny was through and stood up, pointing to the door. "Very well then. You'd best go fetch that basket and get started."

She'd promised herself she wouldn't go crawling to Mama no more, after never getting answers to the letters she'd sent. But now she had something better to tell. And if Mama still cared about her even a little, she'd want to know it.

This time, she didn't put just Mama's name on the letter, but all her sisters' and even her brother's. And thought of adding Papa's, in case it'd make him more likely to let Mama have the letter, but it'd maybe make him throw it in the fire instead.

Dear Family,

I hope you are all well. I haven't heard nothing back from my letters, and hope you don't mind my writing again, as I have some real good news.

I bet you gave up on me finding a husband, or at least one you'd be glad I found, but I think I done it. His name is Tom Barlow, so I'll be Jenny Barlow.

That thought fair made her head swim.

He grew up on a farm, and now he makes pictures on saddles and boots and such. People like his pictures real well.

She'd left out the most important part.

Tom is a real nice fellow and treats me good.

I'm happier than I've been in such a long time, and I wanted you to know. I hope you'll be happy for me. And I hope you'll write back and tell me how you all are.

I hope you can meet Tom somehow.

If that ever looked to happen, she and Tom could figure out what tale to tell about how they met. And that'd be soon enough for her to tell them about Tom's leg.

Or was it? It wasn't like she was ashamed of him for having just one. And maybe he wouldn't know she was hiding the truth, but she would.

And if they thought that was the only reason he'd settle for someone like Jenny, well, they could go ahead and think it. She knew different.

He lost his leg last year when a plowshare fell on it, but he gets around real good on his wooden leg. And he's real strong.

She let herself spend a minute thinking about just how good it felt to have those strong arms around her. She could think on that some more — and on what else felt good, and would feel even better when it was just for the two of them — as soon as she got this letter finished.

Well, that's all I got to say just now. You all take care.

Every time she ended a letter after not getting one back, the words got harder to say. But she'd say them anyhow, one more time.

Love, your Jenny

Chapter 25

TOM CAME home whistling as the sun headed down, birds in the fields and by the creek doing it better. Pa was leaning on a fence smoking his Sunday pipe. He gave Tom a quizzical look. "You've been a long time over dinner, and come back pretty chipper. Anything we should talk about?"

Pa was most as good as Ma at reading a fellow's mind. Tom couldn't grin and whistle at the same time, but now it was time for grinning. "I'm going to marry Jenny!"

Pa's eyebrows shot up. Before he could start asking and warning and lecturing, Tom told him the rest. "We're going to leave town and head south! It'll be a new start for both of us."

Pa took out his pipe and turned it this way and that as if learning it by heart. "Well, if you're going to take such a step as marrying her, that's what you'll need. What do you have in mind?"

Tom explained the plans, including Mr. Jed's leather worker as a place to go if they had to. Pa listened, letting his pipe go out. When Tom ran down, Pa lighted the pipe again, got it going, and said, kind of casual, "How do you figure on carrying your belongings?"

Tom had been pushing that to the back of his mind so it wouldn't spoil his mood. But Pa had to know more about buying wagons than he did. And about borrowing money, if there was any way to borrow it without already having plenty of it, or plenty of things already bought with it. "I'm hoping you can help me figure that out. I'm afeared to think on how long it'll take me to save up for a wagon, even if Finch keeps me on and I get enough side work to fill up every minute left over. But I'm not sure what else to do."

Pa puffed on his pipe. "Well, now, I could talk to Mr. Stewart, couple of miles from here. He's got an old broken-down wagon in his barn, from when his pa came west. They had a hard journey, almost didn't make it, and the wagon barely did. But Stewart and I, and maybe a few other neighbors, could get together and fix that wagon up to where you could use it."

It took some trouble for Tom to swallow the lump in his throat. "I'd — Jenny and I would — take that as right kind of you. And Mr. Stewart and the others. If they're willing."

Pa must've finished his pipeful — he took the pipe out of his mouth again, shook it out, and put it in his pocket. "I'll talk to 'em. Though it'd take some time to fix up that wagon to where you could count on it not to break down and leave you stuck in the middle of nowhere. You'd still have to bide a while."

"That's all right," Tom said, though it might or might not be, depending. "We've both got things to do before we can head out. For one, I've got to scrape up a saddle and do some decorating."

Pa scratched his head. "Well, that might not need much scraping. Your ma doesn't do much riding these days, but she used to, as a girl. And not side saddle, neither. If all you need is a saddle to show your work on, would that do? Mind, it'd need cleaning up."

"Can I see it?"

Pa answered by leading the way into the barn. In a

corner full of rusty tools and mouse-eaten blankets, Pa dug through the rubbish and pulled out a worn dirty saddle. To Tom's relief, it didn't look that different from a regular saddle, only on the small side, and not all that small — which made sense, as Ma was a big woman now and might've been even back then.

Pa handed the saddle to Tom and Tom turned it every way, checking it over. He opened his mouth to thank Pa before he realized he was skipping a step. "Reckon I'd better ask Ma if she minds parting with it."

Pa smiled a little. "Yup, reckon you had."

Ma was hemming an apron at the kitchen table when Tom carried the saddle in. She dropped it and stood up. "I declare, is that my old saddle you've got? Pa must've found it, but whatever for?"

He'd forgot for a minute that he'd have to explain his plans all over again. And he knew what piece was going to be hardest to tell. Sure enough, Ma just tightened up her lips when he said he was marrying Jenny. But when he got to the part about leaving town, she gasped and went a little pale. "Oh, Tom! Leaving? For good and all?"

He put an arm around her. "Ma, we've got to go. You know how it'd be for both of us if we stayed here. And even if I was willing to give up Jenny — which I ain't — it drives me wild working for Finch, and having to hide what I'm doing for cowboys, all because Finch don't give a hoot for how things look and won't admit others might."

Ma picked up the edge of the apron she had on and wiped her eyes. She just stood there up close to him, shaking her head, for about a minute. Then she said, her voice shaky, "I can't rightly speak agin it, not after your pa and me left our own folks when I was little older'n you, to come out west looking for a better life. It's what folks do in this country, isn't it, sooner or later, grandsons if not sons. They go looking for what's better."

Tom held her closer as she choked out, "And I should be glad for you, that you've found a way to do it, with all that could've stopped you. I don't know as I can be, just yet." She pulled away to face him and took his face in her hands. "But I am awful proud of you that you've done it, Tom."

Tom closed his eyes, feeling the warmth of her hands, smelling the smell that was Ma and no one else, a mix of flour and soap and her own self. He hadn't thought until right now that once he left town, it might be months, and more likely years, before he smelled it again.

Tom spent what was left of Sunday cleaning the saddle, getting it ready to work on, and stewing over what to tell Finch in the morning. He couldn't afford the satisfaction of marching in and quitting. He and Jenny would need every dollar he could scrape up. Not that he'd necessarily have a choice — Finch might fire him the second he heard about Jenny, or Tom leaving town, or both.

Finch hadn't had the best of Sundays, it seemed. The minute Tom walked in, Finch started bending his ear about how he'd lost his pocket knife and his dog had puked on his favorite chair. Tom hadn't known Finch even had a dog. If he'd been Finch's dog, he'd probably have puked a lot sooner.

When Finch finally ran down, Tom grabbed his chance before Finch could set him to work. "Mr. Finch, I've got something I need to tell you."

By now he was getting used to summing it up — and while Finch was the furthest from a friend to hear it, he was also the fellow he cared least about pleasing, aside from practicalities. Finch's eyebrows got lower and lower, and seemed to get hairier even, as he listened. When Tom had finished, he growled, "So you mean to tell me you aren't satisfied working here, for all I gave you a job when few others would've?"

Tom waited to answer until he could govern his tongue. "All things considered, Mr. Finch, including what it'd be like for Jenny and me if we was to stay, I don't think it could work my staying."

Finch stared at him for what felt like half of forever. Tom was about to go looking for something that needed doing when Finch said, still in his growl, "Guess you've got more gumption'n I would have, at your age."

Now it was Tom's turn to stare. Which he did until Finch lumbered off toward his work table. But as he went, Tom thought he heard him mutter, "More'n I would've then. Maybe more than I've had since."

Finch didn't have much else to say to Tom that day. But about an hour before quitting time, Finch came up to him holding a deal of leather, finer'n what they used for saddles. "So you're going to make fancy boots, along with fancy saddles? You'd be wasting a chance, then, if you weren't wearing some. Advertise your services, like, everywhere you walk in 'em." He pointed to the stool where he had customers sit for fittings. "Sit down and stick your — your legs out, and I'll take your measure. Reckon I can give you a pair of boots afore you go, like a wedding present. Then you can mark 'em up however you like."

Tom wondered if he'd fallen asleep and was dreaming all this. But his stump pained him like usual this time of day. "Thankee, Mr. Finch," he stammered. "That's a real fine idea, and I surely appreciate it."

Tom could feel the first cooling of autumn coming, and see a leaf here and there just starting to turn, as he left Finch's that evening. He'd hardly had time to figure out which of the thoughts whirling around in his head to catch hold of when he saw the blacksmith standing in front of the forge and stretching. Seeing O'Connor started up a whole new thought, or more like a new sprout on an old one. Tools. He changed course and met O'Connor, tipping his hat. "Not a bad evening, specially after a day of hot work like you do."

O'Connor grinned. "You got that right! The air's most as good as a dip in a nice cool lake. And how's life treating you since I saw you last? Got any more silver as needs melting?"

Word hadn't got around that fast, then. And as interested as the blacksmith had been in Tom's work up to now, he'd enjoy hearing it. "I'm leaving town! Going to go from place to place doing my saddle work. And the same on boots." No need to get into ladies' shoes, which Tom didn't altogether believe yet. And as for his other big news, that was likely to take them off on a detour longer'n Tom felt like taking.

O'Connor stuck out his big hard hand to shake Tom's. "Best of luck to you! It's an adventure you'll be having and no mistake."

Whether that prickly feeling running all through his body was excitement or fear or both, it made Tom feel wider awake than any sunrise. "That it will. And I'll be happy to get started on it. But I've a while to wait yet, and there's something I hope you can help me with in the meantime."

The blacksmith disappeared into the forge and came back out dragging the bench he kept there for customers who felt like waiting for their job. "Let's have a seat out here while you tell me about it. Unless you've got a whole mess of silver to melt ahead of need, I'm guessing this is about which tools you'll be needing."

Tom brought the picture of that Mexican saddle to mind. "I don't rightly know which ones, but I'll need something to make little shapes, pressed into the leather. And another kind of in between that and a knife, to make little curved lines. And one that pushes the leather down in a close-set pattern that makes it look darker, so the rest stands out more."

O'Connor pushed out his lower lip, big as the rest of him. "Well, now. I've never made the like, nor seen any such up close. But I have a catalog that might have pictures."

Back inside he trudged, and came out with a catalog from the Stanley Rule and Level Company. That didn't sound too promising, but as O'Connor started leafing through it, Tom could see all manner of tools pictured. O'Connor stopped at a spread with the swivel knife Tom already had and a few tools he didn't. O'Connor ran his finger from one to the next, saying — to himself, seemed like — "I could do that. . . . And that one, I could come up with something of the sort . . . That'd take some making. But it'd be a nice change from horseshoes and handrails, sure enough!"

Tom felt like his pockets was getting emptier with every picture. He stood up. "Which ones would take the least of your time, and use the least of your stock?"

O'Connor stood up as well. It took Tom a moment to figure out that the low rumble was a chuckle. "Counting your pennies, are you, with all you've got to spend them on? Well, never you mind that. I'd be pleased to give you a wee bit of help getting started."

Tom caught his breath. Could he accept? Well, he'd

better, now that he had Jenny's welfare in his keeping, and tools like these'd help him provide for her. And it'd comfort his pride some if he explained as much, not to mention that he owed it to the blacksmith to let him in on the news ahead of other folk. "That's right kind of you, Mr. O'Connor. And I know my intended would want to thank you too."

O'Connor's head reared back like someone'd punched him. "Your what, now?"

Tom let himself grin. "I'm getting married before I leave town. To the prettiest little red-headed gal you'd ever hope to see."

The blacksmith beamed at him and shook his hand again. "Red-headed, you say! I'm highly partial to red hair, myself." He paused and stroked the dark stubble on his chin. "I've heard tell you had a sweetheart in a place most fellows don't find one. Would that be the lady you're wedding?" He didn't act like he was shocked nor pretending to be, and he didn't wear the kind of leer Tom was all too sick of seeing.

"It would. Her name's Jenny." He found himself wanting to sit back and tell O'Connor all about her. But he'd best not linger to do it. "I'll come by again soon, and tell you more, if you'd like to hear."

The blacksmith clapped him on the shoulder, which made him stagger even though he'd seen it coming in time to brace himself. "Indeed I would, lad! And you can watch me working on your tools, if you've a mind. There might come a time you'll need to tell some blacksmith how they're made, somewhere out west or down south."

Tom doubted he could take in enough information to give any such instruction, but he'd enjoy watching the work, notwithstanding. "Until then. And thank you again for what you're doing for us."

The blacksmith smiled even bigger. "It does the heart good to hear a young man say 'us' about his lady. I'll go and study those tools some more, get to figuring what I'll need to do."

Tom headed toward home, knowing Ma would've been watching for him. But his steps slowed as he looked across the square at Madam Mamie's place. He had someone else watching for him, now — someone with a claim on him. And he'd had an idea come to him that needed checking on.

Mamie saw him come in and came over as quick as usual. "You'll be wanting Jenny, I expect. She's in the kitchen, helping get supper ready. But you can wait in the smaller lounge."

"I'd appreciate that, ma'am. But I also come to ask you about something. I'm going to be working on a saddle, as fancy a one as I can make, to show folks what I have to offer. And some boots. I was wondering if I could bring 'em here to work on some evenings and on Sunday afternoons, so Jenny could see."

"And so you can see her, no doubt." She smiled her knowing smile at Tom's embarrassed nod. "Let me see. There's a table out back you could use when it's not raining. And you'd both be out of the way there. Or for better light in the evenings, you could work in the kitchen once supper is over and cleaned up."

He could just picture Jenny sitting by his side or looking over his shoulder, her hair falling down and glowing in the lamplight. "That'd be most kind of you, ma'am."

She laughed a little. "It is, in fact. The small lounge is off that way. There's books there, if you're a reader. Or you can just dream about Jenny until she's done with her work."

Tom found the lounge, and a good-sized armchair that proved downright comfortable. Sitting back, he set himself to planning out what to put on the saddle and what on the boots. But he didn't get that much planning done, what with thinking on the picture Mamie'd painted for him. It almost startled him when Jenny actually showed up, like she'd somehow come up out of his daydreams. But there she was, every bit as pretty as he'd been picturing her. And once he stood up to greet her, a whole lot more warm and real, and even more welcoming.

As she pressed against him, he realized there was one thing they hadn't talked about. And darned if he knew what she might expect. When she let go of him, he cleared his throat and said, "When I visit you here . . . "

He could tell from Jenny's look that she'd been thinking on the same subject. "You'll probably think it's silly of me. After how we met and all. But with us soon to be wed, and our wanting — *my* wanting to make a new start . . . I'd rather, rather not . . . ."

He leaned over and kissed her, real gentle. "We see eye to eye on it. I won't ask anything of you I wouldn't expect from any other girl before we got married." He chuckled. "Not that every farm girl you'd meet would be all that particular, truth to tell."

She stiffened up a little. "But whatever they'd do, you don't, you won't . . . ."

He kissed her again. "No, I don't, and I won't. We'll have something to wait on and look forward to."

For all that, once he started coming there to work on the saddle, it was a powerful strain walking through those doors and seeing all those girls in their low-cut dresses and their face paint and their scent poured on, and then sitting close to Jenny, trying to pay attention to what he carved on leather. And Mamie seemed to guess it. Catching his eye one day as he was heading out, she beckoned him aside and said quiet, "If it would ease your — mind, we've got an extra bedroom upstairs. You could go there and be private, when you've the need."

Tom's face went hot. "That's thoughtful of you, ma'am. But I'd just as soon not." He could control himself. And if he turned out to need easing, as she put it, he'd rather not have a houseful of giggling ladies guessing as much on the other side of the door.

Mr. Jed and Mrs. Freida had left town for a while, but they were sticking pretty close to Cowbird Creek so's they could get back quick when Mrs. Clara's time came. When he finally figured he'd done enough to the saddle that anything more'd spoil it, he found out when the travelers were next expected and brought the saddle to Doc's place that evening.

Mrs. Freida ran her fingers over every bit of the design. "So clever, so fine, I never saw the like, did you, Jedidiah? Even that Mexican saddle you showed me wasn't better, you'd think Tom had been doing this since the cradle."

Mr. Jed chucked his wife under the chin, which took some reaching, and nodded his big gold head. "This will do the trick, right enough."

Mrs. Clara hadn't come to stand over the table like the others, being inclined to stay off her feet. Tom carried it over and laid it on what was left of her lap. She studied it like she was memorizing it, or was a teacher come to tell him whether he'd flunked saddle making. Then she gave him one of her smiles that brightened up her face so. "It's truly fine work, Tom. You should be proud."

He was, except when he got to doubting things in the middle of the night. He carried the saddle home, along with all the encouraging words, and let them run through his head until they carried him off to sleep.

Next was rubbing the oil in. Jenny volunteered for that job. "Of course, if you think I'd spoil it, I'll leave it alone. But I'd like to know I done something."

He told her that'd be fine. After all, rubbing oil on a saddle was almost the first thing he'd done at Finch's, when he knew just about nothing. As he sat there watching Jenny pour oil on a cloth and rub it in careful circles, seeing the design come sharp and clear, he thought back to that day, and his chest swelled up fit to bust.

After the saddle, he got started on the boots. He couldn't say they fit his feet all that well, but he could maybe ask some other cordwainer along the way to make them more comfortable. And the boot on the wooden leg just had to look good. He sat with the saddle for a good three hours, picking what designs the boots should share and how to change them to suit.

He could almost have worked on them at Finch's, the way things had changed — which confused him plenty. The way Finch had handled the news of Tom leaving, and then given him the boots, didn't much fit with the boss Tom thought he knew. He didn't know whether to apologize for thinking so ill of the man — and wouldn't *that* be a tricky thing to manage — or to hold a new grudge against him for acting so surly before, when he knew how to act different.

He talked to Jenny about it, one of the times she sat watching him work, but she didn't have much to offer aside from sympathizing. "After all, Tom, I hardly know him except through what you tell me." He thought that was all she had to say, but a minute later she added, kind of nervous, "If he'd've been easier to get along with the whole time, do you think you'd ever have wanted to leave town, and your folks and all?"

He put aside his tools to lay a hand over hers. "Finch still would have had me mainly scraping hides and other such chores. Once I learned what I could do as — as used more of me, I'd never've been content working for him. And what matters more, I'd have figured out sooner or later — you'd have taught me — that the way to be with you was to move on out of here. And I'd have wanted to be with you, any way I could."

She grabbed his hand and kissed it before she let it go so he could get back to working.

Thinking over the months of dealing with Finch, what most stuck in Tom's craw was that crack about going to Mamie's when he hadn't. Not to mention calling Jenny a wag-tail, which maybe Tom had no right to resent but did anyhow. He chewed on it for a couple of days, knowing it'd be easier to leave it lie, but one day just before quitting time, he found he was just too sick of holding it in.

"Mr. Finch, sir, I was hoping you could explain something to me, something from quite a while back."

Finch turned around from where he'd been closing the shutters and grunted, "Don't know as I'll remember whatever it is. But go ahead and ask." He turned right back toward the window, like he might not be hankering to look Tom in the eye.

Why had he thought it was worth starting this? He didn't have much choice now but to plow forward. "You said you'd been to Mamie's when you hadn't. At least, J — the girls there say you haven't been since you was a married man."

Finch turned around, slow, and his face had gone kinda red. "I guess I do owe you an answer at that." He seemed to stick right there, until Tom wondered whether he'd had some sort of sudden spell and might need Doc to come. But he finally said, "You're a young man. There's things you don't rightly understand yet."

Tom could hardly argue with that, but it didn't explain much. His face must've spoke clear enough for him, because Finch went on. "When you get older, and see your life stretching out behind you more than before you, it don't always sit right. You can get to envying them as are just finding out what's fine in life, and have plenty more to come. And when that happens, you sometimes take it out on the ones who have all that."

Tom couldn't help gaping. Finch, with two good legs and his own shop — and a pretty wife, if not so pretty and smart and all kinds of special as Jenny — had been envying Tom? At a time when Tom had been envying pretty much every man he saw? It fair made his head spin.

Finch cleared his throat, along with the subject. "How are those boots coming along?"

Come to think of it, those boots might have been meant as a sort of apology, and not so out of the blue as it seemed. "Not that I'm the best judge, maybe, but I think they're coming along fine. I can bring 'em tomorrow, if you'd care to see."

Finch gave a short nod and then opened the door for them both to leave.

When he finally finished the boots, all they had to wait for was the wagon and the wedding.

Chapter 26

PA AND the others had been working on the wagon at Stewart's place when the urgent tasks of the season allowed. He knew that at least some, including Pa, were going short on rest, and wished he could do something about it. But this time of waiting and in-between had to end before he went plumb crazy.

If it was hard on him, it had to be even harder on Jenny, living at Mamie's where everything reminded her of the life she was trying to get away from. Though that was only part of it, from something she'd let drop the last time he went to visit. "The girls look at me different now. Like I think I'm above 'em, or don't want to be their friend no more."

He'd put his arms around her and comforted her as best he could. When he left, she acted like he'd made her feel better. But as he left the room, he heard her say real quiet, like she hadn't meant him to hear, "At least before, I wasn't lonely."

He had to marry her and get her away before she could change her mind.

Finally, on a Saturday night, as Tom dragged in from Finch's, Pa told him the wagon was ready, saying in that way that wasn't far from an order, "You can come to church tomorrow and give thanks, and then we'll show you what you're giving thanks for."

"I'll want Jenny to see it with me." He needed her to know this was really happening, and to be able to picture just how they would ride away.

Doc Gibbs decided to join them. "I'll fetch Jenny after church and bring her along in the buggy. I wish Clara could be there as well, but she's sticking close to home." He looked more fretful than Tom could recollect seeing him. He thought for just a minute about how he'd feel when Jenny came to be expecting and was so near childbed, and then shoved the thought away. He had enough to keep his mind spinning, right here and now.

The preacher had the surprising good sense not to say a word when Tom walked in, though he glared plenty, and his sermon went on and on about impious and prideful sinners getting their fiery comeuppance. Tom fidgeted enough that Ma poked him in the shoulder to settle him down. When they were finally let to leave, he paced back and forth, waiting for Ma and Pa and Doc to make it out the door, and then told Pa, "I'll go with Doc to get Jenny." He didn't want to maybe see the wagon before Doc and Jenny got there, nor to stand around Stewart's place waiting and looking antsy. They'd show up and see it together.

Doc must've stopped by before church to let Mamie know, because Jenny was standing out front when he and Doc got there, bouncing on her toes, her face brighter'n morning. She ran up and took his hand, not even looking around for who might see, and he grabbed it, not even caring. Doc chuckled and followed them to the buggy.

It didn't take long, nor even feel long, before they pulled up in Stewart's yard. Tom didn't see any wagon yet, but he did see Mr. Stewart and Pa and the others who'd done the work, all standing over by the barn. Even Tom's little brother was there. It was the first he'd known of Billy helping. Billy must have kept it a secret on purpose, just so's he could stand there grinning and sticking his thin chest out in pride.

Tom hurried over the rough dirt of the yard, Jenny right behind and Doc following after. The doors of the barn were open wide, and just inside, where the morning light could reach, stood a wagon smarter'n any he'd seen or heard tell of. It wasn't as showy as Mr. Jed's, but it had trim painted green, and shutters on one side to let light in, and all the wood and canvas was new as new.

Pa pointed to a framed space on the side. "You can nail up some leather here, to show off your work. Maybe in the shape of a saddle skirt. And the same on the other side. And there's a hook at the back to hang a pair of boots on, but you'll have to remember to take 'em down when it's fixing to rain or snow."

Billy stood tall and pointed to the trim. "I helped paint that, almost all the way up!"

Tom looked from end to end of the wagon, taking it all in. "I don't know what to say. This is — well, thank you all. We're awful grateful."

Jenny craned forward. "Can we look inside?"

Pa and the other men looked at each other, puzzled. Stewart finally said, "I guess so — but what for?"

* * * * *

Jenny didn't pay much mind to what the farmer was saying, except that it amounted to "yes." She fair ran up to the back of the wagon, which had the flap folded back, and leaned in to look inside.

What there was inside was nothing. No benches. No

bed.

She turned around and wrinkled up her forehead at Tom. "Isn't it finished, after all?"

Tom was opening and closing his fists, and his face was kind of flushed. "It's as finished as it's going to get."

Doc Gibbs made his way through the farmers to join Jenny. "I suspect I know what's confusing you. You were expecting to see furnishings inside? Perhaps a bed?"

Jenny's jaw dropped. Well, *yes*, she'd sort of been expecting they would *sleep* sometime on their journey across half the country. And maybe even sleep *together*, seeing as they'd be newlyweds! . . . But she realized she must be looking quite a fool with her mouth hanging open, and pulled herself together to nod.

The farmer that looked a lot like Tom — must be his pa — said, "Miss Jenny, there's only so much room in that there wagon. It ain't exactly a furnished room on wheels. And all your belongings'll need to fit inside it, including Tom's tools and spare leather and all. Back when this wagon was new, them as used it slept underneath."

Damn it if her lip wasn't quivering, and for all these folks to see.

Doc put his long-fingered hand on her shoulder. "I know you're still getting used to all of this. But you can put quilts down, to sleep in the wagon. If you do sleep underneath some nights, you can put a tarp under the quilts. You'll get used to it sooner than you imagine."

Tom muscled forward and stood looking at her, not mad now, more like pleading. "And we don't need to carry all that much. It's not like we was settlers bringing a farm's worth of stuff with us. So we can maybe put in benches like what Mr. Jed's wagon has, for you to sit on when you don't feel like sitting up where I'm driving."

One of the other farmers said, "We've put in those new leaf springs, so you won't be jostled so much." He looked around at some of the others. "Not like our families were, coming west."

Jenny felt herself bristling. So she was a soft, complaining sort next to their *families*, he was saying. Well, maybe so, but she was giving up a big soft bed and pillows, and a dressing table, and dresses to wear —

What was she *thinking*? She was giving up all as came with being a whore. She'd been wearing those dresses so men she didn't know could stare at her bosom and her legs. And sleeping in that bed after doing everything but sleep in it. And looking in that dressing table so she could make sure she was pretty enough for men to *buy*. And here she was getting ready to gripe about where and how she was going to lie with Tom, and only him?

Jenny went to stand right by Tom's side. "It's fine. I'm sure those quilts'll be right comfy."

Here all these folks who had put in so much work were standing around, and unlike Tom, she hadn't so much as said thank you. And whatever they were thinking of her just now, she owed 'em that. She curtsied, as pretty as if some high-class gentleman had come into a room, and said, "Like Tom said just now, we're very grateful. Thank you all."

But that wasn't enough, was it. She should've known better. Mamie'd seen it coming, somehow, and when would Jenny get to be as smart as Mamie, or would she ever?

"And I'm sorry about how I acted. I've got a lot to learn, and I'm ready to learn it."

All the men, Tom included, and even Billy, relaxed enough so she could see how tensed up they'd been. Mr. Stewart did the answering for them all. "That's quite all right, little lady. I reckon you'll do just fine."

* * * * *

Tom waited for Jenny to be talking to Doc and then went over to Pa. "I hate to be always needing something else, but does Ma have enough quilts to let us have any?"

Pa sent a fond look Ma's way, though she was busy with Mrs. Stewart, unpacking a basket she'd brought in the wagon and setting up dinner, and didn't see. "Ma has that well in hand, son. She already had one she'd made for you, years back, for whenever you set up housekeeping, and she'd started another for Martha, which she could let you have since Martha won't be needing one for years yet. She's set up some quilting bees to get that one finished sooner. The ladies are plenty tickled to get their turn, with all the men so full of themselves for how the wagon come out."

Tom gulped. "But we've waited so long already —"

Pa cleared his throat in that way that meant Tom needed to hush up and listen. "Your ma needs to do this for you. She needs to do something for you while you're here to be fussed over, before she says goodbye like she'll have to. You'll need patience in the life you're planning, and you can just practice it."

Tom couldn't stop the sigh that gusted out of him, but he knew Pa was right. "Yes, sir. We'll wait."

If they were stuck in Cowbird Creek for even longer, he was going to stop worrying about him and Jenny being seen together in public.

He got Finch to allow him some time off after dinner the next day, in exchange for working late, now that he'd got no more leatherwork of his own to do. After, he realized he'd forgot about the saddle-shaped leather for the sides of the wagon. But he could do that later.

When he got to Mamie's, he had to wait — more waiting! — for Jenny to finish washing dinner dishes. And when he explained he wanted to squire her around town, he had to talk her into it, and then wait again for her to change out of the dress she'd been wearing for her kitchen work. Once they were out on the street, she looked at him with her back kind of tense, even though she was smiling, and asked, "Where are we going, then?"

"How about the ice cream shop? We can split a sundae."

She took his arm. "Ice cream it is, then, Mr. Barlow."

He grinned. "Glad to hear it, future Mrs. Barlow." He kept her arm in his as they headed for the shop, and even as he ordered their sundae, until the minute they sat down together. He almost forgot to keep eating, though, along of watching how much she enjoyed the treat. She had to remind him his ice cream was melting.

He was walking her back, arm in arm again, and starting to think about what he'd do on that leather piece once he had time, when a fellow Tom didn't remember seeing before swaggered up and spat tobacco juice on the ground right in front of them. "So Madam Mamie's sending her girls out on the street with fellers now, bold as brass? When's my turn, pretty lady? I'll show you a good time — better'n this one-legged fellow, you can bet on that!"

Jenny had gone real stiff alongside him. Should he defend her honor? Or do like that one-legged soldier had said, and walk away if he could?

* * * * *

Was Tom thinking of *fighting* that man? Did he think

that's what she wanted?

Well, to be honest, she would've liked to think he could. But she sure didn't want him getting beat up on her account. She tugged at his arm. "Let's just go back. Please!"

Tom's jaw was set hard as stone. He stared at the fellow for what seemed an hour, and then said, "I don't need to fight you. So I won't."

The man jeered, "You sure won't, 'cause you can't, you cripple, you!" He spat again. "Now push that girl on over to me, so's I can have my turn."

Jenny's mouth was dry, or she'd have spat back. "No one's taking turns with me, mister, ever again. So you can just keep that nasty tongue in your head and go on about your business."

The man had been doing something between grinning and leering, but now he showed his teeth in a snarl. "That's enough out of you, you little tramp!"

He reached for her arm. Tom shoved her behind him and stood with his fists clenched. The man stared and then started laughing. "Oh, you ask for it that hard, I'm gonna give it to you." He made a fist and swung.

Real quick, Tom dropped down to the ground, hitting it with his hands and knee. For a moment she thought the man had knocked him down, but no, it happened too quick for that. And then, even quicker, Tom lunged at the man's legs and somehow pulled them out from under him. And then he was astraddle the man's chest, punching his head with one hand and holding the man's right arm with the other.

A crowd had come from somewhere, like always happened when men got to fighting. Catcalls and whistles almost drowned out the sickening sound of a fist meeting flesh. Jenny ran toward the two of them on the ground.

"Tom, stop, that's enough!"

The blacksmith came up next to Tom and grabbed the arm Tom was punching with. He looked down at the fellow on the ground, whose mouth was swollen and bleeding, and had a black eye coming. "The young lady's right, don't you think? You've made your point, I reckon."

Tom slowly climbed off the man and let the blacksmith help him to his feet. He faced Jenny, breathing hard, and said, "I didn't fight 'til I had to. You saw that."

Jenny put her arms around him, right there in the street with all those men watching, and murmured in his ear, "I did. I'm glad you didn't let him goad you sooner — and I'm glad you can fight when it counts." She drew back in time to see him smile and swagger a little. "However did you learn to do that?"

He took her arm again. "Let's go our way, and I'll tell you all about it.

* * * * *

It was full dark and getting colder out by the time Tom dropped Jenny off and passed Doc's house, but Doc was sitting on the step even so. He came to meet Tom, looking serious, and said, "I've got some news. I can't say it's surprising, but you need to know it."

Tom nodded, then stood there wishing it was easier for him to shift from foot to foot to warm up. You didn't care about little things like that until you couldn't do them. Luckily Doc went back up the steps and opened the door. "If you have a moment, why don't we talk about it inside. Clara's made hot cider that'd go down nicely, and we've got some shortbread to go with it."

Tom gladly followed Doc in. Clara, sitting in an easy

chair, smiled up at him kinda weakly. "Welcome, Tom. I'd get up and greet you, but that's a major undertaking just now. Joshua knows where everything is."

Once they were sitting at the kitchen table with plates of shortbread and steaming mugs of cider, Doc waited until Tom had taken some of each and then said, "I talked to the preacher yesterday about the wedding."

The shortbread went dry in Tom's mouth. He took a gulp of cider, burning his throat. "He won't marry us, will he. I reckon I should've gone and apologized before this."

Doc looked about as grim as he was able. "Frankly, Tom, I doubt it would've made any difference. Oh, he might have taken less relish in refusing if you'd gone to him. But to be fair, he genuinely believes your marrying Jenny will take you away from the path of the blessed and he'd be failing in his duty to further it."

Tom set his mug down, harder than he should've. "Well, then, we'll just leave town and get married later. Somewhere no one knows us and our stories." Jenny mightn't like it, what with all her new resolutions, but she'd do it for him, and to get their lives started.

Doc fetched the cider pitcher, and filled up both their mugs. "That's always an option, but I hope we can do better. Jedidiah is ready to hit the road again, though Freida will stay behind with us. He'll go to Rushing first and talk to the preacher there. And if that one won't assist us, he'll try farther afield." He looked close at Tom and must have read his mind. "I'd go myself, for whatever that would add to the chances for success, but Clara's time is upon us."

Tom made himself smile. "Don't fret about it, Doc. Of course you should be here — and Mr. Jed is a mighty persuasive fellow. He'll get us a preacher if there's one to be got."

He drank a little more cider to be polite and then excused himself. Time to head on home and tell Ma and Pa.

Ma did some hand-wringing and lamenting, which Tom knew to expect and tried not to mind. Pa just grunted and stroked his beard. After a while he said, "Well, we'll hope for the best from Mr. Jed's efforts, and bide 'til we know."

Ma had gone quiet and seemed to be working up to something. When both Pa and Tom looked at her with their eyebrows up, she looked away before meeting their eyes and saying slowly, "With as long as all this is taking, I do believe it's time your Jenny had somewhere else to stay. We should have her here until the wedding. Assuming she'd like to come."

Pa edged her way and said, kind of quiet, "Hon, you sure you're all right with her being around Martha like that?"

Tom interrupted in spite of it maybe being disrespectful. "Jenny wouldn't do or say nothing to shock Martha or — or tell her anything she shouldn't know. I'm sure of it." Which he almost was. Jenny wouldn't do anything like that on purpose. And she was mighty bright — she'd probably know what not to say.

Ma had her determined look on. "It's the right thing to do, and we're going to do it. Jenny is going to be part of this family, and everyone can just know it and get used to it." She loosened up enough to give Tom a softer look. "Including Jenny, who might find it hardest to credit."

"Very well, Ma," said Pa. "Tom, you can leave word on your way to work tomorrow, so she'll have time to pack up and say her goodbyes, and then bring her home with you in the evening, assuming she don't object."

Tom couldn't talk for the lump in his throat. He just went to Ma and gave her the biggest hug he could, and shook Pa's hand, and went to the kitchen to grab himself a bite of supper before bed.

Where he lay awake, thinking of Jenny under this very roof come tomorrow evening.

*   *   *   *   *

Jenny had been learning to rise earlier, now that she had breakfast to help fix, but Mamie still had to shake her awake some mornings. When Mamie knocked and came on in, Jenny's first thought was that it must be later than she'd figured. But Mamie didn't bustle around tossing her clothes at her and lecturing. Instead, she stood leaning against the door frame, just waiting for Jenny to attend to her.

Finally, when Jenny had got out of bed and was standing there fidgeting, she said, "I've got some news for you, and you might find it frazzle your nerves at first. But it's good news. Real good."

Chapter 27

THE CARDBOARD case she'd had when she first landed on Mamie's doorstep hadn't been worth keeping. Some girls had come with proper trunks, but there was no saying when they might want 'em again. Mamie brought a suitcase for her to use, and didn't say where she got it. Jenny had a sad notion it might have been Amanda Jane's, but she didn't ask.

Not that she had that much to pack. Bessie was good with her needle and had helped Jenny make over some of her dresses so they'd be decent. Jenny was partway done with a brand new dress to wear on the road, out of sturdy fabric as would stand up to use and rough scrubbing, and she packed that to work on at Tom's place. She likely wouldn't have call to be wearing any paint, but she took a little just in case. Cook surprised her with a spare apron, clean and looking almost new.

Way back when Jenny was little, Mama had given her a silver-backed brush and comb from her grandma, and she'd kept it with her since, even when she'd have done better to pawn it. She packed that last of all.

Mamie called Jenny into her office when it got to be almost time for Tom to show. "You make sure and treat Tom's folks respectful. It's a good thing you've been working with Cook — you can be of some help in the kitchen. Make sure you offer, and not just with that. There'll be plenty you can do if you pay attention and follow his ma's lead."

Jenny gulped and said, "Yes, ma'am. What about his pa?"

Mamie shot a stern look at her. "Just you make sure you don't do anything even close to flirting. You'd best be as quiet around him as you can, so no one gets the wrong idea."

A knock on the door, and Trudi stuck her head in. "Jenny's fellow's here to pick her up, ma'am."

Mamie stood up. "You tell him we'll be right there." Trudi closed the door, and Mamie said briskly, "You run and get your things and meet me downstairs. I'll entertain your young man until you come."

* * * * *

Tom sat on the edge of the chair, doing his best to ignore the whispers and giggles coming from every corner of the room. He stood up as Mamie swept in and shooed the girls away. "You give us some room, and no eavesdropping or I'll know it."

When things had got quieter, she steered him toward the bottom of the stairs. Tom couldn't resist a glance upstairs where Jenny must be getting ready to join him.

"Young man."

Tom twitched his head back toward Mamie and folded his hands in front of him. "Yes'm."

"I don't know, and don't really care to know, what you think of me. But the fact is that I take care of these girls as best I can, and consider myself responsible for them, up to a point. Jenny and her ma haven't spoken in years, from what I understand, and that makes me the closest she's got to a mother just now. So I feel called upon to say a few things before you take her off with you."

Well, it wasn't much stranger than the rest of his life had been lately. "Yes'm, I'm listening."

"I don't know how much she's said about it, but Jenny had a rough time as a girl, and on her way here as well." She read Tom's face and added, "I see that isn't news to you."

"Not really, ma'am, though I don't know many particulars."

"You probably know enough to understand that she's likely to have some fears about falling on hard times again. She can picture it, you see, more than a girl who's never been there and might have romantic notions about what hardship is like, so long as you've got *love*." From the twist she gave the word, Tom guessed she didn't have much call to use it. He couldn't tell if she believed in it.

"And you, on the other hand, have known your own kind of hard times, but you've never gone hungry — not *really* hungry — nor known cold without shelter nor blanket, nor wondered when you'd next find shelter. It'll likely come as a shock when you first encounter times like that. So I want you to be ready for it, as much as thinking on it can make you, and to promise — promise me, and Jenny even if she doesn't know it, and yourself for that matter — that you'll put her welfare ahead of yours, and live harder if it means she lives less hard." She gave a half-smile with something of bitter in it. "For as long as you both shall live."

Her words sent a shiver down Tom's spine, as if he could already feel the cold wind of some coming winter, where he'd need to work and struggle to keep Jenny warm. He managed to stand straight and look Mamie in the eyes. "I do. I will."

"You two look awful serious." It was Jenny. Mamie

had had him near to hypnotized, for him to miss her coming down the stair. She walked right up to him and grabbed his hand.

He took the suitcase from her and turned back to Mamie. "We'll be going now, I reckon. Thank you for — for taking care of Jenny like you have, and everything."

Jenny looked at Mamie and did a double-take, which made Tom look for himself and nearly do the same. Mamie had tears in her eyes. No wonder she'd made the other girls keep their distance, not to see as much. She opened her arms, and Jenny ran into them, holding on hard.

It wasn't long before Mamie unwound Jenny's arms and gave her a little push toward the door. "That's enough of that. You go on, girl. Go live the best life you can. Good luck to you."

And with that, she turned and bustled away, leaving Tom and Jenny to stare after her and then walk out the door.

* * * * *

Jenny might've seen Tom's ma, for all she knew, but not to know it. And Ma had likely never seen her. Jenny was all of a shiver as they finally made it to the farm after their long walk from town.

Tom's ma and pa were waiting in the yard, along with his brother and sister. Both his sibs had eyes as wide as saucers. Ma held Martha's hand and stood a little in front of her, the girl peering around her to see better. Jenny wondered if Tom's ma even knew she was doing it.

Mr. Barlow came up first. "Welcome, Miss Hayes. I'm Tom's pa, as you must've reckoned. Welcome to our place."

Mrs. Barlow let go of Martha and joined her husband, smiling like she was nervous, and said, "Welcome. We're glad to have you."

Jenny bobbed a curtsy to them both. "Thank you kindly, Mr. and Mrs. Barlow. I'm right glad to be here, myself."

Mrs. Barlow shook her head, which made Jenny pretty nervous herself until the woman said, "You're going to be my daughter, so you may as well start right now calling me Ma."

Jenny's breath caught in her throat. With all the things she'd been afeared of and all she'd hoped for, she'd never expected that. And here she stood gaping, when she needed to say something. "Thank you, ma'am. I mean — Ma."

The Barlow house was a whole lot bigger, not to mention better kept up, than where Jenny'd come from. She guessed the parents might have a room of their own, and figured she'd be sharing a room with Martha and Billy — and likely Tom, though how she'd sleep with him lying nearby, she couldn't think. But when Mrs. — when Ma told Martha to show Jenny upstairs, they headed down the hall to a room with just one bed, a new-looking coverlet on it and everything spic and span. "This here's our guest room. It's the nicest, even nicer'n Ma and Pa's."

Now she thought about it, it wasn't hardly a surprise that Tom's folks didn't want her rooming with their innocent youngsters. She shook off the twinge of hurt feelings and said, "That's right kind of your folks. It looks lovely."

Martha, ignoring or defying whatever purpose Ma might've had, plunked herself down on one end of the bed while Jenny put her suitcase down on the other end and started unpacking. She looked avidly at every dress Jenny pulled out, probably disappointed every time it wasn't skimpy or bright red or drowning in lace. When the suitcase was empty, which didn't take long, Martha asked brightly, "You've been to lots of places, haven't you? Do tell about some."

Jenny shook her head. "Not that many, and mostly not very nice. Not near as nice as what you've got here. You should feel lucky, and thankful too."

Martha pouted. Then she went thoughtful, tracing the pattern of the coverlet with her finger, and asked, "Are you afraid of going off again? And with just Tom?"

Jenny sat down on the bed and patted Martha's hand. "Not a bit." That might not be altogether true. But the next part, she believed, or more than she would've a few days before. "Tom will take care of me just fine."

Jenny did her best to be useful. She got up and dressed as soon as she heard anyone moving about, hurried to the kitchen, and set to peeling potatoes and frying eggs, even when Ma tried to make her sit and act like a guest. She tagged after Billy as he milked the cows, getting him to let her try it once she'd watched a few. She got most of the milk into the pail, and if she got some on her dress, Ma didn't have to know. Billy probably wouldn't tell.

A few days after she'd moved in, Jenny came down to help with breakfast one morning and could tell that Ma had something on her mind. She wasn't in any hurry to say what, seemingly, so Jenny just went about peeling and chopping up potatoes. What with trying to get the pieces close to the same size, she forgot about how Ma'd been acting until she took the bowl over to Ma and saw that Ma was still looking fidgety. Jenny handed over the bowl and stood there until Ma finally said, "We're having the first quilting bee tomorrow. Over at the Flanders place."

They just stood there with the bowl between them until Jenny said, "You don't want me to come, I reckon."

Ma rocked back on her heels a little as if something had startled her. Jenny had the funny feeling it was something in Ma's own head. "I guess I do. You're marrying Tom, and from what he says, you've been awful good for him. And you seem like a nice girl, at that. But — there's likely to be someone there as'll be less'n welcoming."

The someone might even be Mrs. Flanders, as was hosting the bee. But prob'ly Ma wouldn't be more or less inviting Jenny if she thought Mrs. Flanders would bar the door.

Jenny lifted up her chin and looked straight at Ma. "You're making this quilt for Tom and me, ahead of when you were planning. And I'm still learning what to do with a needle, but I can stitch up pieces and do whatever else you tell me. I'll come, if it won't make things hard between you and your neighbors."

Up came Ma's chin to match. "Not hard enough to matter. And I ain't scared of some busybody looking down her nose. You come with me after breakfast, and I'll show you what I've got done so far, and what you'll be needing to do."

Martha came trudging in just then, sleepy and making sure they both knew about it. Ma chuckled like she'd seen it plenty of times before. "And Martha'll be going with us, so you'll have two of us there to take your part."

Jenny could just imagine Martha answering someone back and getting a reputation as disrespectful — if she didn't have one already. "Thank you for that, ma'am — Ma. But I'd just as soon no one say anything. Knowing as you're there, that'll be enough."

There was more'n one busybody, and Jenny had to bite her tongue a couple of times, before she got caught up enough in the work that she could quit listening. Martha opened her mouth once like she planned to answer back, before Ma put a hand on her arm like she was holding her down.

But the quilt looked to turn out right fine.

* * * * *

After Jenny helped Ma and Martha get dinner the next day, Pa leaned back, rubbed his belly, and said, "Soon as I digest this fine meal, I'm taking the wagon into town to pick up a few things. Would either of you ladies like to come along?"

Jenny couldn't stop her eyes from bugging out. Pa was willing to be seen with her, and to have Ma seen with her? She'd go with, even if she had nothing much to do in town. She could maybe get some store-bought handkerchiefs, and some sweets to give Tom's brother and sister.

And — she could gather up her courage and go see whether she'd got a letter.

Jenny barely got back to the wagon before Ma and Pa did. She hadn't reckoned on having time to read the letter stuffed in her pocket, but she'd hoped for enough to pull herself together. As Pa helped Ma up, she sat on her hands to hide their shaking.

Her mama wouldn't have wrote back just to say something hateful. That wasn't her way. Or it hadn't been.

Ma looked close at Jenny's face as Pa set the horse pulling for home. "You're a bit flushed. Did anything happen in town? Someone being unkind, like?"

Jenny shrugged, and then hoped Ma and Pa didn't hear how it made the letter crinkle. "Nothing much. You saw how it was at the quilting bee — about like that. It's better than what men get up to."

Pa's jaw got tight. Jenny looked away. It wasn't hard to find something else to think on out here away from town, with all manner of clouds scooting across the sky, and the prairie gold-like where the sun hit it between clouds, and a breeze poking under her hat and tasting sweet, and a red-tailed hawk riding the breeze higher up.

She'd thought it'd feel like forever before they got back and she could go read her letter. But when Pa pulled the wagon into the yard, she wasn't so eager after all. She made a point of helping carry the provisions in and putting things where Ma wanted them. And when Ma thanked her and told her it'd be a while yet before they started supper, she almost asked for some other chore to do. But whatever was in the letter, it wouldn't get better with waiting.

She climbed the stairs with her heart in her throat, it felt like, and pushed open her door — only to find Martha sitting cross-legged on her bed, playing a game of knucklebones and singing to herself. She looked up and grinned as Jenny stood in the doorway staring. "I wanted to see what you got in town, and not to have to unload the wagon. Hope you don't mind my being on your bed."

Jenny had to laugh, though it kind of shook coming out. "That's all right. I got some handkerchiefs, see?" She came over near the bed and pulled them out of her pocket, just managing not to bring the letter with them.

Martha crawled forward on the bed and looked them over. "They're nice, I guess. I thought you might get something fancier. Or maybe scented."

Jenny pushed aside a mix of feelings, some hurt and

some huffy. No surprise that Martha'd expected the kind of handkerchief Mamie's girls would flutter at a man in the street. "I'm going to be your sister, so I figured I should get the kind of handkerchiefs your sister would."

"Is that *all* you got?"

Jenny's face got hot, and she could just imagine how that looked. She had better say something quick. "I got a letter. From back home, I think, but I ain't read it yet."

Martha started bouncing on the bed. It must be nice to feel so safe you could act like a little kid, just a few years shy of being a woman. "Did you write about Tom? I bet you did! Did you write about me too?"

Jenny couldn't help but smile. "I did. All of that."

Martha clasped her hands and beamed. "Will you read the letter out loud?"

Time to act like a big sister, which Jenny hadn't done in longer'n she wanted to think on. "No, I won't. This is private, and you need to leave me be for a while."

Martha's face fell, but she slowly climbed off of the bed and slumped toward the door. Jenny'd said the right thing, but it didn't feel altogether good, so she added as Martha reached the door, "If they say anything about you or send you a message, I'll be sure and tell you."

Martha turned and gave her another quick grin before heading down the stairs. Jenny made sure she kept going before closing the bedroom door and pulling the letter out.

The writing wasn't Mama's.

Jenny fell back against the door, the letter shaking in her hand, blinking tears out of her eyes. She tottered on shaky legs over to the bed and plopped down on the edge.

Dear Sister,

This is Agatha. Mama told me to write, along of her eyes give her trouble these days.

Jenny breathed a huge sigh of relief.

But really, I think it's because she starts crying whenever she tries to write back, and enough time's gone by already.

We're all real happy you met a fellow you like as wants to marry you. When I say all of us, I mean us girls and Joey and Mama, because Papa died last winter when he drank too much and got lost in a blizzard, between the barn and the house. Joey found him froze stiff and with ice all over him.

Jenny put the letter down on the bed, folded her hands, and closed her eyes. Could she pray for Papa, as mean as he'd been, as much trouble and hurt his meanness had caused her? She wouldn't've asked the preacher, not if he was standing right there in front of her. For some reason the face that drifted into her mind was Doc. She wasn't sure just what he'd say to her, but it'd be something kind. And he'd expect her to have kindness in her, even about Papa.

She squeezed her hands and her eyes tight and whispered, "Dear Lord, please forgive Papa his sins, as I hope you'll be forgiving mine. And please give him the chance to repent, even if he didn't think on it when he was freezing to death. Amen."

She opened her eyes and picked up the letter again.

Charity got married to the new wheelwright right after harvest time last year. He's some kind of handsome, and we was all real happy about it. We had the grandest party, which he paid for, along of money's pretty scarce here even without Papa drinking it all away.

Since your fellow's good with pictures, we'd sure like it if he could draw a picture of hisself, maybe standing next to you, for you to send. It could be on leather like you say he does, or any other way he'd rather. We're all powerful curious what he looks like. What color hair's he got? Has he got big muscles? Charity's wheelwright does.

Jenny could just picture Agatha's mouth flapping with all her questions.

Mama says to tell you she's real glad you're all right and getting married. She's been afeared for you ever since you left with that oily fellow. You don't say what you've been up to all this time, and Mama says I'm not to ask you, so I won't.

Which meant Mama had a pretty good notion. The letter took to shaking again.

Mama says maybe you and Tom could come see us after you get married. We're all wanting to meet him, and to see you again.

Maybe they could head that way, sooner or later. There might not be so much call for saddles there, but men'd still want boots, and they could go through places where ladies wore fancy shoes. She could talk to Tom about it later, whenever she felt up to showing him the letter.

Mama says to make sure I tell you she loves you.

Jenny barely had time to put the letter out of reach before she busted out crying. At least she had a new handkerchief to use.

Chapter 28

WHEN TOM came in all of a hurry that evening, she thought at first he was that eager to see her, before he called out, "Mrs. Clara's time has come! I saw Doc running full tilt down the street so's his hat fell off, which he didn't stop to get, and Mr. Hawkins come into the shop and told us."

Ma got up and grabbed her coat off the hook. "Jenny, Martha, can you get supper? I'm going to go see if I can help. I don't know as Doc would admit it, but it never hurts to have a woman there as has helped a few babies into the world."

Jenny hurried to put on her apron. "Of course, Ma. We'll take care of everything. Tom, why don't you go wash up while we get supper on the table."

Tom grinned at her being so domestic, but he didn't hold it for long. He must be worried about Mrs. Clara. She was kind of old for a first baby, after all. Good as Doc was at his trade, she was glad Tom's ma knew about birthing and was going there too.

Meanwhile, Jenny had supper to tend to.

Ma didn't come home until morning. By then, both menfolk were pacing around muttering to themselves, and Martha and Billy had been popping out of bed all night, creeping downstairs and asking, "Ain't Ma back *yet?*" Jenny got what rest she could with her head and arms on the kitchen table, so she'd be right there if something came up as needed her to run over to Doc's.

When Ma came through the door, a few rain drops on her hat catching the first rays of sunshine, she looked fair wiped out, but even more happy. "A girl, and healthy. And Clara's doing fine." She chuckled. "Even Doc's doing all right. He was brave and strong the whole time, until the baby came and all was well. Then he fell into a chair all of a tremble, and cussing under his breath. Mrs. Freida made him drink some brandy. It was a fair treat, listening to her tell him to drink it down."

Ma yawned. "I'll just have a bite of breakfast and then lay down for a bit. Tom, Doc says you and Jenny can come see the baby this evening. I'll likely come along with you, and bring some of my calf's foot jelly. It's wonderful strengthening, when a woman's lost blood like you do."

Tom went a little pale at the thought, and Jenny decided to be nice and not tease him over it. She just went and put her arm around his waist, giving him a little squeeze. He'd do, when the time came. Though he might resort to drinking earlier'n Doc had.

Mrs. Freida opened the door, talking before she even saw them. "Such a day, a new baby, a new life! And Clara, so brave, not that she didn't yell when she needed to, no point holding it in, she had more important things to think about. Come in, come in!"

By that time they were in already, Doc coming to take their coats. He looked as happy as a tired man could, and as tired as a happy man could. Tom and Pa took turns shaking his hand. Meanwhile, Jenny and Ma looked around for Mrs.

Clara and the baby.

A lusty wail gave them the clue on where to go. Mrs. Freida led them to the room where Mrs. Clara was in bed, propped up with pillows and holding the squirming, red-faced baby. Mrs. Freida shooed them in, saying, "You go, look all you want, I'll have plenty of chances, I'll go see to the menfolk." She bustled away, leaving the doorway open for Ma and Jenny to file on in.

Mrs. Clara looked up from the baby and gave them a quick smile before looking down again, mainly taken up with putting the baby to her breast. "There, now," she murmured, "that wasn't so hard, was it? We've got this almost figured out. That's right, just like that, you bring your mama's milk in, then it'll be easier all round."

It'd been a long time since Jenny saw a newborn babe. She'd forgot how little and wrinkly they were. Mothers were supposed to think their babes were beautiful, but from the look on Mrs. Clara's face, fond and amused both, she saw plainer'n most.

Now the baby was sucking instead of screaming, Mrs. Clara lay back carefully so's not to unsettle her and gave the visitors a weary smile. "Welcome, and thanks for coming. After this major an achievement, I'm eager to show off the result." She looked at Ma and went teary-eyed. "And Mrs. Barlow, thank you so much for all you did for us last night. I'm more grateful than I can say — at least until I get some sleep and my mind is clearer."

Ma came close and looked down at the baby, her own eyes moist. "You're most welcome, and I'm glad I could be here. Isn't she an angel!"

Mrs. Clara's mouth twitched like she'd have laughed if she had the strength to. "It's rather early to say. But if she turns out at all angelic, she'll have her father to thank for it."

She looked over at Jenny, who was hanging farther back. "It's all right, Jenny. Come close and look your fill."

But looking wasn't all Jenny found she was wanting.

When the baby's sucking slowed and then stopped, the little mouth falling half open with a bubble of milk on the lips, Ma and Mrs. Clara hushed at the same moment. Mrs. Clara freed a hand and crooked her finger at Jenny, whispering, "Would you like to hold her? If we just wait a minute or so, she'll be deep enough asleep that she's unlikely to wake."

Jenny crept up to the side of the bed and sat down as cautious as ever she had, then scooted closer. Clara slowly shifted the baby over into Jenny's waiting arms and settled her there.

And there Jenny was, holding a baby for the first time since she was a woman grown.

She heard Doc's voice, real low, from the doorway. "Now that's a real pretty sight to see, and I wish Tom had come with me to see it." He came up to the bed and kissed Mrs. Clara on the forehead. "Tom and Mr. Barlow would like to see the baby, if it's not a bad time."

Jenny bit her lip, then let it go quick before Doc could see, finding a smile for him instead. "It's high time for her pa to take her, don't you think? I'd hand her to you, but I'm that scared of waking her."

Doc laughed real quiet. "No more than I am. But boldly into the breach!" He squatted down 'til his arms were level with Jenny's and lifted the baby out like she weighed no more'n a dumpling. Bringing the baby up to his face, he gave her a kiss on the forehead, much like he'd done for Mrs. Clara, and made his careful way out of the room.

Mrs. Clara sank back against her pillows, her eyes closed. Ma patted her hand and said, "I'll be back to see you tomorrow morning. You get your rest, now."

Mrs. Clara said nothing. It looked to Jenny like she was already getting that rest Ma had ordered. They went back to where Doc was showing the baby to Tom and his pa. Jenny went up to Tom and snuggled into him. He turned to smile at her, which gave her the chance to say, "I held the baby! And it went fine."

Tom gave her a quick kiss and said, "Of course it did."

Ma headed to where Mrs. Freida had put their coats. "We've stayed long enough, I reckon. Like I told Clara, I'll be back in the morning. You all take care, now."

She was just handing Jenny her coat when there came a commotion from outside. The door flung open, and there stood Mr. Jed, blowing on his hands to warm 'em and smiling all over his face. "Well, here's a merry crowd and no mistake! The more the merrier, to make our guest welcome. Tom, Jenny, come and meet him. I've brought you a preacher."

Once everybody had brought everybody up to date, and Mr. Jed had made introductions all round, and then took the waked-up and crying baby from Doc's arms and bounced her 'til she stopped, the preacher followed Ma and Pa and Tom and Jenny out the door. Tom shook the preacher's hand for the third time and asked, "Sir, how long are you able to stay? We didn't figure on all this happening when you showed up. And we owe Doc a powerful lot. We'd like him at the wedding if he can get free while you're still in town."

The preacher, a skinny fellow well along in years, gave them a big smile. "Young man, this is the first trip out of town I've had in too long. I'm in no great hurry to be home again. Do you think three days from now will be soon enough?"

Ma had come up to listen, and said, "So long as Clara and the baby stay well, I expect so. But we need to talk about the ceremony."

Jenny'd forgotten to think about where it could be. Not in the church, that was sure and certain! It could be at Tom's house, and that's maybe what everyone was expecting. But an idea come to her, strange maybe, but lodging in her head and taking hold. She looked around at them all and said, "Excuse me if I'm interrupting. And I'm not going to be making any trouble about where, nor when neither. But I'm wondering, given all that's happened and how we come to this point, whether we might do something kind of different."

* * * * *

They had, as planned, bought two horses. Tom hadn't had to use every bit of his savings after all. Mr. Jed and Mrs. Freida, and Doc, and Madam Mamie, and even Finch had chipped in to help. So he and Jenny would have something to live on for at least the first part of their journey.

They'd been keeping the new horses separate in a stall apiece, but now Tom grabbed a couple of carrots from where they stored them, and Pa fetched the mare and led her to the pasture where Cochise was grazing. He turned her loose, watching close. "That gelding'll do fine here biding with us, pulling the plow and the wagon. Let's see how the mare gets on with your old friend."

The mare and Cochise got busy smelling each other. The mare put her ears back and swished her tail; Cochise backed away a couple of steps and lowered his head. Pa chuckled. "Looks like that mare is showing Cochise who's boss. Don't let her give Jenny any ideas, now!"

Some other time, Tom might've bristled at the joke, but he had other things to think about. He whistled to Cochise, who left the mare to come trotting up, though she followed after. Given how Cochise and the mare had started out, he figured he'd better give her the first carrot, which she snapped up like he'd kept her waiting for it. Tom stroked Cochise's mane and fed him the second carrot, saying, "Looks like we get to go adventuring together, after all, don't we, boy? We won't be herding cattle nor riding ranges, but we'll see plenty of cowboys. You ready?"

Cochise blew a warm breath in Tom's face and nuzzled his shoulder. It was a good enough answer. Tom faced Pa, almost too choked up to talk, and said as best he could, "Thankee, sir. For letting me have Cochise and taking on the new one instead."

Pa clapped him on the back. "I'm happy to make the trade." He added with a chuckle, "And I'll feel better somehow, knowing that when you're out who knows where, you've got Cochise there to keep an eye on you. Now let's get back inside and get dressed up proper. We've a wedding to go to."

As if Tom didn't know. But what with the horses, he'd almost managed to forget for a minute, and breathe normal. Now the air turned back to treacle. Fighting through it, he followed Pa into the house.

He wasn't to see Jenny before the wedding, which had meant plenty of awkward maneuvering and being sent out of rooms and down halls. But by now, Jenny and Ma and Martha were on their way to town in Doc's buggy. As soon as Pa and Tom got into their best Sunday duds, Pa helping Tom with his collar when his fingers wouldn't work right, they set out in the wagon to catch up, the new gelding getting them there in good time. It only seemed like it took hours. Except when they arrived, and it felt like it had took only seconds.

They pulled up outside the cemetery where the preacher was waiting, his lips moving like he was practicing. Ma and Martha and Doc and Mr. Jed, and Madam Mamie and 'most all her girls, were standing in a clump in front of him, but all Tom could see was the little figure with the pretty red hair, bundled up in a fine long coat, gazing back at him.

He strode up to her as fast as he could walk without tripping. She held her hand out, to grab his as soon as she could reach, and pulled him close, whispering, "Mrs. Freida wanted to lend me her coat. I'd have looked like a bear! but Mamie gave me hers. She said I can keep it! And I've got the prettiest dress under it. Sorry you can't see it until we get back to your place for the wedding breakfast."

She was talking almost too quick for him to understand her, and shivering along with it. At least they were both scared silly. He looked in her eyes, trying to see if scared or no, she was as sure as he was — about getting married, about him, about all they'd planned.

Her eyes shone back at him like the Christmas star.

The preacher cleared his throat and pulled out his book. "Dearly beloved, we are standing here by the grave of our departed sister Amanda Jane, who we know is with us in spirit. We are here this day to join this man and this woman in holy matrimony . . . ."

The words seemed to fade in and out, but Tom managed to follow well enough to hear when the preacher said, "And now, do you, Thomas Barlow, take this woman, Jennifer Hayes, to be your lawful wedded wife . . . ."

Tom blurted out, "I do!" before the preacher had quite

finished saying, "so help you God." A laugh made its way around the crowd, but Tom couldn't have cared less, not with Jenny gripping his hands tight and smiling up at him. And then it was her turn, and she said, "I do!" at just the right time, looking at him like she maybe, finally, could believe what was happening.

And then it was back to the house, all who chose to come — which turned out not to be Mamie and her girls. He shook hands with them, every one, and stood aside while Jenny collected one last round of hugs, Mamie's last and longest. Pa took Ma and Martha in the wagon this time, so Tom could take his bride home in style, as Doc put it, in the buggy, Mr. Jed's wagon with Freida following after.

Jenny's dress was every bit as pretty as she'd said, a peach sort of color with crystals all over and lace at the breast. But he didn't have all that long to see her in it, not if they were going to be ready to leave as soon as the wedding breakfast was over. They both went upstairs to change after Mr. Jed gave his toast, and were back down in good time to hear Pa's.

Guests started to say their goodbyes, wishing Tom well and congratulating him on their way out, bowing to Jenny and wishing her every happiness. Tom fetched the sample saddle and put it on Cochise, for passersby to see and, he hoped, wonder at. Maybe he'd make one for the new mare, in time, or maybe he'd let Cochise be the only one with such finery.

They'd already loaded the quilts, and Tom's tools, and such clothes and other odds and ends as they were taking. Everything was stowed and ready. Pa was already getting the horses harnessed. Doc walked out with them, making sure Tom knew everything to do for his stump and to keep his leg in working order.

Ma ran out to give Tom a final hug, and he held her tight, feeling her shake and knowing she'd cry the minute he was gone. Martha was already sniffling behind her, while Billy was looking on with envy writ all over him. He'd be a handful for a while. But Ma and Pa were up to handling him.

Pa gave Tom a big, man-sized hug, and helped Jenny into the wagon while Tom pulled himself together. They'd managed to fit in a bench after all, almost like the one in Mr. Jed's wagon, and Jenny would ride there later, maybe, but for now she'd be sitting up with Tom. He was going to show her how to drive.

Tom took one more long look around, at his family, at Mrs. Freida calling out some stream of wishes he couldn't rightly hear, at Mr. Jed in his smart coat and hat looking mighty satisfied, and finally at Doc, looking up at him with no trouble on his face, like he knew Tom was ready for whatever lay ahead.

He shook the reins and chucked at the horses, and off they went to meet it.

THE END

Author's Note

Writing a novel, especially any kind of historical fiction, involves innumerable decisions. I'm highlighting a few of those here, in no particular order. If you're curious about what considerations led to any other detail, please see the "Connect with the Author" section, following, and ask me!

Given Jenny's level of literacy and her concerns about spelling, it would have been more accurate for her letters to include some spelling mistakes. I gave that a try, but I found the result distracting enough that I thought it would pull some readers out of the story. I ended up hoping the lurking inconsistency would be less disruptive than the misspellings would have been. I was also far from certain I could figure out, or find sources to instruct me, what errors Jenny would be likely to make.

I used customs and labor statistics from the late 1860s and 1870s (see Acknowledgments) to establish that commercial hair dyes were available during this period. I posited, for my purposes, that such dyes included the color red, and that they could be ordered in some manner from Nebraska.

I based Jenny's idea for helping Tom's phantom itch on the much later development of the mirror box, invented by Vilayanur S. Ramachandran in the 1990s. Jenny's a smart woman, and I thought she might just come up with the idea on her own.

Tom, as a boy much interested in the doings of Indians,

named the horse Cochise after the principal chief of the Chiricahua Apache. Cochise led an uprising against the U.S. government from 1861 until 1872, and Tom would have heard news of him.

I considered having both Tom and Jenny regularly drop their gs at the end of gerunds like "talking" and "standing," in dialogue and/or in internal monologues. However, such words appeared quite often, and as a reader, I find frequent dialect references distracting. I decided, as I often do, to write what I'd prefer to read, with just a few uses of missing gs and constructions such as 'em (for them) to give the flavor of the characters' speech.

When in doubt, I try to confirm that words and phrases I use were current at the time, using the resources mentioned in the Acknowledgments (immediately following). Sometimes I proceed with something less than solid reassurance. For example, the first recorded use of the phrase "soft in the head" may have been in 1775. I chose to assume it was current before it was "recorded." I also found few uses of either "leatherworker" or "leather worker," but the latter appeared earlier, and I chose to use it.

Joshua's brief mention of increased difficulty obtaining "French letters" is a reference to the 1873 Comstock Act, which (among other things) prohibited manufacturing, selling, giving away, mailing, or possessing for distribution any item to be used for contraception. Aside from the provisions affecting use of the U.S. mail, these restrictions applied anywhere in the District of Columbia, U.S. territories, and anywhere the federal government had "exclusive jurisdiction." Exactly what if any effect this federal statute had within a U.S. state, unless and until that state passed its own similar law, is a legal question at which I've only taken a quick glance. Simple possession of contraceptives wasn't criminalized in that statute, so I'm assuming for purposes of this book that Joshua has quite a stockpile of French letters, and also that either his giving some to Tom wasn't a crime within Nebraska, or that Joshua doesn't care enough about any potential legal jeopardy to leave Tom unprotected.

Magpies may not, as is commonly thought, collect shiny objects, but Jenny would probably believe they did.

The process of editing a draft includes deciding what interesting historical tidbits, pleasing bits of dialogue, and vivid images to include, and which ones must be omitted to keep the narrative from dragging. I could probably struggle with that balance forever if I didn't, at some point, force myself to call a halt. For example, I first cut and then added back the scenes where a cowboy comes off a cattle drive wanting saddle decoration, and where Clara reads Freida's letter. On the other hand, I first added and then cut a scene with Mamie and Jenny where the two of them discuss what happened to any babies that came along. I also cut some details about the tools the blacksmith makes for Tom. I may eventually put some of these deleted passages on my website in the "Deleted and alternate scenes" section (http://www.karenawyle.net/deleted_scenes.html).

Acknowledgments

An introductory caveat: I consulted so many websites that I may well have missed a few in putting this section together, most likely those consulted for late revisions. My apologies to the omitted! Those I have managed to include are presented in no particular order — and it's a long list.

I consulted Wikipedia so often that I haven't bothered to mention every time I did so.

This time around, I had a new resource for checking whether a word or phrase was already in use during my time period, namely Google Books Ngram Viewer (at https://books.google.com/ngrams/). One selects a time span, sources to be searched (e.g. American English), and search term, and can see a graph showing the percentage of times the word or phrase was used in the appropriate section of the enormous Google Books collection. I also made frequent use of the Online Etymological Dictionary.

My go-to source for last names is *Behind the Names*, though I also consulted others I neglected to note. For likely names of ranches, I took inspiration from a "Travel" article on the online Fox News channel.

When I needed something to fill the sacks Tom Barlow was loading into a wagon in March, Jordan McBride, member of the NaNoWriMo Facebook group, helpfully pointed me to Laura Ingalls Wilder's novel *Farmer Boy*. As for facts about covered wagons, I consulted *History Daily*, *The Oregon Territory and its Pioneers*, and a website whose title I couldn't find at https://www.learningabe.info.

The following sources helped me shape Jenny's and

other prostitutes' experiences at Madam Mamie's:

—Angela C. Fitzpatrick's 2013 dissertation, *Women of Ill Fame: Discourses of Prostitution and the American Dream in California, 1850-1890*;

—excerpts from Anne Butler's *Daughters of Joy, Sisters of Misery: Prostitutes in the American West, 1865-1890*, provided in a review whose author I unfortunately neglected to note;

—Phillip A. Snyder's Foreword to *Upstairs Girls: Prostitution in the American West* by Michael Rutter;

—*Women of the Old West: Prostitutes and Madams* by Emma R. Marek;

—"What Sex Was Like in the Old West," by Jacoby Bancroft;

—"Wild Women of the Wild West - inside the brothels worked by the 'white doves'," by Matthew Growcott and Jane Alexander;

—"A Brothel Reveals Its Secrets," by Amy Laskowski;

—"Victorian Era Feminine Hygiene," by Kristin Holt;

—"The Soiled Dove Takes Flight: The Introduction of Prostitutes into Common Western Mythology," by Mirya Rose Holman;

—"Labor of Love: Prostitutes and Civic Engagement in Leadville, Colorado, 1870-1915," by Darby G. Simmons;

—"Red Light Ladies in the American West: Entrepreneurs and Companions," by Alexy Simmons;

—*Lengends of America*.

For period slang for "penis," I consulted *Timeglider*. As for other slang, I found more options than I could find uses for at *Mess No. 1, NPR History Department, The Long Riders Guild Academic Foundation, Rootsweb* (maintained by Ancestry.com), and *Legends of America*. An article at *The Irish Times* provided guidance about forms of address an Irishman might be likely to avoid.

My sources on various issues related to lower limb amputation and phantom pain included:

— "The prevalence of phantom limb pain and associated risk factors in people with amputations: a systematic review protocol," by Katleho Limakatso, Gillian J. Bedwell, Victoria J. Madden, and Romy Parker;

— *Prosthetic Restoration and Rehabilitation of the Upper and Lower Extremity*, by Mary Catherine Spires, Brian Kelly, and Alicia Davis;

— *The Textbook of Clinical Sexual Medicine*, edited by Waguih William IsHak;

— "Sex and Intimacy After Amputation," by Erin Deegan;

— various articles by various authors in the compendium "Post Amputation Chronic Pain Profile and Management," edited by Craig Murray;

— "People with lower limb amputation and their sexual functioning and sexual wellbeing," by multiple authors, published in *Disability and Rehabilitation*, April 2014;

— and finally, a thread on Reddit.

Concerning the availability of commercially produced hair dyes, I consulted:

— "From 1500 BC to 2015 AD: The Extraordinary History of Hair Dye," by Deven Hopp (on the Byrdie website);

— *Hair: An Illustrated History*, by Susan J. Vincent;

— "United States, Commission on Philadelphia Custom-House, January 1, 1877";

— "The Annual Report on the Statistics of Labor, Massachusetts Dept. Of Labor and Industries, Division of Statistics, 1878."

For how horses show affection and liking:

— "How Do Horses Show Affection?" by Franklin Levinson;

— "How To Read Your Horse's Body Language," by Jennifer Williams, PhD, on *Equus*;

—Various threads on Quora.

For how horses interact with each other, including hierarchical behavior, I checked websites including:

—"How to Introduce Horses," on *The Horse*;

—"How Horses Interact and Communicate," on *Veterinary Practice*.

Concerning observance of the Sabbath:

—*Sunday Rest in the Twentieth Century* (whose longer title I failed to note), edited by Alexander Johnson, which includes many references for the latter part of the 19th century;

—"Second Great Awakening," author not indicated, on the Ohio History Central website;

—"Mormon Sundays," by William G. Hartley;

—"Church Building and Community Making on the Frontier, A Case Study, Josiah Strong, Home Missionary in Cheyenne, 1871-1873," whose author either was not indicated or whom I failed to note, via JSTOR;

—Another JSTOR article I failed to record, dealing with Sabbatarianism.

Concerning fighting with one leg:

—"The One-Legged Wrestler Who Conquered His Sport, Then Left It Behind," by David Merrill, on *Deadspin*;

—"One-legged fighter Matt Betzold just wants a chance to get punched in the face like anyone else," by Shaun Al-Shatti, on *MMA Fighting*;

—"One-legged German kickboxer wins world title," by Mark Bergmann, on *Bloody Elbow*.

Concerning laudanum overdoses:

—"What Is Laudanum?" by Brittany Tackett, M.A., on *ProjectKnow*;

—"'The laudanum evil': Maryland's 19th century opiate epidemic," by Christina Tkacik, on AP News.

My sources for bird facts included *Gilligallou Bird Inc.* and *Sciencing*.

I double-checked the likely availability of pumps (for water) at *Illinois Archeology*.

I gleaned information about wages from *Hathi Trust Digital Library, Outrun Change, Cowboy Kisses*, and *Semantic Scholar*.

An article on *Curbed* told me to use coal rather than wood in the stoves at Mamie's.

I confirmed that I could include a cattle drive (peripherally) at *History Nebraska*.

Sources for photographer equipment and techniques of the period included an online library article from Oregon State University.

Various YouTube videos helped me with the basics of Western saddle making, as well as techniques for embellishing the same.

I found some non-medical remedies for stress on *Legends of America* and the *Huffpost* blog.

Sarah Wassberg Johnson of *The Food Historian*, Catherine Lambrecht from the Greater Midwest Foodways Alliance, and historian Rachel Laudan kindly answered my questions about the availability of lemons and lemon juice (and hence the likelihood of lemonade at particular times of the year).

I found ideas for Tom and Jenny's sleeping arrangements at author Theresa Hupp's blog. That information led me to seek expertise in quilting. Beta readers Wendy Teller and Dedaimia Whitney were both helpful in this regard. Dedaimia referred me to quilt historian Janice Frisch, who in turn passed me on to the

International Quilt Museum in Lincoln, Nebraska — where Communications Coordinator Laura Chapman and Collections Manager Sarah Walcott gave me the rest of what I needed.

I once again owe a multitude of thanks to cover designer Kelly Martin of KAM Design, and to all those who helped me choose between several gorgeous alternatives, including my daughters Livali Wyle and Alissa Wyle, husband Paul Hager, Debora Frazier, and the members of the April Moms Facebook group. Paul also helped me with my protagonists' likely word usage by pointing out that any word used in the King James Bible would probably be familiar to them.

And of course, I am extremely grateful and much indebted to my beta readers for this book, Jennifer Bourgeois, Steven Karel, Linda Lizenby, Glenda Morris, Nik Parker, Wendy Teller, and Dedaimia Whitney.

Finally, given how much this book builds on the research I did for its predecessor, *What Heals the Heart*, I once again thank all those who assisted me so much in that research.

About the Author

Karen A. Wyle was born a Connecticut Yankee, but eventually settled in Bloomington, Indiana, home of Indiana University. She now considers herself a Hoosier. She and her husband have two wildly creative daughters. (Return readers may notice that I no longer claim to have a sweet though neurotic dog. She left us in June 2019. We miss her.)

In addition to writing fiction (science fiction, afterlife fantasy, and now historical romance), Wyle is an appellate attorney, photographer, and politics junkie. Her voice is the product of almost five decades of reading both literary and genre fiction. It is no doubt also influenced, although she hopes not fatally tainted, by her years of law practice. Her personal history has led her to focus on often-intertwined themes of family, communication, personal identity, the impossibility of controlling events, and the persistence of unfinished business.

Connect with the Author

Learn more about Karen A. Wyle by looking her up on:
her author website, http://www.KarenAWyle.com;
Twitter, at https:/www.twitter.com/KarenAWyle;
Facebook, at https://www.facebook.com/KarenAWyle;
Goodreads, at https://www.goodreads.com/kawyle;
or her blog, , at http://looking-around.blogspot.com.

Like the book? Please tell readers!
Online book reviews are enormously helpful —
and old-fashioned word of mouth is terrific as well!

You can sign up for Wyle's monthly newsletter,
Including news of upcoming releases as well as looks
at her writing process and frequent extras
like excerpts and cover reveals,
at Wyle's newsletter signup link, available
on the main page of her author website.